FATAL FLIGHT

By

J. Howard Speer, Jr.

ISBN: 0-75962-044-X

This book is printed on acid free paper.

1stBooks - rev. 4/10/2001

1.

"Come on, Andrea, come to Daddy." He stooped as his preschool daughter ran to him. Catching her under her arms, he raised her high over his head, gently shaking her side to side. He smiled up into the happy face, surrounded by golden curls. Her legs dangled while he held her close to the ceiling. She giggled as he lowered her to his chest to hug her.

"You be real good for Mommy while I'm gone." He nuzzled her neck. "Ma belle petite chére," he kissed her cheek, "I'll be home soon, you'll see." He hugged her again, then placed her on her feet. She grabbed his leg with both arms.

"Daddy gone long?" the little voice asked.

"Not for long." He bent and rubbed the curly head. "I couldn't stay away from you or Mommy for long. You know how it goes: I go away for a little bit, then I'm home, and you're prettier each time I get home."

"You don't tell me that," his wife pouted.

"Aw, Jackie," he looked up, "you're the pretty she's going to be."

She fluffed her dark brown hair.

"Jim, are you sure you won't have trouble taking the rifle on the plane?"

"We've been over this at least five times. I have all the federal forms here. I look up a Mr. Streyling at the Interstate counter, and he takes me, my pack, and the rifle into a special screening room. The rifle, ammunition, and the hunting knife are all packed together, and they will lock them up in a closet on the plane. Then he will hand search the pack, and I'll carry it onto the plane and stow it in a closet in back. And I do the same thing at Denver after the lecture, at Pocatello starting home, and at Salt Lake when I change planes. It's all set up, honey."

"I just wish you wouldn't be gone so long. How come you don't do your hunting in the fall like everyone else?"

1

"You know how busy I was last fall. I couldn't even get whole weekends at home. I've never been winter camping before, and this neat deal on the private ranch came along—"

"I know, I know. But...but Andrea and I get lonely without you. You travel too much." *And someday you may not come home,* she thought in fear.

"That comes with the job. I can't help a few days here and a few days there—"

"But this is ten days, Jim."

"Aw come on, honey. Ease up. I don't want to leave and have a hassle to remember you by." He stooped to pat the girl's head, "Come on, Lilliput, let go of Daddy's leg so I can say goodbye to Mommy."

He pulled his wife to him and hugged her tightly as he kissed her. Jackie pulled her head back.

"You want something to remember me by? I'll give you something."

She pressed her abdomen into him and kissed him with fiery passion. In the five years since their wedding night, Jackie Hoskins had learned well how to turn her husband on. She pulled away from his mouth.

"You want more," she panted, "you get your buns home!" She teased him with the hand hidden from Andrea's view.

"Maybe I could take a later flight."

"Maybe you could just stay home," she countered, still fondling him.

He tried half-heartedly to stop her. "Whoa."

She whispered in his ear, "I don't want an empty bed for ten days."

The doorbell rang. Jim released Jackie and went to the door.

"Mr. Hoskins?" the airport shuttle driver asked.

"Yes. Be with you in a minute," Jim responded, bending to hand the driver his garment bag and a briefcase. He kissed Jackie again, "Je t'aime beaucoup."

After putting on his all-weather overcoat, he ran an arm through the shoulder straps of his pack, lifted it, and picked up

2

the rifle case with the other hand. A well-worn pair of insulated boots hung by their laces from the pack.

"Bye honey," he said to Jackie, "I'll call you from Boulder tonight."

"Bye sweetheart," he nodded to Andrea. "I love both of you." He struggled out the door. Jackie stood in the doorway, holding Andrea's hand as they watched him get into the shuttle van. A cold February rain was starting.

"Bye, Daddy," Andrea called, sadly waving her free hand.

The door closed. Jackie hurried to the bathroom. She felt moistness, a remnant from last night's and this morning's lovemaking. Feeling that he was spoiling Andrea, she wanted another child to divert some of his attention. Her panties were damp. Oh, to hell with it; they'd dry soon enough.

She suddenly began to cry. "Damn me! Why do I have to put on a scene every time he leaves?" Her open hand pounded against the sink in frustration. When he was gone a prescience of disaster pressed down on her.

"Mommy hurt?"

She knelt and pulled her daughter close and hugged her, "I'm sorry, Andrea, I don't like Daddy to be gone. I—I—" *just don't know what I'd do without him,* she finished to herself.

Why do I do this to myself? Why don't I trust him. He's never given me reason to doubt him, never a penny missing from his paycheck. Jackie, you have to stand up and be strong. No woman is going to take him. And look what he has to remember me by: a dependent, clinging wimp!

He was far more than she could have hoped for while she was growing up, and she lived in constant fear another woman would take him away. There had been several other women in his life before he met her, but, aside from Lori, who had also become her best friend, he kept no liaison with any of them. He had no interest in them, except he could never forget his high school sweetheart, Su Lin. But she had disappeared long ago, and Jackie felt no threat from her.

3

She couldn't complain, really, having a handsome husband, a modest home in a nice, if older neighborhood, and a sweet daughter. Jim was fixing up the home. *He's not procrastinating*, she thought, noting the bathroom wall still awaiting wallpaper. *He's just too good at his job. But that means bucks, and we can sure use them.* An engineer in the Los Angeles aerospace industry, he had been rapidly promoted. He was also honored by two professional societies. This trip was also a well-earned honor: The University of Colorado at Boulder had written his company asking if they would sponsor him to give a guest lecture to their engineering students. His boss, Mike Mitchelson, had insisted he go, and arranged an Idaho camping and hunting trip as well. Mike would meet him in Pocatello for the week in the wild.

If she needed anything while Jim was gone, she could always call Lori, and the guys in Jim's carpool had promised to drop by every couple of days and check on her. *No, damn it! I'm not helpless. Why do I have to feel this way when he's gone?* Panic struck her. *What if he doesn't come home?*

Jim looked at the house as he settled his six-one frame back into the bench seat of the van. The smallish three bedroom house was just south of the Santa Monica airport near an elementary school. The price had not been too stiff, a bargain, really, but he noted wearily that the trim and shutters required painting, the shrubs pruning, and the front lawn needed rebuilding. Was there ever an end to the work the house exacted from him?

The van was rolling down the street.

"What airline?" the driver asked.

"Interstate." *Monday, and I'm flying again. Fourth time in a month.*

"Okay. I've got two others to pick up."

"Don't sweat it, my flight's more than two hours away. I have a long check-in." *I must be stupid. I've hardly been home since New Years.*

"Figured that when I saw the rifle and pack. This ain't no time of year t' go huntin'."

"Hunters, like golfers, are a stupid lot. I have a special deal up in Idaho." *This is the last for a while. It'll be good to stay home for a change.*

"You gotta be stupid; it's downright cold up that'a way. The snow's—"

"Deep," Jim finished. "I know. I read the papers. The garment bag has a lot of insulated clothing in it."

The driver lapsed into silence; Jim returned to his thoughts. *Jackie's been hot for sex lately. I wonder what's on her mind. Another baby?* They always had made good love, particularly after the honeymoon when Lori had coached Jackie on the finer points of sex. Jackie had been the only virgin he had ever experienced. He smiled. *I'll never forget our wedding night, baby.* She had developed an almost insatiable appetite for the pleasures of marital sex instantly. *I guess I made it good for you!* But he was aware of Jackie's fears. *I don't know why you worry; I could never leave you for someone else.*

She was pretty, not the most beautiful woman he had loved, but she had many of the qualities he had searched for, and her shyness reminded him of his own and Su Lin's. Su Lin had been by far the most beautiful woman he had ever known. Lori was the most confident and competent. He had asked Lori to marry him. She turned him down, but they remained close friends, no longer lovers. Lori also befriended Jackie and was like a second mother to Andrea. She had admitted to Jackie the worst mistake of her life had been not marrying him. He counted on Lori to bolster Jackie while he was gone.

Jackie could really get along by herself he guessed. Her lack of self-confidence was her one big flaw. His years of searching for love, a love like he had never experienced after Su Lin, had taught him that all women have good features and bad. Perfection in women is as illusory as it is in men. He certainly did not consider himself perfect in any way, nor could he expect Jackie to completely fill his specifications of the perfect woman.

5

She loved him—passionately to say the least. Thirty-three, his junior by two years, she was faithful, an attentive, concerned mother, a good housekeeper, and a warm companion. She liked his kind of music, the outdoors, most of his friends, and she shared his concerns about the quality of life available to them. Most of all, she tried to be her best for him. He could ask no more.

Jackie had given him Andrea. One of her precious giggles could drive the knottiest problem from his mind. A smile on her face could light an otherwise dreary day. A hug, a wet kiss...instant cure for the aerospace blues. She was a happy child. And the more he loved Andrea, the more he loved Jackie. To play with this little girl, to teach her even the simplest things was recreation, reward of the highest value, satisfaction unknown at his job. The cruelty of his trade was the more successful you are, the less you see of your family.

The van stopped and a trimly-suited woman climbed in next to him. The driver opened the back of the van and heaved a suitcase in next to the pack. A slam of the back door, another of the sliding side door, and yet another of the driver's door and they were rolling again. The lady shook her small folding umbrella free of excess water and sheathed it.

Jim smiled shyly at her. "Not too great a day to fly."

"I'll try to catch up on some sleep," she replied, smiling, as her expensive perfume barely reached him. Class, he thought, everything in perfect taste. A hint of eye shadow, a touch of rouge, a conservative shade of lipstick, blonde hair neatly in place, she radiated executive manner.

At the next stop a pudgy man with a dark beard brusquely crowded past the woman to the back seat. His armload of hand luggage dragged across her shoulder. She slid across the seat nearer Jim. He smiled again and barely shook his head in understanding agreement of her unspoken opinion of the newest passenger. The door slamming routine was once again executed. They were headed for the freeway and the airport.

"You're going to—?" she asked Jim.

6

"Denver. And you?"

She frowned at his answer. "Boston."

Too bad. She seemed like an interesting person.

* * *

At Los Angeles International Airport by an Interstate Airline gate two men walked under the wing of the airplane parked waiting for the morning's flight. Rain was coming down hard as they put up a ladder and opened an access hatch on the underside of the fuselage. One ascended the ladder and began working on an engine controller box.

"I don't know, Steve, the self-test works. What do we do now?"

The man called Steve took his cap off and scratched his balding head. "Run it several more times."

Several minutes passed.

"Ah-ha, failed on the sixth try," the man on the ladder called down.

"Pull it out. I'll get a new one. He turned and left, using the wing as an umbrella for as long as he could.

Steve returned a few minutes later with a carton under his arm. He opened the box in the shelter of the wing and removed a black box which had many electrical connectors on one face. Keeping the clear plastic bag over the box, he called up to the other mechanic, "You got that thing out yet?"

"Keep your shirt on. This ain't the easiest place to work, you know."

"I know. That's why you're up there and I'm down here."

"Thanks," came the muffled, grunted reply from within.

After several minutes, the man on the ladder handed down the faulty box and took the new one from Steve's reaching hands.

"Hey, this is a different make. Where's the FAA certs?"

"Super said to use it."

"What do I put on the plane's maintenance log?"

"I'll take care of it. Shut up now. Here comes the flight Captain." He turned to the approaching flight officer. "Hi Captain, what can I do for you?"

"How's it coming?" the Captain asked, gaining shelter under the wing.

"It'll be a while yet. Had to change out a box. Damn bitch of a place to work, and he has to reconnect everything and safety wire all the connectors. Then he has to let it warm before he can run self-test. 'Bout an hour I 'spect."

2.

At the Airport Marina Hotel near Los Angeles International Airport a girl looked with a frown at the clothes her mother had laid out on the bed.

"Aw Mom! These clothes are gross!"

"Penny Ferguson, you settle down. It's very cold in Chicago and you're going to need that snow outfit. You don't have to wear it to the airport, but you'll need it when we get off the plane. Here, stuff it into this bag." Maude Ferguson's patience with her daughter was near its limit.

"And the boots?"

"Wear them onto the plane; it's pouring outside."

"But we're taking a limo."

"Wear them!"

"Aw Mom!"

"The ski sweater looks very nice on you. I like your selection," Maude tried a new tone of voice. She reached to her daughter's head and brushed the dark curls covering her eyes aside. "I don't see how you can stand your hair in your eyes."

"I'm part Cromagnon." That had been one of her father's favorite replies, and she knew it would cut her mother to hear it now.

Maude stopped her final packing to look sharply at her daughter. "Get your raincoat on." She went into the bathroom checking that nothing was left on the counter. Returning, she looked around the room. They had stayed at the hotel near the airport this night because the movers had come yesterday and packed up the household. California was no longer their home.

"Did you brush your teeth?"

Penny stared sullenly at her.

"Well, did you?"

"Mom, I'm eleven years old. I'm not a baby any more."

"Okay, then answer me. *Did you?*"

Penny sighed in disgust. "Yes."

"Okay, pick up your handbag and the bag with your snowsuit. Let's go." She put on her fur coat, wrapped her rain cape around her shoulders, shouldered her purse, and collected her overnight case. She stopped short. "Penny! Put on those boots *now!*"

"Aw Mom!"

Maude's heart was no more in this move than Penny's. With her husband dead and her parents in frail health in Chicago, she had little choice but to sell her house near Palos Verdes and head for Chicago. The bank had taken much of the proceeds. The insurance companies were hassling each other. Her mother and father needed help, and she and Penny needed a rent-free roof over their heads. She could identify with Penny's reluctance, but she didn't need the foot-dragging to make it much harder. Until recently, Penny had been a very tractable girl, but the sudden tragic loss of her father, plus the loss of her friends, had made her recalcitrant.

* * *

Marina Del Rey luxury apartments overlook the preferred anchorage of the yachts of the super wealthy, the rich, and the nouveau riche of Los Angeles. The apartments are affordable. The yachts are not. Tania Richards scurried around her apartment, hurriedly packing her overnight flight bag. Her uniform raincoat lay over the back of the white leather couch, a black strap purse cluttered the chrome and glass coffee table. A brilliant yellow, red, and blue modern art picture hung on the wall opposite the window overlooking the docks.

"Lil," she shouted, "I've left my revised flight schedule for the rest of the month on the table by the phone. Would you call the dentist and see what you can do to reschedule my appointment?"

"Don't sweat it," came the reply from a bedroom. "I fly out later today, so don't look for me 'til Thursday."

"Okay. I'll be back tomorrow night. Why do they always call me to fill in for Pearl when she's sick?"

"Beats the shit out of me."

"Lil!" Tania complained.

"...Okay, I don't know."

"Better. I'll make a lady out of you someday."

"I hope not."

She closed the case and stood it on its collapsible cart. Deftly wrapping the bungee cords around, she clipped the hooks over the vertical bars. Passing by a picture mirror, she stopped to check her uniform, brushing lint off the jacket. Five-eight, trim, and very attractive, she nicely filled the uniform. Rushing back to the couch, she scooped up her coat, snatched at the strap of her purse, and towed the suitcase toward the door.

"I'm gone. See you Thursday night," she yelled.

"Have a good trip," Lillian yelled from the bedroom.

"You too." Tania closed the door behind her and hurried to the elevator. She had worked for Interstate Airlines for seven years now, and this was not the first time they had called her on short notice to fill in for one of the flight attendants. Her roommate, Lillian Bromley, was also a flight attendant and her dearest friend.

"Let's see," she muttered, reviewing her scribbled note in the elevator, "Flight 238. Denver. They put on someone else. I stay overnight, then take 636 to Salt Lake and 523 to LA. The OT will pay for some nice clothes. Okay." She brightened at the expectation of a shopping spree. "No, maybe I'll get that chrome lamp." Her expensive tastes meant extra dollars never languished in her checking account for long.

Tania rushed to her car in the rain, quickly stowed her suitcase, and slipped behind the wheel, closing the door. "Hey," she recalled, "238's Danny's flight. All right!" Then a dismal thought occurred as she started her engine. "He'll be taking it on to Chicago." Captain Danny Farrell was her current beau. He was ten years older, mature, and fun, fun, fun.

She snapped on the radio.

"...weather outlook east of California is dismal for the next several days. Blizzards are raging in upper Nevada, Utah, and throughout Colorado. They will move on to the plains this evening. The new Pacific storm over Oregon and northern California is following close behind, giving little relief for the mountain states until the end of the week. Flight schedules are being disrupted..."

"Damn," Tania commented, anticipating delays throughout her scheduled itinerary. Maybe she wouldn't see Lillian on Thursday night after all. She checked her dark mahogany hair in the rear view mirror while she waited at the light at Lincoln Boulevard. "Come on idiot," she muttered at the driver in front, "right turns against a red are legal...Moron." She tapped her hands on the wheel in time with the windshield wipers. The light changed. Slipping the gears into first, she hit the accelerator, and whipped her red Acura around the slowpoke.

At the apartment Lillian finished ironing her uniform blouse. Tania was special to her. She was her companion, her mentor, her dearest, dearest friend, and Lillian worried every time Tania left the apartment that—heaven forbid—one day she might not return. She was concerned maybe Tania and Danny might soon choose to be married. She couldn't fault that, but she needed Tania as her roommate to support and guide her, feeling weak and uncertain in how she faced her life. And she needed to feel Tania's love, love freely given, love Lillian tried to return twice over without resorting to sex. Sex as she had known it was sometimes exciting and pleasant, yes, but so far without real love, love like she and Tania shared.

* * *

Tania greeted the small knot of flight attendants gathered near the boarding gate. Her spirits were picking up.

"Tania!" one of the women screamed in delight, "It's been so long since we've been together."

12

Tania hugged her with her free arm. "You're looking good, Cherise." She nodded and smiled to another, "Perry."

"It'll be a good flight with you aboard," a third chimed in, "Welcome to our little group."

"Hi, Sharon. Are you the lead?"

Sharon nodded. "You and Cherise will work the back; Perry and I will cover the front. You can lock up a rifle that's going with us today. We'll be late departing."

"Oh? Why?"

"Mechanical. Engines."

"Oh great!"

"Danny's out in the rain watching them work on it."

"Getting soaked, I'll bet."

"No, he's under the wing staying nice and dry."

"There's no one I'd rather fly with," Tania said.

"Or sleep with?" Perry asked, mischievously.

"Yeah, Tania, when are you two going to admit you're in love and get married?"

"Oh, come on you guys." A round of giggles greeted her protest.

Bill Coates, the second seat, and Frank Morrison, flight engineer, arrived with their flight bags.

"Well, aren't we lucky," Bill smiled at Tania. "The weather's always smooth with you on board."

Tania gave him a quick hug. "I think my charm ran out today."

"Wrong. You're always charming." He hugged her back. "I'll bet I do most of the flying today; the captain will have something else on his mind."

"Not this flight. I'm going to be busy with the tourists in back."

"And you'll be busy on your back—"

"Frank! Let's keep it clean. I'm only going as far as Denver."

"That'll be enough to put Danny in a bad mood, for sure."

"I don't think he's too happy right now," Perry said.

"He'll get them to hold this bucket together. It goes in for a major soon. In fact, I think they pull it out of service in Chicago," Bill said.

"And a new interior!" Sharon added. "I don't like the service area amidship." She unlocked the door to the jetway.

The group went onto the plane, closing the door behind them. Tania was a popular member of any flight crew. She was cheerful, helpful, shared the work, and accepted any duty assigned to her. There were few men who did not admire her, and few women who were jealous of her. On her regular runs, she was the lead, but when she filled in, she was just one of the other girls. The airline used her natural friendliness to pair new girls to work with her and learn the ropes. Two of this crew had been her protégés.

* * *

Jim struggled down the aisle with his pack. Cherise led the way to a closet in the back of the cabin. He dropped his briefcase and garment bag off at his seat near the back on his way. Pushing a coat aside, he carefully slid the pack sideways into the closet.

"That looks heavy," Cherise said, smiling.

Jim smiled shyly back, "About fifty pounds." He liked her cheerful spirit. Tania had taught her the value of a pretty smile. It worked on him. *Oh, isn't she cute!* he thought as he watched her all the way back up the aisle, then opened the overhead compartment to stow his garment bag and overcoat above his seat. As he made himself comfortable, two women with small children settled in. Other passengers began to board the plane.

Maude and Penny stopped a couple of rows short of him. Cherise took Maude's fur coat to the closet in the rear, winking at Jim as she went by. She had taken a liking to him—quiet, a little shy—but she sensed there was a lot to know about him.

Penny assisted her mother in stowing their hand luggage in the compartment, then settled into the window seat and wrestled with her boots until they were off. Maude placed them above and sat on the aisle.

"You should check out the guy who came on with the pack," Cherise confided to Tania. "I think he's pretty neat."

"If he's that good, why are you telling me?"

"You're safe. You have Danny."

"You're naive if you think any unmarried woman isn't interested in what's available."

"He's not your type."

"Oh?...What is my type?"

"...I guess I don't know."

"Neither do I," Tania confessed. "Come on, let's get everybody strapped in and button up the overheads. I'll check him out while I'm back there." They moved out of the service area and started preparations for take-off.

Jim returned Tania's smile when she passed by checking seat belts. *She's not bad, either.* The aisle seat next to him was vacant. A seasoned traveler, he had already raised the arm rest to make extra room. *Field and Stream* was in his hand, and he started leafing through it while the emergency procedures announcements were being made. Tania, halfway down the aisle, was annoyed at him for his inattention. Penny paid careful attention, this being her first flight. The plane was already being pushed backwards from the gate. Penny's nose went to the window as the announcements ended.

"What do you think?" Cherise inquired. Drinks had been served; it was now time for the meals.

Tania looked up from unloading the service cart. "Two to one he's married."

She lifted the ice bucket onto the counter, cleared the plastic glasses and other paraphernalia from the top of the cart and stowed the cart under the counter. Cherise unloaded the entrees from the oven into the food cart and pulled the cart into the aisle to make more room.

15

"Mom, I've got to go," Penny announced.

Maude looked up from her murder mystery, stared at her daughter, then unloaded her drink onto Penny's tray, pushed her tray up and secured it, then released her seat belt and stood in the aisle. Penny scooched out from under her tray, reached the aisle, but didn't know which way to turn.

"In back, I think," Maude suggested. Penny bounced down the aisle, full of youthful vigor.

Jim was amused at Maude's look of fatigue as she watched her daughter. *Why am I laughing? I'll bet Andrea will be just like her.* She already was a lively little girl. The article entitled "Winter Fishing Techniques" pulled his mind back to the magazine. He doubted he'd soon have use for them, but fishing was one of his loves.

* * *

The meal was over and the remnants had been picked up and tucked away. The flight attendants were refilling coffee cups when one of the engines coughed and began to spin down. The cabin began to depressurize, and the oxygen masks suddenly dropped. Tania and the other attendants hurried to the service area to get their portable oxygen units. Sharon, after installing her mask, grabbed the intercom and instructed the passengers to immediately put their masks on. The second engine increased in power, coughed and popped twice, then quit. The aircraft nosed down as the captain avoided a stall. The relative silence of the wind noise was eerie as Tania struggled up the sloping aisle checking passengers. Depressurization was such a rare event she had never experienced it except on training flights. She installed a mask on a mother who had disobeyed orders and placed the mask on her child before herself. The mother was now unconscious.

Tania felt very nervous; the oxygen problem was masking the more serious problem; without engines the plane would not fly for long. She knew from a brief visit to the cockpit earlier they were approaching the mountains of Colorado. No place to try to land a large jet in a blizzard. She tried to concentrate on her job.

"Flight Attendants, please instruct the passengers on emergency landing procedures," came the terse announcement.

There were shrieks of fear from the passengers. The one from Cherise behind her, however, did more to unsettle Tania.

"Frank," Danny yelled in the cockpit, "What the hell is going on?"

"I don't know, but I'm trying to restart."

"Bill, get on to air traffic control in Denver and let 'em know we're in trouble," Danny commanded.

Bill picked up the microphone. "Mayday, mayday. Denver ARTCC, this is Interstate 238. We've lost all engines. Over."

"Interstate 238, this is Denver ARTCC. Repeat your status. Over," the cockpit speaker squawked with scratchy interference noise.

"All engines dead, descending through thirty-one thousand, trying air restart," Bill intoned, "Is Grand Junction open for emergency landing? Over."

"Interstate 238. Negative on Grand Junction landing. Status—closed. Ceiling one hundred feet, visibility fifty feet, blowing snow, cross winds to seventy knots. No landing aids. Montrose also closed. Same conditions. Nearest open fields, Albuquerque, Pueblo, Colorado Springs, Denver. Over." Bill looked at Danny. Danny shook his head.

"ARTCC, 238. Can't make any of them. Vector me to Albuquerque in case we get an engine back. 238 over."

"Interstate 238, roger. Your vector is one...ah...forty-nine. Your status please. Over."

"Interstate 238. Turning to heading one-forty-nine. Engines still out. Descending through twenty-four thousand. Over."

"Goddamnit, Frank," Danny complained, "We're running out of sky. Can't you get even one of those suckers to go?" Helplessly he watched the altimeter unwind.

"Trying. It's my ass in this, too, you know."

"Bill, crank on some flaps; we'll have to try to keep this bucket from dropping so fast," Danny commanded. Electric motors answered his command almost instantly. "Kill the cabin lights to save the batteries."

"Cabin lights...off." Bill responded. "How much flaps do you want?"

"Ten degrees to start with."

"Ten degrees," Bill repeated. The flap motors stopped.

"Can't see a thing," Danny complained, tense and sweating. "Damn blizzard!"

"Twenty-two thousand," Bill called out.

"More flaps," Danny commanded. "Better get them all the way down."

One of the engines started to wind up.

"I think I've got number two back!" Frank shouted. But his elation was soon crushed as the engine ignited, started to supply power, and died.

* * *

Tania's heart ached to hear the sound of an engine again. Though she tried to appear calm to her passengers, her throat was taut. "I'm going to die," kept running through her mind. She found Jim kneeling at his seat, facing the rear, holding onto his seat belt, and leaning back against the seat in front.

"Sir!" she screamed, "You must get into your seat and fasten your seat belt!" Grasping the arm of the aisle seat to steady herself, she quickly brushed the dangling oxygen mask next to him out of her way.

"No! That position will kill in an impact," he replied in a firm voice.

"Please!" Her voice climbed an octave. She was about to move on and leave him to his fate.

"Prepare for impact!" the intercom announced. Tania noted the panic in Bill's voice.

"Save your own life! Get down here quick," Jim shouted over the screams of the passengers. He sucked in a deep breath. *I've thought this scenario through*, he reminded himself, *It should work.*

She would never know why, but something authoritative in his manner convinced her. Kneeling quickly at the seat next to him, she was barely settled when the plane suddenly pulled nose high, climbing, then settled sickeningly and crashed, breaking apart aft of the wing.

Meanwhile, in the control room of the Denver ARTCC, operators stared at their screens as Bill's voice was suddenly heard screaming, "Frank, there's a mountain ahead! Pull it up!—" then moments later static hissed from the loudspeakers. Silence gripped the stunned operators as the blip that was Interstate flight 238 disappeared. Outside, the blizzard howled around the center, angry, malicious, unrelenting.

3.

Pain. All Tania could sense was pain; pain in her head, pain low in her back; dull, aching pains. She continued her inventory: left leg—a sharp pain...What was the matter with her leg? Is death supposed to be so full of pain? Shouldn't there be some relief from the awful things she had just been through? She tried to review her life; it had been reasonably free from sin—well, maybe not so free, but had she earned all this pain? Was she damned to an eternal Hell of pain?

"Are you all right?" the archangel asked. A quiet voice, masculine, nearby.

She moaned, "I don't think so. I feel so much pain." Her eyes were tightly shut, trying to shut out...what? Where was she? Was she at the gates of Hell?...Could she maybe be entering Purgatory? Oh eyes, please open. Her hands. Her hands were grasping something tightly...The seat belt? Was she still in the plane? Was she still alive?

"Duck your head and let me get out to the aisle," the voice said.

She opened her eyes as he completed stepping over her to the aisle. She was still on the plane, and she was alive.

"Here, take my hands and let me pull you out of there."

With light dancing wildly about the cabin, she reached for his outstretched arms and took hold of him. He began to pull her to the aisle.

"Oh God! Please stop," she said, her face contorted. The pain in her leg had suddenly increased. "Let me roll over." Slowly she rolled to her back. There was definitely something wrong with her left leg. While he reached up to the overhead compartment to remove some blankets, she looked at her leg. She was dizzy, light headed. What she saw didn't completely register. "I never saw so much blood." Her voice sounded strange. "Will I die?"

He looked down at her, then dropped to his knees beside her. "You will if we don't get *that* stopped!" He grabbed her leg, roughly, at the pulsing wound. Looking wildly around, he grasped at the white cloth covering the headrest of the seat next to him. A smart yank and it came free of it's fastenings. "Here...ah—"

"Tania...Tania Richards."

"...Tania." He grasped her left hand and pushed it into her groin, "Push down here."

The blood began to flow as he released his grip on her leg.

"Harder." There was patience and urgency in his voice. "Hard enough to stop the bleeding."

She put her right hand on top of her left and pushed harder. The bleeding almost stopped. He fully released his grasp, quickly folded the cloth into a long, narrow bandage, and wound it twice around her leg at the wound.

She screamed as he worked. "Please, you're hurting me."

"I'm sorry. I can't help it." He finished tying the bandage. "I hope this will hold. Try letting go." He watched closely as she removed the pressure.

She shivered. This was the first she realized she was cold. Very cold. A bitter wind was howling into the broken fuselage. She could see flames, whipped wildly by the wind, eating away at the forward section of the plane which was lying crushed and ripped many yards away. When the flames leapt toward the after section, the smells of burning rubber, fuel, plastics, and flesh overwhelmed her. Sickening. She looked up at the man. If she was alive, what about the others? Danny—

"Let me move you as far out of this wind as I can." He grasped her under her arms and towed her up the down-sloping aisle toward the rear of the cabin.

"My leg's broken," she said, the pain calling attention to the strange bend below the knee.

He grunted as he pulled her up to the back wall of the cabin, "Yeah...both bones. Ugh...That's what got the artery." He

propped her up against the closet doors. "I'll get some blankets."
He took a deep, shaky breath.

She watched as he returned to his seat to retrieve the
blankets he had dropped there. Some overhead compartment
lids had sprung open, spilling luggage out. There was debris all
over the aisle from broken hand luggage which had flown out at
impact. Reaching across slumped over passengers, he opened
other compartments and gathered more blankets and several
pillows. Returning to her side, he knelt and covered her with
the blankets and placed a pillow behind her head.

"Thank you...ah—"

"I'm sorry. Jim. Jim Hoskins."

"Jim...Did anyone else get through it?" She hoped somehow
others of the crew had survived.

"I'm going to find out now."

He opened another compartment, pulled a blanket out,
wrapped it around his shoulders, then started down the aisle,
checking the slumped over passengers on both sides for signs of
life. At a couple, he stopped to take their pulse, but moved on
again. In spite of finding so much death, a feeling of elation
began to replace his trembling. *It worked, Goddamnit!* he
thought. *It worked! She's alive and so am I!* Several seats had
torn from their mountings to the floor. A clutter of tubing for
oxygen hung from the overheads. *She's alive—maybe—if I can
keep her that way.*

Danny, she thought watching Jim, *Oh God!* The flames were
telling her what she didn't want to know. Could anybody have
survived? She pulled her hands to her face hoping when Jim
abruptly leaned into a window seat.

"Hi, honey. Where do you hurt?"

Penny, doubled over, moaned. She turned her head toward
him, "My stomach hurts real bad...Please help my mother."

He placed his hand on Maude's neck. No pulse. He gently
lifted her head, only to find a broken neck. Penny sensed from
watching what Jim knew. His face was grave as he tried to find
words to console her.

22

Oh Jesus. How do I tell her her mother's dead? What can I possibly say that has any meaning at all? She knows. Look at her eyes; she knows. But what can I say? He slowly shook his head.

"I'm sorry. I can't—"

Penny stared at him. "No!" she flopped across her mother's body. "No, she's not dead!...She's not *dead!*" She rocked back and forth, pulling her mother's limp body with her. Her cheeks glistened in the erie light as she cried, "She can't be dea-ea-ea-ead!...NO!"

Never had he felt so helpless. But a sense of urgency prevailed; he had to bring this to a halt; other matters were more important. He placed a hand gently on her shoulder. She looked up at him seeing only a blur.

"I—I know how I—how I would feel if she were my mother. What's important right now is that you're alive. We have to try to keep you that way."

"NOooo! I don't want to live!"

"Honey, how—how is anyone to know—to know what a fine person your mother was if you don't live to show them?"

Remembering watching the girl put clothing away, he reached up to the overhead compartment. The door was jammed. Trying again, he banged on it with his fist. No go. *How come the one I want is jammed, and others just popped open?* he wondered in frustration. With a pry at a corner, he tried the latch again. The cover finally swung up out of his way. He lowered her boots and the bag of clothing down, pulled a blanket out to add to his collection, and dropped another pillow into the aisle.

"Here, please put your clothing on quickly before you freeze."

He gently pried her hands loose from her mother's body.

"NO!" She swung her fists wildly at him.

He caught her arm as it swung by him and grabbed at her two wrists. She struggled but soon realized he was too strong for her. Each effort hurt her already sore abdomen. Her resistance suddenly ceased.

"P-Please let me go, " she cried piteously, "If Mom's dead, I want to die-ie-ie-ie."

The battle over, his voice remained calm. "Please, I need your help in back. What's your name?" He slowly released her hands.

"P-P—Penny."

"Penny, I'm sorry if I've hurt you— The stewardess in back will bleed to death if you don't help me. I need your help right now...Will you help me? Please?" He waited as she sobbed, then smiled at her when she nodded. "Fine. Now get into your clothes; I need a steady hand. I can't use someone who's shivering." He placed his hand behind her head, looking into her eyes. "I care, really I do."

Jim waited as she started to get into her snowsuit, then resumed checking the remaining passengers. He collected every blanket and pillow he found on seats or in the overhead compartments. Finding no other survivors, he returned to Tania.

"Find anyone else?"

"Yes, the girl who was sitting a couple of rows in front of me. Her mother died." He wrapped her uninjured leg in a blanket, then carefully put pillows under her broken leg. She grimaced in pain as he moved the leg.

"Is that all?"

"That's it. I told you that position would kill."

"How did you know?"

He lowered her leg gently onto the pillows. "Later. We have more important things for now. I want to get my pack out of the closet; let me slide you over." He pushed her body sideways, avoiding moving the leg more than necessary to gain entrance to the closet. "Here, put this on," he said, handing out Maude's fur coat.

"What's the pack for?" She started to struggle to put the coat on, trying not to move her leg. He paused to help her with a sleeve and to restore the pillow behind her head.

"I was going on a winter camping and hunting trip in Idaho." He propped the pack up against the back row of seats. Opening one of the pockets, he pulled out some thermal underwear and socks.

"But we were going to Denver."

"I know. I was going to enthrall two hundred and ten engineering students in Boulder with a guest lecture, *then* go hunting."

"I'm impressed...The rifle we have locked up back here, is it yours?" She studied him as he went to his seat and pulled the garment bag from the overhead compartment.

"Yes. It's back here? Good, we may need it."

After retrieving his garment bag, he started changing clothes. Off came the dress shirt, on went the thermal underwear and a warm flannel shirt from the bag. His pants followed, and he was soon garbed in heavy jeans and ski pants. Thin socks joined the pile in the aisle as he pulled the thermal socks on. A long down jacket with a hood and a wool cap completed his change. He returned to the pack and released the boots from it. When finished, he took the blanket which had been around his shoulders and draped it across her injured leg. From the pack he removed down booties and an insulated hood. He put the hood on her head. The warmth was almost instantaneous. The booties soon warmed her feet, but her injured leg was getting colder and beginning to be numb.

"Thank you."

"I use the hood while sleeping to keep my sinuses warm. Was there a first aid kit on the plane?" He removed a large flashlight from the pack.

"In the overhead back of the galley."

"Great. I'll get it and the girl."

Reaching Penny's row of seats, he put the flashlight down on the floor.

"Ready?"

"I couldn't get my boots on." Her faint voice caught on the words. "My stomach hurts too much."

"That's okay, Penny. Your back doesn't hurt, does it?" He took the boots from her. They joined the flashlight on the floor.

"No, just down here." She moved her hand across her lower abdomen.

Damned seat belt! "Okay. Grab hold of my neck while I lift you out." He grasped her hips firmly, then lifted her slowly over her mother's body, standing her in the aisle. She stood bent over. "That's a nice warm outfit. Where were you going?"

"To Chicago. My Dad was killed in an accident—" she began to cry, "a few m—months ago. And my Mom an-and I w—were g-g—going—"

Impulsively he pulled her to him, wrapped his arms around her, and held her. "Jesus! I'm so sorry, Penny."

Tania watched as he held Penny for several moments. There was a lot she liked about this man. Part of it was the compassion he was showing the girl. The first aid he had rendered her was textbook. There was no sign of panic in his actions. Cherise had been right...Cherise! What had happened to her? She had been in back with her before the crash. Where was she now?

The girl and Jim were coming up the aisle; she stooped over in some pain, he carrying her boots and urging her along with a gentle hand on her back. The girl looked up.

"Hey, that's my Mom's coat!"

"Yes," Jim admitted, "I gave it to Miss Tania to keep her from freezing to death. It's still your mother's, or yours, and I had no right to give it away. I would hope your mother told you about helping others in need. Miss Tania's clothing was in the forward portion of the plane."

"Please, would you allow me to wear it...ah—"

"Penny," Jim supplied.

"Penny?" Tania finished.

Penny looked uncertain and rebellious. That was her mother's coat! Jim took his hand from her back.

"Stopping the bleeding in Miss Tania's leg won't do much good if she's going to freeze to death soon afterwards." Tania admired the calm patience in Jim's voice. "She's not going anywhere in that coat you're not going. You'll have your eye on it at all times. She really does need it, and having it in a closet seems such a waste. Okay?"

"Okay," Penny sighed.

"Thank you," Tania replied.

"That's the spirit. You snuggle up to Miss Tania while I get the things we're going to need."

Penny sat next to Tania, who put an arm around her shoulders. Jim covered them with more of the blankets he had liberated from the compartments. He went down the aisle and into the snowy gloom. They watched him, silhouetted against the flames as he searched for a suitable piece of wreckage to make a splint for Tania's leg.

Jim's gaze was riveted on the flaming fuselage, now bent and twisted from the crash and the inferno raging inside. Many seats he could see near the broken end were ripped loose and piled up, blocking any escape possible survivors might have had. It was like looking into the open door of a coal-fired furnace. *This must be what Hell is like.* "Oops, what's this?"

He bent, then knelt in the snow melting from the heat. Moments later he lifted a body to his shoulder and brought it back to the cabin, placing it gently on the floor.

"Cherise!" Tania gasped, "Oh no!...Oh nooo!" She twisted in her agony, sickened as she watched Jim climb onto the floor, lift the body and move it up the aisle to an interior seat. There were few persons, aside from Danny and Lillian, she liked more. Her feeling of loss was overwhelming. A high pitched wail she could not recognize came from her mouth. Penny's eyes blurred again. Tania held Penny tightly, having to hold on to something.

Jim left the cabin again and soon returned bearing a couple of long metal strips. He stopped at the galley to locate the first aid kit, and rejoined them, stomping snow from his boots and pants legs. "These are hat sections which used to reinforce the skin. The whole front section has been ripped apart," he said as he set the strips down next to Tania. He went to his pack, and using his flashlight to search, pulled out a sewing kit in a zip-lock bag and an X-acto knife with blades in another. He also pulled out a butane cigarette lighter.

"Where are we?" she asked.

"I don't know; it's snowing too hard. Can't see more than fifteen feet except for the fire." He rubbed his face as he checked his equipment, "That snow is like fine sand, and the wind is driving it like little bullets. It stings."

"What are you doing?"

"I'm getting ready to fix your leg."

"Can't it wait until we're found?"

"No. You might lose your leg or your life if we wait."

"I don't like either option," Tania said, her eyes wide and her face taut.

"Neither do I," he replied, kneeling next to her. He pulled the blanket off her leg. "What I've done so far is buy us some time, but not much. We still have a panic here."

"I don't understand. Can't we hold out until tomorrow? They'll be looking for us tomorrow," Tania added hopefully "In a blizzard?—"

She suddenly recalled the horrid weather report she had heard on the way to the airport.

"...Come on!" he continued, "The forecast for the mountain states is at least two more days of this. From all I can tell, we are on a mountain."

"Danny...ah...the Captain said we were coming up on Grand Junction, Colorado, when I was in the cockpit a little before the engines quit."

"Okay, we are probably on some mountain in Colorado. We're not going to be rescued very soon. We have to do more for your leg. How's it feel?"

"Sore, cold, and it's getting numb."

"Right. That bandage, while it's keeping you from bleeding to death in a few minutes, is also strangling the circulation in your lower leg."

28

"My head's killing me and you're telling me this?...What do you think you should do?"

"I want to set the leg and try to patch the artery."

"Cut me with a knife or something?" She grimaced at the thought of more pain.

"Yes."

"No way!"

"But—"

"No WAY!"

He started searching through his pockets, a resigned expression on his face. "Give me a quarter and I'll go down to the corner phone booth and call 911 for the paramedics."

She closed her eyes in pain. "Be serious."

"I *am* serious. If you don't let me try to patch the artery, the leg could die before morning. Then we might be faced with gangrene and possible amputation to save your life. One legged ladies don't do much for me. Personally, I'd prefer to mess around with the artery, than to hack your leg off at the knee."

"Pearl, why the *hell* couldn't you have taken this flight?" She moaned. Her eyes were still closed.

"Who's Pearl?"

"The regular attendant with this crew. She called in sick...sick of work, if you ask me, and I'm filling in for her. I was supposed to be in a dentist's chair this afternoon."

"Well, you just got into the wrong office. I'm Doctor Quack." He waved his arms. "Look, I'm no surgeon or doctor; I'm an engineer—"

"That's no qualification to cut my leg."

"I'm an assistant scoutmaster, I've taken the Red Cross first aid courses, and I've taken a backpack awareness course."

"So?"

"Red Cross first aid is based on medical help being only a short time away, say an hour. What do you do when you're in the wilderness with some kid's emergency when help is two or three days away?" He gestured with his hands. "Well, you have to act—beyond what Red Cross teaches you. Sure it's a risk, but you have no choice...All I want to do is find some way to patch you to hold out until we're found. If it doesn't work, we're back to where we are now."

Tania's patience was at an end. She could see his point; her leg was worth the risk. "Okay, do it. It's numb."

"You're an important part of the operating team," Jim said. "You must control the bleeding at that pressure point. I'm going to stop several times to let you release it so we can keep the leg alive. I'll hold the wound closed while we refresh the blood in your leg. Okay?"

She nodded her understanding. He turned to Penny. "Your job is to hold the flashlight on the wound. You'll have to move it around as I work to keep the shadows down. I may need you to help hold the wound open while I'm working. Can you hang in there? Can you do it for me and Miss Tania?"

Penny stared at him.

"I'm very serious, honey. We really need your help here," he pleaded. "I know you're hurting, too...Please?"

Penny finally nodded her assent. "Okay," Jim continued. "The two of you sit tight while I fix up a splint and get all the materials we'll need together. He went into the lavatory and collected paper towels and several sanitary napkins. Going down the aisle, he pulled every headrest cloth free from the seats. Ready at last, he settled onto his knees beside Tania.

"I'd like you to pull your skirt as far up as you will allow so I can fit the splint to your leg," he requested.

Without hesitation she pulled her skirt and slip up to bare her leg to the groin. He cut away the panty hose above and below the bandage and pulled it off as gently as he could. Laying one of the spars on the inside of her leg, he found it was way too long. Gripping it just beyond her foot, he took it to the lavatory door and bent it about 90 degrees. He made a second bend, another 90 degrees, about one fist's distance from the first to form a U. The metal was cold against her skin as he brought it back to measure a second time. The outside leg of the U was too long. He bent it back against itself.

With a quick tear, a blanket, folded double and laid along side her, became the same length as her leg. He wrapped it around her leg near her groin, noting the excess width. Another tear and refolding produced a two-layer wrap which just encircled her thigh. Carefully, he raised her leg enough to slip the blanket piece underneath. Tania frowned in discomfort but said nothing.

Next he folded the many headliners diagonally into long narrow bandages. He slipped these under the blanket at spaced locations from groin to ankle. Finally, he placed two pillows into her crotch, which brought a quick protest. Ignoring Tania's complaint, he shifted his position to sit at the end of her leg with one of his legs between hers.

"Penny, get over on the outside here." He motioned with his arm. She stepped over Tania's legs and knelt down next to her knee. "Okay, Tania, clamp down on the pressure point."

When she applied pressure, he quickly untied the bandage covering the wound. "Penny, when I pull her leg out straight, you feel the shin bone on both sides of the break and guide it together as I relax."

"I don't know what you mean," she whined.

"Okay. Run your hand along her shin. Feel the break?"

Penny gingerly felt Tania's leg. She nodded.

"Feel the offset or misalignment?"

"Yes."

"We want to get rid of the misalignment. So you use both hands to guide the loose end of the bone into place. Up and down and side to side. Okay?"

She nodded. He put his foot into the pillows in Tania's crotch and pulled the leg out straight, using a grip around her foot and ankle. Tania closed her eyes, sucked in her breath, and pulled a fist up to her mouth.

"I know it hurts but keep the pressure point closed," he reminded her as blood began to pulse from the wound. "Hurry, Penny." Penny's hands pushed the bone around. "Okay?" he asked. Penny nodded. He slowly relaxed his grip. "That's one," he announced, checking the alignment, "Great!"

He retied the bandage at the wound. "Let go, Tania."

"Okay, Penny. The next bone will be harder because you can't feel it as easily. There's a lot of muscle in the way. I'm going to bend the leg sideways to open things up and you'll have to do the best you can. We'll hope we don't disturb the one we've just set." He brought his foot out of Tania's crotch and placed it opposite her knee. "Okay gang, ready?" He untied the bandage again as Tania pressed her hand into her groin.

"I can't feel the bone," Penny complained.

"I know," he replied patiently while holding the leg bent slightly inwards against his foot, "Just grip the area of the break as tightly as you can and we'll hope it will be close enough."

A minute later he retied the bandage around the wound, wrapped the prepared blanket up around her leg, placed the splint in place outside the blanket and began tying the bandages to hold the splint to Tania's thigh. He carefully wedged a couple of pillows between the splint and her ankle, then tied the bandages around the lower leg to secure the splint. Two sanitary napkins, packed between the blanket and her leg adjacent to the wound, held the blanket away from the wound area.

He poured antiseptic into a shallow cup, then prepared a curved needle from his sewing kit by heating it with the cigarette lighter until it was red hot, bending it with the blade of his knife. He heated the knife blade enough to sterilize it. From his pack he obtained some fine fishing leader which he threaded into the needle. He trimmed off a long length of leader and coiled the needle and leader into the antiseptic to await his later need. Finally, he handed the flashlight to Penny, had Tania shut off the blood once more, and mopped the area around the wound with antiseptic, finishing by cleaning his fingers with the liquid.

"Let's have a look at that artery," he announced, spreading the wound with his fingers. He peered into the wound, mopped some blood out with a paper towel, and looked again. "Hmmm." He retied the wound and stood up.

"Do you have something like a large drinking straw in the galley?"

Tania looked puzzled.

"Not the little straws like you hand out with the cocktails. One more like you'd use for a malted milk?"

"Oh, yes. They're in a drawer under the counter. There's only a few."

"One's all I need." He hurried off.

Tania surveyed her leg. The numbness was deepening, a blessing she guessed, knowing what was to follow. "I'll say this," she commented to Penny, "he seems to know what he's doing. I'm not looking forward to the next episode, though."

"What's he want the straw for?" Penny asked.

"Beats me."

At the counter Jim took a deep breath. *Pull yourself together; quit shaking.* He returned, a straw in his hand. Removing the paper wrapping, he cut a short length of the plastic off with his knife and set it swimming in the antiseptic cup with the needle and leader. He pulled a toothpick from its wrapper and dipped it into the cup, standing it up where he could grasp it. Straddling Tania's leg, he knelt, and looked at the two faces staring at him.

"What are you going to do?" Tania asked.

"I cut a plastic water pipe when I was planting a tree in my yard. They sold me a kit with a piece of pipe which would just fit inside of the broken one, and it had two stainless steel clamps to clamp the broken pipe to the patch—"

"I'm not some old water pipe."

"What is an artery, if it's not a pipe for blood?" He looked into her eyes. With no answer he continued.

"Okay, here's the way it's going to go. I'm going to use the toothpick to determine the direction the artery runs on both sides of the break by sticking it part-way into the artery. I'll carefully slit the muscle back along the artery on both sides of the break to gain access, then insert the straw into the artery and secure the artery to it. I'll then try to spot sew the two halves together. I don't think, with my limited skills, I can sew the artery up tight enough without the straw. If I can tie the artery to the straw, like those clamps, I think I can keep it from leaking. If it works, I'll sew the wound up and we'll all say a prayer that it won't infect. Okay? Everybody understand?"

Tania began to feel he wasn't completely crazy. She nodded. Penny looked at him; her abdomen was hurting, but she was with him.

"I'll probably be pretty slow because I don't want to do more damage than necessary, so we'll stop fairly often to let the blood circulate. But once the straw is in place, we have to keep going."

Although Tania had a throbbing headache, and her arms were becoming fatigued holding her groin, she watched in fascination as his hands, skilled from many years of model airplane building, carefully followed the plan he had outlined. Penny, usually ill at the sight of blood, was no less fascinated. She helped by holding the incision open and kept the light fully on the opening. The numbness in the leg kept Tania from experiencing much pain, although the power of suggestion as she watched made her think she ought to feel pain.

In what seemed an eternity for all three, he finally leaned back on his haunches.

"Okay, Tania, let's give it a try," Jim sighed, his back aching.

She slowly released the pressure point.

"It's bleeding!" Penny's disappointment almost got to Tania.

"No, no!" Jim exclaimed, excited as he sponged the blood slowly filling the cavity with a towel, "That's bleeding from the muscles around the cut. Looking good! Let it go completely." He stretched muscles so cramped, they had given up complaining long ago.

He smiled at Tania. "I think you can plan on walking around on that leg for a good long time. Okay gang, let's close it up."

Tania leaned back against the bulkhead, relief creeping throughout her tense body. He picked the needle out of the cup and began to close the wound. He hummed some gay tune while he worked.

"Do you think I could get a sewing merit badge?" He pulled a stitch tight.

"Sacré bleu! Je suis très stupide," he muttered.

"What's the matter?" Tania was suddenly tense again.

"I think I'm becoming attached to you."

"What? We hardly know each—"

He tugged at a finger holding the wound closed as he was sewing. "I think I sewed my finger to your leg."

Penny giggled as she watched.

Tania was concerned. "Couldn't you feel the needle?"

"My hands are so cold I can't feel anything...Does this mean I won't get my merit badge?"

Weak from fatigue, Tania laughed hysterically. "Poor baby!"

He freed his hand. "It was just a loop of leader." Another knot and he was finished.

"The leg's beginning to tingle a lot. It's cold, too."

"Good sign," he smiled. "We didn't have the blood shut off too long. Okay, Penny, let's rub the leg down to help circulation. You take the thigh, and I'll take the lower end around the break."

As the rubbing proceeded, pain became the dominant sensation. Tania leaned back and took a deep breath.

"I think I prefer the leg numb," she said through clenched teeth.

Jim wiped Penny's and his hands with a leftover towel. Penny got to her feet and hurried to the front of the cabin. He turned off the flashlight.

"Jim, weren't you hurt?" Tania asked.

"A few bruises. My right elbow and shoulder where I was thrown around against the side and a bump on the back of my head." He started slowly down the aisle after Penny.

While she watched Jim trail Penny down the aisle, the pain in Tania's leg was joined with pain in her mind as she began to grieve for her lost friends, for the passengers she had served so briefly, and for the loss of the plane.

Danny! Oh God, what happened to him? Trying not to believe what her eyes told her, she remembered their last time together. A party. They had gone to a party together, danced, laughed, sung some stupid songs, then gone back to his apartment to make love the rest of the night. Love. Yes, they were in love. They both knew it, but they were in no hurry to get married.

He had been so different from other men who had come on to her. They had shared drinks at a hotel in New York after their first flight together, but there had been no intimacy or an attempt at intimacy on his part. They had enjoyed each other's company. He dated her back in Los Angeles, always fun, always a gentleman, always patient. They had gone to movies, to concerts, dancing, sailing, to parties, to the zoo to see baby leopards, to Olivera Street for a Mexican fiesta. She had many memories of pleasant times. After one particularly lovely evening, she had taken him back to her apartment. Lillian was out of town, and she had led him on into their first intimacy. He was a superb, gentle lover, giving her many ecstasies before satisfying his hunger for her. Now she was helpless, staring numbly at his funeral pyre. A wave of nausea swept through her, moisture dripped from her jaw.

* * *

Kneeling at the edge of the broken floor, Penny vomited into the snow. Jim waited patiently until she seemed finished. The panic with Tania over, Penny was now his chief concern. How badly injured was she? There was little he could do for internal injuries. He hoped she was only bruised. He knelt beside her, turned the flashlight on to examine her vomit and then turned it off quickly. He put an arm around her shoulders as she knelt, her head hanging down, breathing deeply.

"Good," he said quietly, "no blood...How old are you?"

She began crying, "E-eleven."

The wind screamed around them viciously, driving stinging snow pellets into their faces.

"Is your stomach settled now?" She nodded. "Then let's get back out of this wind," he said, helping her to her feet.

She stopped by her mother's body and knelt on the floor, crying. He knelt with her and held her close to him.

"Crying's okay," his voice so soft it was almost lost in the howl of the wind.

The fates had been cruel to her, he reflected. Yet, cruel or not, she would have to put these experiences behind her and carry on. He searched for some way to put it all into some kind of perspective. After some minutes, he stroked her hooded head with a hand.

"I think she's very proud of her daughter," he said.

Penny looked up quickly, "But she's dead."

"Yes, this body before us is dead...but *she,* your mother, isn't."

She wiped some tears from her eyes, "I don't understand."

"Her spirit. Her spirit is still very much alive. And is it ever proud of you." He shifted around a bit. "My knees are killing me. Could we sit back here while we talk?" She nodded, so he flopped back against the seat behind him and stretched his legs across the aisle. He held an arm out for her, and she settled back into its protective space.

"Let's talk about spirits a little. Some people who have been dead—that is, their hearts stopped and their breathing stopped—who have been revived have reported 'seeing' everything that was done to revive them, seeing as though a portion of them left their bodies and floated up where they could see what was going on. Some, who technically died on operating tables, have accurately described seeing emergency equipment being rushed down a hall to the operating room to be used to revive them. Others have described the actions of paramedics and their family members during the period they were not breathing and had no pulse. So, some evidence suggests something we might call a spirit of a person may exist which can see what we do, even though the person is dead. Do you follow me?"

Penny looked up at his face and blinked, "I—I think so."

He pulled her close with his arm, "Okay, if that is true, then your mother's spirit watched what went on back there a little bit ago, and right now she is probably saying to the other spirits of persons who died here this afternoon something like, 'That's my big girl! Did you see what she just did? Did you see her help those people?' And in my book, she has a perfect right to brag. You were super. So, wherever her spirit goes from here, it goes with pride, pride in the person she left behind." He looked into her upturned face and smiled.

"But you did the operation," she said.

"Oh no, honey, *we* did the operation; you, me, and Miss Tania. I couldn't have done a thing if you hadn't held the flashlight and held the wound open with your fingers, and I couldn't have done anything if she hadn't kept the bleeding controlled and held still. She put on a hell of a performance, too: not one scream or moan or complaint. And it had to hurt."

She blinked again. Something was missing. "You said Mom was alive."

"No, not quite. Her *spirit* is alive. That's what I meant to say."

"The spirit you just talked about?" She was confused.

"No, this is a little different. This spirit is the part which is in you."

She wriggled around in his arm to turn and face him. "In me?"

"Sure, in you."

"I don't see— Would you explain it to me, please?"

He smiled at her. "What is it that makes up this person we call Penny? Is it the pretty head of curls, the sturdy body, or what?" He took her head in both of his hands, "Your physical being is a minor part of what is YOU. YOU is inside this head I'm holding; it is your brain, or more specifically, it is how your brain is wired up, which is different from everybody else's." He released her head.

"Why aren't my arms and legs and...and body part of me?"

"Well, they are, really. But they don't determine what you think or how you behave. Your leg won't tell you to be nice to Miss Tania or to yell at me. Your brain does that. See?"

"I guess."

"I'm trying to talk about you, the sweet character, rather than you, the body of a pretty girl. Can you see the difference?"

She nodded, "But this is about me. I thought we were talking about my mom's spirit."

"We are. Just let me lay it out for you. Okay?"

"I'm sorry."

"No. You have to ask questions so it will be clear to you. Your brain has many billions of cells. Things you know or can do are represented by patterns of interconnections—"

"Interconnections?"

"Well, just connections. Okay?"

She nodded.

"Everything you learn is represented by new patterns of connections: A new word, a new athletic act, such as jumping on one leg, anything—"

"Like breathing and talking?"

"Exactly. The brain is pretty complicated and Man does not completely understand it yet, but it's fascinating to study." He smiled again, a soft smile, a smile she liked. "Back to your mother's spirit?"

Penny wriggled around to face him more directly and to get a little more comfortable. Her hand rubbed her abdomen gently. She nodded, "Yes, please."

"So, what do the interconnections presently in your brain represent? Just who is this girl? Well, I suspect her attendance in school has added many interconnection patterns. That's what school is for. But the most important ones are those she has absorbed from living with her father and mother, ones she is not even aware of because they have grown with her. To be sure, she has added some which are purely Penny." He hugged her lightly. "You should never try to copy anybody completely because nobody's perfect. But you see, these patterns you don't even realize are in you?—" She looked at him expectantly. "They are your mother's and father's spirits living on...in you!" His voice rose in excitement. "They are a large part of what is YOU! They're built into you, and they will be with you every day of your life."

She looked puzzled, "Could you, maybe, give me some examples?"

"I don't know if I can because I don't know you very well yet, but I'll try to help you look for their presence. What I'm trying to show you is, that you have already done something positive toward keeping your mother's spirit alive by the help you gave. If you loved her, then stand tall and let others help you. They will. You'll see."

She looked at him for several moments, sniffling. "Will you help me?"

"For as long as you'll let me...For starters, when you were home, you had a room of your own where you could go and close the door and shut out the world. Right?"

She nodded.

"You could climb onto your bed, put your face down in the pillow, wrap your arms around it and pull it close to you, and cry or think things through."

"Yes," she said, tears building.

"I suspect you might like to be able to do that here." She nodded again. "But there's no place for you to hide away in, is there?" She shook her head. "So I'm going to make a place."

Wide eyed, she stared at him. "How?"

He smiled back. "When you need a private place, you just come to me, pull my arm around your shoulders, and close it down tight, like you're shutting a door. Put your arms around my chest, and pull it close, and cry, or think, or rest. When you do that, I won't talk to you, nor will I let anyone else bother you; that is your private place. If you want me or anyone else to talk

40

to you, you'll have to open the door first. If I want to talk to you, I'll say 'knock knock,' but I'll have to wait for you to open the door. Okay?"

She looked a little bewildered.

"Okay, let's try it." He opened his arm holding her. "Take my hand and pull my arm around you."

She grasped his hand and pulled it around her shoulders.

"All the way to my chest," he prompted. "That's it. The door is closed. Now put your arms around my chest and pull it as close to you as you want."

She responded. He held her for several minutes without talking. At first, she thought he was joking with her, but as the minutes wore on, she realized he was serious. Comfortable with a warm, close feeling, she liked that she was protected, that she was not alone. It was all too much. She began to cry again. But as she cried, she remembered what he had said about her mother and about what she had to do. Alone and afraid, now she had a friend, a friend who seemed to be reading her mind and understanding her.

While he held Penny, Jim agonized about how Jackie would receive the news of the downed airplane. Would she panic completely, or could she pull herself together and carry on? Would she have some faith in him? It would test her mettle like it had never been tested before. He silently prayed for strength for her.

His thoughts were interrupted by Penny twisting to grasp his hand and pull it away from his chest.

"Well, what do you think? Can we make it work? I know there isn't much room, and the pillow is kind of hard and lumpy."

Smiling through tears still rolling down her cheeks, she reached up to pull his head down and gave him a quick kiss on the cheek. He smiled at her and patted the back of her head with his free hand. She rubbed the wetness on his jacket.

"I'm getting you all wet," she sniffled.

"That's all right...But tell me, was that *you* worrying about my jacket...or really your mom?"

She blinked at him in surprise, "Ah...Mom, I think."

"See?" he said brightly, then, soberly, "Would you like to say a prayer for her?"

"Yes."

They got up on their knees and bowed their heads. Penny looked at her mother for several moments, then said a brief prayer in Hebrew, haltingly as she tried to remember the words.

4.

Jackie carefully spread the man's shirt she had finished ironing on a hanger. As she smoothed the shoulders down, she imagined the shirt filled with her husband's shoulders, broad, strong. She smiled at her handiwork. *Her* husband would wear neatly pressed shirts and radiate executive appearance even though he was only a group head.

She turned on the TV and settled back into the corner of the couch. The news would be on as soon as the commercials ended. Andrea was happily playing on the carpeted floor with some of her dolls and a wooden wagon. Jackie expected to hear from Jim soon. Her method of coping with Jim traveling was to clean house compulsively. She had soiled her jeans crawling on the bathroom floors with a wet sponge, and dampened her tee shirt with sweat vigorously cleaning windows. And now she was catching up on ironing.

The newscaster smiled as the musical intro ended.

"Good afternoon ladies and gentlemen, this is the four-o-clock news. Interstate Airlines just announced their flight 238 from Los Angeles to Denver and Chicago experienced engine trouble over western Colorado. It changed course to try to get out of bad weather and hasn't been heard from since—"

She was suddenly tense. Try to remember, was that Jim's flight? Oh God! It had to be!

"...plane is presumed down somewhere in southwest Colorado. Local authorities hold little hope for any survivors because the severe blizzard which is expected to last two more days—"

43

Her eyes wide, she pulled her clenched fists tight to her mouth. "OH DEAR GOD! Oh dear God, *NO!...JIM!*" The news babbled on but she heard no more. She rocked back and forth on the edge of the couch, sobbing convulsively.

Andrea stopped her playing and came to her mother. "Mommy hurt?" the anxious little voice inquired.

Jackie looked dumbly at Andrea, tears blurring her vision. What had she said? "What is it, honey?"

"Mommy hurt?"

"Oh, no. It's much wor—" No! She couldn't tell Andrea. Oh, what to tell her? She wiped the tears from her face with the back of her hand. "Yes, Mommy's hurt." she said, unsuccessfully trying to control her voice.

"Where?"

Helplessly she took Andrea in her arms, unable to explain where or why Mommy hurt. She was trying to regain some form of composure when the phone rang. Putting Andrea down, she hurried to it. Maybe it was Jim. Maybe it wasn't his plane after all.

The receiver was in her hand on the third ring. "Hello?"

"This is Jackie...ah, Mrs. James Hoskins...Yes, I just saw the news...Did the plane land safely?"

The person didn't know; they had heard nothing further. Jackie slumped, her hopes fading.

"Then— But— Uh huh...But you don't *know* it crashed or that he's dead?...Yes, I see." She began to cry again. "...We h— have one little g—girl...Andrea...Sh—She's just four...Yes, that's right. You're—?"

Jackie picked up a pencil near the phone. "W—Would you spell that, please?...Of Interstate Airlines?" She snuffed as she wrote rapidly. "Uh huh. I h—have the n—number...Call you if I need any h—help?" she asked, incredulous. "I need my *HUSBAND!*" Letting the phone fall into the cradle, she slumped to the floor.

"Mommy? What's dead?"

44

* * *

Lillian stood watching the news telecast, the handle of her luggage cart forgotten in her hand. She was tall and angular. Her short, semi-curly blonde hair was swept back in a near masculine fashion. Yet she was attractive and feminine in her flight attendant's uniform, ready to hustle out to her flight. But now time stood still. She was in shock. She could remember nothing but what she had just heard on the television. The sound rattled on, the images changed, but in her numb state the TV might just as well have been off. Tania was gone! There was the sound of bells. Were they tolling her death so soon? Oh, God, the phone! She broke out of her trance, dropped the cart handle and answered on the fourth ring.

"Lillian Bromley." Her voice was very weak. She choked and coughed. "...I just saw it on TV...Tania was on that flight." The news stunned the other party. "She got a call early this morning to fill in for Pearl. I had to change her dental appointment...Danny, Frank, and Bill?...Oh shit! Who were the others?—" She winced at each name. "A mechanical hold for *ENGINES?*...Oh God!...Oh, Jesus! I've got a flight in an hour and a half. I don't know how the fuck I can do it...Look, Sybil, I've got to barf. 'Bye." She threw the receiver in the general direction of the cradle and ran, pale, to the bathroom.

* * *

There was a small crowd of men around her petite frame. They were studying a drawing one held and listening to her remarks. Lori Cranston was the lead engineer, a position she had earned, even in an aerospace company noted for its foot-dragging compliance with the Equal Opportunity Act. She was five-two, one hundred and twelve pounds, and a ball of drive and energy. She wore tight fitting clothes which accented her diminutive but firm body. The men who knew her kept a respectful distance; she was completely confident and competent and not interested in fooling around with the office staff.

"Lori, phone," the voice came from her office.

Taking the phone from her officemate's hand, "Thanks," she put the receiver to her ear, "This is Miss Cranston...Oh, hi, Jackie...*What?*" She paled as she listened, slowly sinking into her chair. Her hands began to tremble. "Oh God!" she murmured at last. "They— Uh huh...Look, Jackie, I can hardly understand you. I'll be right over. Traffic's a bitch right now, so give me a little time. Okay?...I—I love you. 'Bye." She fumbled with the phone, dropped it on the floor, retrieved it, and finally cradled it. Never had she felt so weak. She put her head down on her arms to cry.

"Lori, is something wrong?" the tall, curly, redhead asked solicitously.

She turned to her officemate, bawling. "A close fr–friend of mine was traveling today. Hi–his plane is overdue...T–Terry, could you cover f–for me? I might not be in t–tomorrow." She got up, took her raincoat from a hanger, picked up her purse, and started for the door. A bulky woman blocked her way.

"You can't leave yet, Lori, we have these EO's to get out before quitting time."

"T–Take your f–fuckin' EO's and sit on them...endwise!" She pushed past the person and ran, blurry eyed down the corridor.

"What's got her ticked off?" the woman asked Terry.

"I don't think I'd push it, Zari, a friend of hers may be dead."

"But, we have to meet the schedule."

"If Lori had died from food poisoning at lunch, what would you have done?"

"Well...I don't know." Zari was flustered.

"I'd suggest you find out and do it. Otherwise, I think she gave you a fine suggestion."

"The shop needs these Engineering Orders," the woman insisted.

"When it comes to your death, I'll personally see that all the damned EO's get signed before anyone can go to your funeral.

And if you don't get out of here, that day might be a lot sooner than you think." He pushed her aside to find their department head. How could the woman be so insensitive?

Lori boosted herself three feet up into the cab of the off-road four-wheel-drive pickup. While the engine warmed, she tried to dry her eyes enough to drive. The all-news station completed the rundown of the freeway tie-ups which lasted almost three minutes; rain always brings on a rash of accidents on Los Angeles' freeways. The station repeated the news item concerning the plane. There were ninety-eight persons missing, presumed dead. She slumped briefly at the wheel. Then, remembering Jackie, she slipped the transmission into reverse and engaged the clutch to back out.

She loved Jim, loved him more than anyone she had ever known. Through her own silly stupidity, she failed to take the opportunity to marry him when he had asked her. Find herself! What a stupid— Braking behind a car, she failed to find a satisfactory word. She also loved Jackie, and she adored Andrea. They needed her strength now. But just where was all this strength when *she* needed it?...Like now.

Lady, are you going to sit there all day trying to figure out which way to turn? Lori blew her highway horn. *That ought to get her ass moving.* It did. The car in front leapt into action. Amused and satisfied she laughed while turning and heading toward Jim's house.

Oh, why the hell couldn't she have been civil to Zari? The woman was just trying to do her job. She would try to remember to apologize.

She tuned in her favorite Country Western station; the news was too depressing. If she had to creep in traffic, she might as well do it to a beat.

Almost seven years since they graduated, and she and Jim were still competing. They worked in different companies, but both were excelling in their field, both were making about the same money, and she had just received a nice promotion to bring her about even with him again. But he was better known nationally due to his recent creativity, the articles he'd written, and the honors he'd received. She didn't envy him; she respected him. She always had.

And she respected his marriage. She had blown her chance at him and couldn't fault him for moving on to find someone else. Maybe Jackie wasn't her idea of the kind of woman he should have married, but it was his decision, his life, and not hers. Okay, having made friends with Jackie, she could drop in and see him anytime. She and Jackie had become quite close. The relationship between all three was based on mutual trust, something Jim held sacred, something Lori admired and honored. But Lori doubted she would ever again find the satisfaction she had in bed with Jim. Lucky Jackie...Except now.

* * *

There was an air of panic in the Interstate Airlines parts warehouse along the south side of Los Angeles International Airport. Men were rushing about, pulling certain boxes from shelves and carrying them to a pair of vans.

"Get all these goddamn phonies out of here before the NTSB starts poking around here," a man, plainly a supervisor, yelled, waving his arm at the shelves. "I hope the plane's log burned, 'cause our ass is going to be in one big goddamn sling if it didn't." He walked over to another man, "Harry, do we have any legit parts on the shelves we can say we been using?"

"Yeah, Mel, we're fairly well covered...But not on those engine controllers."

"Shit! Not even one?"

Harry shook his head.

"Get on the phone and see if we can't get a couple from one of the other bases on a flight tonight," Mel said.

"That'll fool them inspectors maybe ten minutes. We won't have the receiving paper to cover them, an' then they'll track 'em to the other places an' know a cover-up is goin' on."

Mel stood, looking at Harry for two minutes, then turned and walked back into his office with glass windows overlooking the warehouse area. He picked up his phone and tapped out several digits. "Hello, Stu. Mel. We had a bird go down somewhere in Colorado...You heard, huh?...Yeah, well we been taking care of you pretty good, so like now we need you to cover for us with your FAA buddies...Whadayou mean, you can't help?...Crap! Is that right?...From Washington?" He clapped his free hand to his forehead.

"...Well, yeah, we're sanitizin' the place, but that ain't goin' to cover the paper trail...Hey, it wasn't my idea! Them high an' mighty goons in Dallas was the ones that said use 'em...Yeah, like as not they're covered an' it's yours an' my butts hangin' out all lily-white an' shiny for the Feds to kick...Oh, sorry, I forgot, yours ain't white...Well, I ain't goin' to go quiet like. I'm gonna take a few others with me, you can bet on that...Oh, yeah?...Well ain't that sweet." He laughed dryly. "Gonna have some company from some other airlines, too...Why am *I* laughin'? It ain't gonna help *my* butt...You're goin' fishin'...in Uganda? Big help you are...'Bye." He slammed the phone down and looked helplessly around. Tomorrow morning the FAA and NTSB would be crawling all over this place asking questions he couldn't answer. What a way to start the week!

5.

The blizzard continued to rage around the plane. Tania could feel the cabin moving as the wind buffeted it. The inky blackness of night was becoming dark gray. She could make out the snow-covered remains of the forward section of the aircraft. The floor near the broken edge was over a foot deep in snow. The tops of the front rows of seats had at least six inches. She was chilled, her nose and face were cold, her injured leg was cold, but pain and ache overwhelmed cold. Her head was still throbbing; a concussion was Jim's opinion. He was asleep on her left shoulder. Penny slept under the protection of her right arm. Every blanket Jim could find covered the three of them. There was a time yesterday when she had not expected to see this dawn. Gray and nasty as it was, she rejoiced.

"Thank you," she whispered, looking upward.

During the night when she hadn't been able to sleep, she had again mourned the loss of Danny and the others. Why she had been selected to survive she could not fathom. Frank and Bill had families. So had Sharon. How were those families going to carry on?

Perry and Cherise. She remembered the first flight for each, new, fresh out of flight attendant school, eager, green, and herself putting the finishing touches on each. Her heart ached to experience the gaiety of those flights again, of laughing over the silly mistakes the girls had made. Cherise was her pet. Of all the girls she had worked with, Cherise had been the brightest, most cheerful person she had known.

What was the cause of the accident? Had Danny neglected his duties? No, he was much too careful. Maybe the ground crew had neglected something. Why had the engines quit? She had no answers, only questions. Although crowded by her companions, she felt alone.

Lillian. Did she know yet? Would she go on a binge when she found out? Tania hoped not. She hoped she had put enough backbone, enough self-esteem into her that she might be able to cope with this.

She prayed again. Prayed for support of the families, prayed for strength for Lillian, a place in heaven for Perry and Cherise, for Danny, and finally, prayed for a speedy search for the plane. Thanking her maker for the skills of this man next to her, she asked help for the girl on the other side. She rallied herself to face this day so she might be given yet another.

Who was this man named Jim? There was no question she liked him. The change in Penny's outlook when they had returned to her was so startling, she couldn't believe it was the same girl. Oh, she still hurt, but she seemed no longer afraid, no longer rebellious. The man could work miracles. And why wasn't he hurt more than a few bruises? He certainly must know something more than she did. Confidence, competence, concern, affection, all seemed to describe him. Solid.

Tania looked at Jim as he stirred around, his muscles as cramped as hers. He twisted against the hard floor and bulkhead, pawed briefly at her chest as he attempted to turn, then woke, embarrassed.

"I'm sorry," he whispered. "I didn't mean—"

"Don't sweat it," she cut him off quickly.

"How are you?"

"My leg's cold and aching. My head still aches. I didn't get much sleep."

"There's not much I can do for the pain."

"I'm not complaining. Christ, I'll never be able to thank you for what you have done."

He pulled a hand from under the blankets to rub his eyes. "How's Penny?"

"Asleep. She was awake a couple of times. She's hurting."

"I hope it's only bruises. I can't do much for internal injuries or bleeding."

"I've been doing a lot of thanking and praying all night."

"I hope it works. We need all the help we can get." He turned to face down the aisle. "Will you look at all that snow!"

"Yeah," she said dryly, "I've been watching that, too."

"We have to get out of here today."

Tania was amazed, "How can we do that?"

He shrugged, "I don't know at the moment. Are you cold?"

"Yes, but I've been colder."

"These blankets weren't made for winter nights, only to keep patrons toasty warm in a sixty-eight degree cabin. I think I'll make something warm for us." He uncovered and rolled away from her to his knees.

Standing, he put on his overcoat over the down jacket and pulled some gloves out of a pocket. At his pack he began pulling various items out. There was a pot, a zip bag full of instant cocoa and cereal envelopes, a small stove and a kit of tools for the stove, and an aluminum bottle of fuel. Penny groaned as he was gathering up his materials. Jim put everything down and went to her side.

"Hi, how are you this morning?"

She opened her eyes to look at him. "My stomach hurts. My feet are cold," a small voice informed him.

"Welcome to the club," Tania put in brightly, "so are mine, and, if he'll admit it, so are Jim's."

He smiled at her and placed a reassuring hand on her shoulder, "Still hanging tough?" She nodded. "Good. I'm going to make some hot breakfast."

Penny started to uncover herself.

Tania glanced quickly at her, "Stay here and stay warm."

Penny looked embarrassed, "I've got to go."

Jim restrained her with his hand. "The toilet seat is very cold, so put a couple of paper towels between you and it or you'll freeze to it and hurt yourself. I want you to examine whatever you do. Let me know if you see anything that looks different...And take it easy on the toilet paper; that's all we've got. Okay?" He released her shoulder. When she stood, he hugged her.

As he started to pick up his materials again, Tania chuckled, "I've been thinking..."

52

"Oh?" He turned toward her, "What about?"

"Do you know what I think would be real nice about now?"

He shook his head.

"A nice big, woolly Saint Bernard with a keg of brandy."

"Saint Bernards don't carry kegs of anything. They just find people and snuggle up to them and lick their faces to keep them warm."

"Okay, I'm easy. I'll take one without the keg."

"Oh, I thought you wanted the keg."

"No, I want the five monks who were following the dog to take us to the shelter of their monastery."

He grinned, "Smart lady!" and left, going down the aisle to the galley.

Jim pumped his stove to pressurize it and then propped it level on the sloping counter of the galley. Wrapping some heavy aluminum foil taken from his pack almost around the stove to protect it from the wind, he lit the stove. While it was warming, he went to the edge of the cabin and filled his pot with snow and placed it on the stove. He closed the aluminum foil around the pot. With the snow melting, he pushed two of the service carts out of his way, pulled open drawers, poked into cabinets, and pulled the lower cup-boards open to find unused dinners, frozen soft drinks, and miniature bottles of liquor. From the unused dinners he took several plastic cups and three sets of stainless ware. Checking the pot, he added more snow to refill it. Penny came to the entrance of the galley.

"Mr. Jim?" she asked anxiously.

He turned and smiled at her. "Just Jim, honey. Something wrong?"

"Is it bad?...Is blood real bad?"

Concerned, he squatted to her eye level. "Blood? Where?"

"In...in my pee."

"Damn!...None in your stool?"

"I didn't go that way."

He took a deep breath. "Be sure to look when you do. Did it hurt to go?"

"Kind of...Will I live?" She searched his face for reassurance.

He reached out and drew her close to him, holding her by both shoulders. "I certainly hope so. Bleeding is not a good sign. It means you were hurt inside where I can't do anything for you. I want you to take it very easy for the next several days to allow things to heal. We'll give you lots of liquids to keep you flushed out. You and I are going to believe you will heal up fine. Okay?" he said, trying to sound cheerful to cover the anxiety inside. He stood to check his pot.

Penny grabbed him about his waist, "I like you, Jim."

Jim stooped to hug her, "That's the nicest thing anyone has said to me today. I like you, too." He hoped he wouldn't have to watch her die.

Picking up the tray on which he had placed the stainless ware and cups, he turned to Penny. "Do you suppose you could take this up to Miss Tania?" After handing her the tray, he tightly gripped the counter edge with both hands. *Great! It wasn't bruises. Now what do I do? They're counting on me; I mustn't show my uncertainty. Steady, Jim, don't panic. Keep it up beat.* He forced himself to release his grip and straighten up. Taking a deep breath, he turned off the stove, took the handle of the pot, and followed Penny up the aisle. *Gotta break the tension.* Grinning at Tania, he waited for Penny to put the tray down and get covered up again.

"On the first morning of our honeymoon, I thought you might like breakfast in bed."

"You nut! What's for breakfast?"

"Dark brown gook and light brown gook." *The Scouts call it babyshit,* he mused to himself.

Penny giggled. Tania attempted an exaggerated proper air.

"Sounds appetizing."

"Oui, zee very finest in haut cuisine, instant cocoa and instant oatmeal, cooked to perfection at your table," he announced in a lofty French accent.

He tore open an envelope, emptied it into a cup, and poured the steaming water to fill the cup. Bowing low, he handed her the cup and a set of stainless ware.

"Mademoiselle," he intoned gravely. "Compliments of Chef Swiss Miss."

"Merci, " she nodded in reply. She took a sip. "Mmmm."

After he had handed out Penny's portions and filled his cup, he got down on his hands and knees in front of Tania and started panting like a dog.

"What in the world—?"

"Woof!" he replied and handed her an airline miniature of Courvoisier.

She laughed and patted his head, "Nice doggy. Now, where're the monks?"

"I ditched them five miles back," he panted.

She held up the miniature, "I don't think I should with this headache."

His expression turned serious, "You're probably right. Keep it and use it when you're better."

"It's the thought that counts. Thank you." She smiled.

They ate rapidly before the frigid air could cool the food. Finishing first, Tania put her arm around Penny's shoulders and pulled her close. It was instinct with her; she had always been sympathetic to persons who had suffered losses.

"Let's stay close and keep each other warm." She hugged Penny briefly.

While Penny looked into her cup to get the last spoonful of cereal, Jim nudged Tania and silently mouthed, "Orphan." Tania closed her eyes. Though incapacitated, she would find some way to help the girl through her crisis. Her arm tightened around Penny a little. Awash with grief, she had to get her mind off of death.

"What's next?" she asked Jim.

"I don't know." He'd been thinking about their plight, too. "We have to get out of here; it's too cold."

"How can we with this?" She glanced at her leg. "We should stay with the plane; they'll be looking for the plane."

"If we do," he replied coolly, "we'll be just as stiff as the others when they find us. We have to leave."

"We should stay," her voice began to rise. "In flight school they taught us to stay with the plane."

"Did they just happen to discuss the relative merits of staying alive versus being found? In my book, staying alive comes first, being found dead doesn't cut it."

"Why would they tell us—"

"Hold it!" he interrupted. Getting to his knees, he crawled to his pack and held out a tag on one of the pack's zipper pulls. "This is a thermometer. It reads three above zero. When the clouds leave, it'll drop to twenty-three below zero. Did any of your instructors have to contend with that?" He was displaying more hostility than he intended. *Way to go, dummy. That sure eased the tension.*

Tania took a deep breath, softened her voice, and stared right back into his eyes. "Okay, Doctor Quack, how the hell are you going to get me out of here?"

"I'm sorry. I don't know; I'll think of something."

He squatted in front of Penny, "I know this might be a sensitive question; do you have someone who will care for you when we get out of here?"

She looked at him, eyes beginning to water, "We...we were going to-to Chicago to my grandparent's place. I—I know their names, but I don't know th—their address." She was crying again.

He put his hand on her shoulder. "That's all right," he soothed.

"We were going t—to take care of them b—because they were real weak. Now who's g—going to t—take care of me?" Penny bawled.

Jim continued to hold her shoulder, "Do you remember what I said last night? Hang in there. I'm your friend. I will see you are well cared for." He patted her shoulder, "Now, would you mind if we looked through your mother's purse for a letter or something?"

Penny shook her head as Tania pulled her close. He stood and went down the aisle to retrieve Maude's purse. Returning, he handed it to Penny.

"Why don't you look through it? That's better than having some stranger snooping in it."

She wiped her eyes with her hands and started looking into the things, crammed into the purse.

"She won't need these anymore." She held up a prescription drug bottle.

Jim was interested. "What are they? Does it say?"

Penny turned the bottle around to read the label, "Tetra...ah," she began to spell, "t-e-t-r-a-c-y-c-l-i-n-e."

"Oh yeah?!" Jim exclaimed, excited. "Great! Put those in your bag. What did she use them for?"

"After Dad was killed she got this real bad intestinal infection. Yesterday, she went and got all her per...*prescriptions* refilled."

Yesss! Break number one. "Okay! What else is in there?"

She looked some more, pulling out another bottle, "Oh, just her headache medicine." She handed the bottle to Jim as she continued to look for a letter from her grandparents.

He read the label. "Hey, you're mining gold!" He handed the bottle to Tania. *Break number two! We're on a roll!*

"Tylenol and codeine," Tania enunciated, "For my headache and the pain in my leg?"

"Right on," his mood was climbing rapidly.

"What do we need the tetracycline for?" Tania asked.

"This morning she told me she was bleeding. She's been injured by the seat belt. I couldn't do anything about it until now. The medication was used to fight intestinal infection, which is exactly what I've been concerned about. Now, if she isn't bleeding too badly, and I don't think she is, we can fight back." He swung his fist in a big arc and lightly tapped Penny's cheek, "Now, you *are* going to get well. I'll get some more water thawed." He went down the aisle swinging the pot, humming, while picking his way over debris.

Tania turned to Penny, "For better or worse, he's all we've got. We're lucky so far. I hope he can get us out of this."

Penny smiled, "He's neat!" Moments later she scanned a letter from the purse. "Here, this is from my grandparents." She handed the letter to Tania.

"Eric Jacobs," Tania read, "and here's the return address on the envelope. Okay! What's your grandmother's name?"

"Miriam."

"That's pretty. I like your name, too. Put this in your handbag...Is there a comb in your mother's purse you and I might be able to use?...Maybe something for our lips, too?"

Jim returned with the water, and Penny and Tania swallowed their medications. A sudden glare of light streamed through the aircraft windows.

"Hello Sun!" Jim enthused. "I think I'll have a look around." From his pack he withdrew a compass. He was quite relieved. Badly needed medication had surfaced, and now he could look the situation over. Stopping by his seat, he opened his briefcase, and removed a small pad of paper and a pencil, jamming them into his overcoat pocket. He put on a pair of sunglasses, and went to the edge of the floor. Stepping out, he promptly sank almost two feet into the new snow.

"Whooooa!"

*   *   *

Lori carefully rolled away from Jackie and dropped to her knees next to the bed. She glanced at the clock above the pillow on the headboard. "Shit," she muttered and hurried to the phone in the living room. She punched a few buttons and waited for the ring.

"Extension 6943, please." She tapped her fingers nervously. "Terry?...Hey, look, this is Lori. I'm at this friend's house with his wife. I'm in no shape to come in today, so put me in for sick leave...Thanks...Yeah, *that* plane...We still don't know." She twisted around and back, stretching while she listened.

"Look, tell Dan to get the actuator drawing out today. Pull Zari aside and tell her I'm sorry for the way I talked to her yesterday. Paul should look at her EO's before they go out." She listened while her officemate talked.

"Terry, this was the only guy I've ever really loved; it socked me right in my appetite. I hope I'll be in tomorrow. His wife and I have been taking turns crying on each other's shoulder...We're good friends; we slept together last night...No, it's nothing like that! We're more like sisters. We each needed someone to hang on to last night, that's all...Look, it's a long story. Get me drunk enough at some lunch, and maybe I'll tell you about it...Yeah, I know; I don't drink, but maybe I will now...Okay, thanks. 'Bye." She put the phone gently back into its cradle.

It was still raining outside. She looked for her umbrella, opened the door, put the umbrella up, and ran barefooted in her panties and bra to snatch up the plastic wrapped newspaper from the driveway. Running back across the lawn to the front door, she stepped in, folded the umbrella, and closed the door. Anxiously she scanned the article on the missing plane. Learning no more than she already knew, she threw the paper down on the table.

"Shit!" She turned on the TV at a very low volume and watched the morning news reports. Her irritation increased as other items were covered before the plane. There was no change in the information available, except the airline had admitted the flight had been late taking off because of problems with the engine systems. She hung her head in her hands, shaking. "Oh God!"

"Hi, Aunt Lori," Andrea's bright, happy voice cut into her mood. "You and Mommy all well?"

Pulling the child to her, it pained her to know that sooner or later she and Jackie would have to find some way to tell her that her father was never coming home. She was her godmother, and she loved Andrea as much as Jackie or Jim did.

* * *

Tania and Penny watched Jim climb back into the cabin. He stomped some snow off his pants and boots and came up the aisle. After retrieving a calculator from his briefcase, he rejoined them.

"Well, where are we?" Tania asked.

"I don't know where in the United States we are, but we're near the top of some mountain. Peak's over that way," he pointed diagonally through the lavatory. "We're on a ridge, pretty high up, if my shortness of breath and the lack of trees mean anything." He shivered. "It's cold out there. That wind is more than I ever experienced when I was growing up in the Middle West."

"Could you see anything? How about the front section of the plane? Could someone...?" She paused.

He shook his head slowly. "It's less than half its original length. The snow's covered everything up. We're going to be hard to see from the air. This section is wearing almost two feet of snow on top."

"Could you see anything else? Is the storm over? Are there towns near-by?"

"I couldn't see any signs of towns or roads. The ridge we're on slopes gently down for quite a way. It's really barren—mounds of snow with rocks underneath. There is a lake to the north of us with trees around it. I took some bearings on it and some of the other terrain features. I hope I can calculate the distance to the lake." Referring to his notes, he started punching buttons on his calculator.

"The weather?"

"We have a few hours of clear weather, but more snow is on the way. I can see the line of clouds off to the north and west. If we're going to make a move, it has to be now." He continued calculating.

Tania's annoyance with him returned. "Other than cold, why should we leave?"

He looked up from the calculator. "Trees. We get shelter, which we have here, but we get wood so I can make a fire. With fire I can cook better than with my little stove, and we can signal search planes. Wildlife. With my rifle, I can hunt and provide more food; our supplies here are limited. Lake. I have a collapsible fishing pole so I can fish for food. And, it's two to four degrees warmer for each thousand feet in altitude we lose. The wind should be less down in the canyon than it is here. We have at least two more days before they can search for us, and maybe more before they might find us." He returned to his calculating.

"You still haven't said how you're going to get me out of here."

"I'm still working on it," he muttered while punching buttons.

He'll probably come up with some harebrained scheme he'll want me to buy into— But the other schemes had saved her life!

He finished the calculation and looked at the result. "Lake's anywhere from five to ten miles."

He looked at Penny. "I don't like asking you to move around much, but do you think you could help me strip this plane of anything we can use?"

"I think so."

"Okay. We're looking for anything edible—chewing gum, cookies, candy, fruit. We're looking for scarves for everyone, toilet paper, paper towels, newspaper, cigarette lighters, matches, lighter fluid. I'll get a bunch of seat cushions, and clean out the galley. If you find any sunglasses, you and Tania could use them to protect your eyes from the glare and the wind. I'll hand things down from the compartments, you sort through them."

Penny uncovered and went into the lavatory. Tania looked up at him.

"What is it you're not saying?"

He grimaced. He had hoped she wouldn't get too inquisitive. "Okay," he sighed, "it's going to be kind of hairy getting down."

She bit her lip tentatively. A frown crossed her face.

6.

"Tania," Jim said as he carried her down the aisle, "do not look at the other flight attendant; it's not something you want to remember." She looked up at him. He stopped. "I'm serious. Just close your eyes and remember her as she was before the flight: cute, pert, bright, full of life."

"You noticed her?"

"I noticed her. I looked her over pretty good."

"Her name was Cherise."

"I didn't know her name. I think I'd like to have known her."

"I trained her. She was so special to me."

He shook his head. "Such a waste. So many good people died. The ones back here didn't have to, but good or bad, they're gone."

"What do you mean; they didn't have to?" Tania bristled. This man seemed to be suggesting she or Cherise had done something wrong.

"Ask me some other time. I'll tell you why they didn't have to die. It wasn't your fault, so don't get upset. Okay, close 'em up." He moved on when he saw her eyes closed. He would never forget Cherise's bashed-in face and head. She had struck a rock when she was thrown from the broken plane.

He placed Tania onto the makeshift toboggan crudely fashioned from a closet door. It was already covered with numerous seat cushions laid neatly over his ground cloth. When asked, Penny climbed on top and sat between Tania's legs. With her settled, he piled food, towels, blankets, and other salvage from the plane on top and then pulled the ground cloth up and around the two passengers. Nylon parachute cord he had carried in his pack secured the ground cloth and the load to the door. Tania looked around while he went back to the plane to put his pack on. She could see other white peaks in the distance in all directions.

"I don't like having the rifle against my leg. What if it goes off?" Tania said.

"It can't. It's unloaded, disassembled, and the bolt is in my pack."

Tania pulled the scarf up over her nose and put on the plastic sunglasses they had found in a purse. Penny had already protected her face. The hood on her jacket was pulled up tight and tied.

"I see what you mean about this wind," Tania gasped.

Jim picked up the handle made of wire rope control cable and started to tow the toboggan around the wreckage of the forward sections of the plane.

One wing stood up at a crazy angle, supported by a huge rock. The engine had been ripped off and lay many yards away, badly smashed and partially covered with snow. The other wing had been ripped completely from the plane and lay almost even with the aft section in which they had survived. The center section had much of its skin missing and the framework stood above the snow like a charred skeleton. The interior was mercifully covered with snow. The forward section including the cockpit had collapsed to less than half its length, as if someone had stepped on a giant beer can.

Tania looked at what little was exposed from under the covering of snow and said a quiet prayer for Danny. She wept under the glasses and scarf for the others.

"I just want to be on record as not being in favor of leaving the plane," she shouted against the wind. "But I'm glad you at least left some notes telling the search parties where we're going. I don't feel right about this at all."

"I don't like the way the cabin is moving about in the wind. Mush, you Huskies!"

He was dressed in all the clothes he could put on. Outside he was wearing his yellow Goretex-lined rain suit to keep him dry and to break the wind. He had given Tania his gloves, and he was wearing some heavy mittens from his pack. His pack was lighter from the clothes he was wearing, but they had been replaced with salvage from the plane.

The terrain was barren white with large boulders exposed. The going was slow because the footing under the snow was rough and uncertain. Jim stopped to rest frequently. During one of the stops Jim pointed out the lake. He also showed her how far down timberline was. Tania asked him how high he thought they were.

"I guess about thirteen thousand feet. Timberline is generally somewhere between ten and eleven thousand feet."

"How about the peak?" It glistened with sunlit snow.

"Mmmm, maybe another thousand feet."

"And the lake?" She could see it partially covered with ice.

"Maybe nine thousand. Maybe eight."

When she looked to the west, she could see the advancing storm. Jim hurried along as best he could; he didn't want to get caught in a white-out while they were sliding down the ridge.

About a mile from the plane they came to the end of the gentle down-slope. Jim took off his pack, untied a seat cushion he had secured to the back of the pack, and strapped it to his rear with luggage straps he carried in the pack. He shouldered the pack again. Meanwhile Tania was surveying the downhill ahead of them. It was steep.

"Well...ah...it's all downhill from here," he panted.

"Are you sure we should try this?" she asked with fear evident in her voice.

"Toboggan rides are supposed to be exciting," Jim said. She could detect an edge of uncertainty in his voice.

Calling up all his courage, he pushed the toboggan to the edge and took a deep breath. *Oh God, is this going to be hairy! Don't let them see your fear.*

"The USA Olympic bobsled team is poised for their run. They need a good time to beat the Russians. There they go!"

He pushed the toboggan over the edge and sat on the cushion behind the sled. "Wheeeeee!"...*Holy shit, is this fast! Hang on.*

Tania's heart almost stopped as they raced down the slope. Suddenly Jim started digging in his heels...*What the— A cliff!!*

"Whoa!" he shouted in panic, "Whoa damnit!" He dug deeper with his heels and strained against the tow cable, leaning back as far as he could. Snow flew in all directions from his feet and pack. They halted mere feet from the edge of a precipice.

"Holy mack'rel!" he exclaimed peering over the edge. Tania was frozen with fear. He quickly scrambled to his feet and started to pull the toboggan up away from the edge. A piece of the cornice of snow dropped silently away.

"Oh dear GOD!" Tania uttered in terror.

He pulled the toboggan up and over to one side of the cliff. Slowly, pausing every few steps for breath, he dragged them up the side of a low ridge bordering the cliff and finally stood on the top. The lake was easily visible in the distance. The other side of the ridge presented a shallower slope inviting another slide. He wanted to use as much as gravity would do for them; hauling the toboggan was hard work.

"Try to be more careful this time," Tania said as he prepared to start the slide again.

"Yes, ma'am!" he replied with feeling.

They were off again, but this time Jim controlled the descent with his heels. They approached trees, and he steered between them. Tania was still terrified, but Penny, with Jim's improved control, was beginning to perk up. Trees flashed by, getting larger as they lost altitude. The toboggan finally halted a few feet from a large rock.

"All right!" Penny cheered.

"Hey, that was so much fun," he said, happy to have covered so much downhill, "I think we should go back up and do it all over again." *Yeah, right!* he thought. *Not in this lifetime!* "...I wonder how much lift tickets are."

Tania took the first deep breath since they had started. "Are you crazy? It'll be weeks before I stop shaking."

Penny laughed.

"Second floor," he announced. "Ladies lingerie and toddler's and infant's clothing. Watch your step, please. Step aside and let the ladies out, please."

Tania stared at him, "I think your bell is cracked!"

An ominous rumble from above erased the levity. Jim grabbed up the tow cable and started running with the toboggan toward the shelter of a large rock outcrop. When they were all safely behind the rock, he dropped to his knees, exhausted. The avalanche tore down the hill behind them and around the rock. Two rocks, bigger in diameter than Jim's height bounced off the rock outcrop and sailed just overhead, crashing into trees just beyond them and taking them out with a loud snap. Instinctively Tania ducked, but the rocks were long gone. Other rocks sailed by. The ground shook under the toboggan, and Tania could hear nothing above the horrific noise. The trees they had been among were no longer there. Small stones and debris pelted them while they covered their bowed heads with their arms. Grit and dirt and snow were everywhere. Although covered, they were not buried. The tumbling of rocks and snow stopped as suddenly as it had started. Jim brushed the debris from Tania's face, then Penny's.

"Are you all right?" he panted.

"I—I think so," Tania replied, "Penny?"

Penny shook her head vigorously to remove more grit and snow. A frightened tiny voice came from under the scarf, "I don't know."

"I don't blame you," Tania replied.

Jim purposefully got to his feet. He removed his pack and the seat cushion and stepped out from behind the rock. Tania could see him shaking with fear. He faced uphill, raised his fist in defiance and began yelling.

"If we're supposed to die, why didn't we die with the rest of the plane?" His voice echoed around them. "Why do we have to go through this special kind of hell?...We need HELP...not some damn shower of rocks!"

"I think he's lost it," Tania said quietly to Penny.

"You mean freaked out?"

"I guess. Everyone's got his own breaking point. Try to back me; we've got to get him on track again."

"Ease off, damnit!" Jim shouted uphill, "We're doing the best we can!"

A smaller avalanche drove him back to cover. He cowered on his hands and knees while the rocks tumbled by. Light snow flurries started falling again.

"All right," he muttered in awe and defeat, "I'll shut up."

Tania reached from the toboggan to grab his wrist. "Jim, we're still alive. What's so terrible?"

He rolled from his knees to a sitting position facing her.

"Five minutes ago we had smooth snow and downhill. Now," he paused and shook his head, "now we have a boulder field on both sides of us, and the visibility is going to hell. I—I've forgotten what direction I last saw the lake. How am I going to get this rig up over all that sharp rock?"

"There's a lot of day left," she soothed.

"It's going to take a long time to get the next hundred yards. What if those were not the last of the avalanches?"

She sighed, "Okay, okay. Let's take a rest. You calm down and think things over. I'm sure you'll find a way."

She searched his eyes for some sign of the return of his confidence. He put his head down on his arms crossed on his knees.

Tania wriggled around, "Could you untie us so I could have Penny's weight off me while you rest?"

Deep in his thoughts, he moved to the toboggan, removed his mittens, and began to struggle with the frozen knots. Unwrapping them, he piled the goods from Penny's lap onto the opened ground cloth and helped Penny to stand and step out. Penny tried to stretch, but was limited by her sore abdomen. Tania wriggled around to make herself more comfortable.

"Do you suppose you could lift me off these cushions for a few minutes?"

He knelt beside her and lifted her up, standing her on her one good leg on the toboggan. He kept an arm around her waist to steady her. She stretched muscles she hadn't used for almost a day.

"Could you carry me across the boulder field?"

He surveyed the terrain. "I don't know. It would be pretty risky."

Tania's eyes flew open, "Like what we've done so far wasn't risky? Good God! Wouldn't it be easier than dragging that whole thing?"

He looked reflectively at the rocks, "Without my pack it wouldn't be too hard, I guess."

"Take your pack across and check it out."

Penny tugged at his hand. "I could drag the toboggan."

"We'll take it across together." He smiled at her.

He bent, still supporting Tania, grabbed at the seat cushion he had used, and pitched it to the base of the rock outcrop, then picked her up and carried her to the cushion.

"Want to stand or sit?"

"I'll stand, thank you."

He set her on her good leg. Leaning against the rock for support, she was grateful she had Maude's rain cape to protect the fur coat. Tania rejoiced as Jim and Penny set about crossing the rock debris with his pack. They returned, testing different rocks as they went, then struggled to carry the toboggan across the rocks. Going was slow and footing was treacherous, but Jim seemed to be in command of himself.

The snow was falling quite heavily when he returned for her. Penny went in front, testing footing; Tania rode his back across the rock slide. He placed her on the toboggan and loaded up the goods on top of her. Against his better judgment, Penny wanted to walk for a while. After a brief rest, they were off downhill again.

Some time later, he stopped. He walked around behind and some distance up their trail. Taking out his compass, he sighted along their trail, and pocketed the compass again.

"I think we're still on track from what I remember before the avalanche."

"What's that sound I hear? It sounds like water gurgling," Tania asked.

"Yeah," Jim replied, looking around, excitement building. He walked down a slight incline, then poked with his foot. The snow fell away into a small stream which was otherwise covered. "Yeah," he breathed. "We'll just follow this to the lake."

"Aren't you tired?" Tania asked.

"Yes." Every muscle in his legs ached.

"How about stopping here?"

"We need some place more sheltered from the wind. I wish I could see better. Penny, I think you've walked enough."

Although she was tired and she hurt, she was adamant, "No."

"Look, honey. I'm worried about your injuries. This exercise is not what you need."

"No, I want to walk."

He stared at her for several moments. The toboggan was easier to pull without her, and the altitude was taking its toll, but he was uneasy about letting her walk on. He picked up the tow cable and began trudging along again.

Half an hour later, the lake became visible through the murk of the storm.

"Hallelujah!" Tania shouted.

"Way to go!" Penny added. Carried away in her enthusiasm, she tried to jump. Pain doubled her up. Jim and Tania exchanged worried glances.

He towed the toboggan under a large tree, took his pack off, and put the seat cushion down next to the toboggan.

"You sit on this," he commanded Penny.

Without argument, she sat. He covered her with a blanket from the toboggan.

Looking around, Tania saw a beautiful grouping of icicles in an opening in the snow cover over the stream. The beauty of it struck her as odd in the midst of the howling storm, but she wished she had a camera to record this little jewel of nature. The clarity of the water gurgling over rocks enticed her. "Jim, could you get me a drink from the stream, please?"

Taking a cup from his pack, Jim went to the stream to fill it. Chilling her teeth, the water was more refreshing than Tania had imagined. Her thirst required another cup, reminding Penny she too was thirsty, and Jim, after filling the cup several more times finally had to take his fill as well.

"That is absolutely the best water I have ever tasted," Tania smiled.

Jim grinned. "I'll look for a suitable camp site," he said, turning to leave.

"What's the matter with here?" Tania was tired of traveling.

"We can't stay under big limbs for long. If they break from an overload of snow, they'll kill us. I'll look for a tight grove of new growth where we'll get protection from the wind and snow and not so much danger."

"Still a Boy Scout?"

"Guilty, " he acknowledged as he left them, heading for the lake.

When he was gone, Tania patted Penny's arm, "Thanks for the help back there. He's with us again."

"I hope he hurries. I'm getting cold."

"Are you still hurting?"

Penny nodded. Tania frowned, "Don't overdo it, please."

Jim wasn't gone long, and Tania fretted, noting his obvious signs of fatigue.

"I think I've found a place for us, " he announced, picking up the tow cable.

Penny picked up the cushion and kept the blanket wrapped around her.

"Is it far?" she asked, following along side him.

"Nope. Just a little way down the shore and back up into the trees."

They came to a large rock with a grove of young coniferous trees growing, tightly packed, near it. The ground between the rock and the trees had but a few inches of snow. The wind howled in the upper branches, but the snow drifted aimlessly downward in this small area, unaffected by wind. Jim broke off a couple of branches with needles and he and Penny set to sweeping an area free of snow to pitch his tent. He unwrapped Tania and the goods, took the wetted seat cushion and placed it near the rock, and stood Tania on it. Unpiling the things on the toboggan, he pulled the ground cloth to the cleared area, and, with Penny's help, erected his tent on the cloth.

Sending Penny inside, he handed her the many seat cushions they had brought and instructed her to cover the floor of the tent with them. He passed in some blankets.

"Start with one blanket over to one side of center. Then lay another on the other side." He waited for her to comply. "Good. Put a third across both of them in the center." He watched her spread the blanket. "Now take this one and put it down on the end with the fold across the tent...That's it."

He had her repeat the process a second time, then handed her several more to be stacked in a corner temporarily. The toboggan had been heavy because he took as much as he could find to keep them warm.

"Okay, honey, get out while I put Tania inside."

Penny scrambled out while Jim went to Tania and picked her up. He took her to the tent and helped her inside, asking her to make herself comfort-able in the center of the tent. He took the rain cape from her and draped it over the tent for the moment. When she was settled, he had Penny enter the tent, take off her boots, and stash them in the corner near the entrance. While she was struggling with her boots, he removed his sleeping bag from under his pack, unrolled it above his head, and shook it to fluff the synthetic insulation material, carefully keeping it out of the snow. He passed it in to the women and requested they unzip it and spread it on top of themselves. Finally, he passed in several small pillows they had brought from the plane.

He went about breaking dead wood from nearby trees to build a fire. Using newspaper they had brought from the plane, he soon had a fire going. Some of the airline dinners began to cook while he continued to prepare for the night. He laid out three cups and three baggies of stainless ware in front of the tent.

Soon, using a kitchen mitt from his pack, he handed a steaming dinner to Penny, then another to Tania. "Save the foil; we'll need it again," he cautioned.

Penny and Tania took their medications, washing them down with melted snow. Jim crouched on a small rock, trying to shelter his food from the snow, to eat. When finished, he collected the plates, foil, stainless-ware, and cups, placing them in one of many plastic trash bags he had collected from the plane. Tania could see he was weary as he worked. The trash bag was carefully secured to the pack and another was pulled over the pack after he had removed his flashlight and some toilet paper to put in the tent. He put his rifle bag inside the tent along the outside wall.

Lying beside them at last, he took the spare blankets and interleaved them on top of the sleeping bag, overlapping the blankets Penny had offset on the sides to completely cover their bodies. The blanket at the foot of the tent was interleaved so there was no open zone for cold air to reach them as they slept. An extra blanket was spread down at their feet and tucked in along the sides. Satisfied, he wearily sought his pillow and was asleep in moments.

Tania took the flashlight and turned it off. She pulled the entrance of the tent closed. Turning to Penny, she kissed her on the forehead, then lay on her back.

As she had watched Jim laboriously remove his boots and rain suit before lying down with them, it was evident to Tania the gauge on his energy tank was on empty. Each move seemed to be the last he was capable of. Although she hurt from her injuries, and she grieved for her friends, her thoughts this night were filled with him.

She whispered, "Thank you, Lord."

7.

The phone was ringing on the spartan desk. There was little cluttering the desk other than a pad of paper and a well-chewed wooden pencil. A picture of several men grouped together with a basketball hung on the wall near the desk. Close to the end of his shift, Sergeant Able Thurston was in no hurry to answer the phone. The insistence of the phone outdid his patience; he picked up the receiver.

"Forty Twenty-Ninth Recce Squadron, Beale Air Force Base, Sergeant Able Thurston speaking." He suddenly sat straight up and reached for a pencil, "Yes, sir, General...Will you hold, please, while I locate Colonel Higgins?...Thank you, sir." Pushing the hold button, he scurried from his desk.

It was Tuesday evening in Washington. What did the General want with the Colonel at this time of night? It didn't sound like a social call. The Colonel's car disappeared down the road to the gate just as the Sergeant reached the parking lot. He sauntered back to the phone, not wanting to have to rush a call to the gate to intercept the Colonel.

"General?...I'm sorry, sir, but he just left the compound for the day. May I take a message?"

Writing rapidly, he acknowledged the information with a series of grunts.

"Uh huh...got it...uh huh...okay. We're to fly a mission to find—" his pencil was flying. "Yes, sir...Denver ARTCC...location...ah, weather clears—" Suddenly sitting straight up, "Yes, sir! I'll tell him...Promotions...New plane...Ah, General, I'm sure the Forty Twenty-Ninth will make you proud. We'll find it for sure...Yes, sir. Thank you, sir...We'll get right on it." Slowly he hung up the phone while reviewing his notes. Because of his hasty scribbling, he erased a couple of items and overwrote with corrections.

Picking up the phone, he dialed a number.

74

"Hi, Jason. Able here...Yeah? That's your fantasy, buddy. You guys are in for pure punishment. We'll beat you by thirty points, easy...Come on! How're you going to stop the Stilt?...Come on! You guys don't have anyone over six-one; we've got four over six-four...Yeah? We'll see who has the best team on Saturday night, creep." He laughed at the response.

"Oh yeah, with mirrors and midgets, huh?...Hey, look. The General called a few minutes ago. He wants us to get an SR-71 mission going over Colorado and the nearby states to locate that civilian airliner that's missing...Yeah, the one that's been on the news...As soon as the weather clears...I know; it won't be until Thursday, but you guys need time to lay on a mission...He says to forget the booms and get the bird down lower. He thinks it may be hard to find because of the snow."

His pencil tapped on the desk as he listened. "Yeah, yeah. We have to refocus the cameras and reset the intervalometers—" He stared at the ceiling in boredom. "Yeah, and the ground speed compensation, too...So, it's a big pain. Stripes are in this boy; yours and mine. We put on a good show and the budget boys in Congress don't hack us to death...Well, yeah, that's the way the Old Man put it to me...Okay. You guys in Mission Planning will need all the time you can get; that's why I called tonight. The Colonel will make it official tomorrow morning, so get your fannies in gear so you can look sharp tomorrow...I don't know. Why don't you call Denver ARTCC? They were the last ones talking to him...Hey, anything for a buddy."

He grinned as he listened, "Saturday, you creep...Fifty bucks...Gotcha covered. Why don't you and Miriam plan on going out after the game with me 'n Eva?...Okay, see you there. 'Bye, sucker." He hung up.

He laughed, shaking his head wonderingly as he began to lock up for the evening. "Fifty bucks the jerk went for." At the window he noted the rain had finally stopped.

* * *

It was dark in Montrose, Colorado. Snow swirled around the almost deserted streets as the wind howled in the power lines overhead. Street lights carved out cones of sodium yellow in the falling snow. The cars parked in the county sheriff's office lot wore more than a foot of new snow. Inside, Deputy Sheriff Lieutenant Warren Baker answered a complaining telephone. He was long and lanky with curly black hair and mustache. His voice and manner were deceptively soft and smooth.

"Montrose County Sheriff, Lieutenant Baker. May I help you?"

Shorthanded, this was at least the hundredth call he had fielded this day, and it was hard to be warm and cheerful. He was weary. "Oh, hi, Bert. How's the weather in Denver?...Yeah, same here," he sighed, "can't see the street from the office...Just a minute, I'll get him on the line."

He pushed the hold button and turned toward an open office door. "Hiram," he raised his voice, "the Governor's office is on line three."

"I got it," the reply came from within the office.

When the blinking light on his phone stayed on, Lt. Baker answered yet another call.

Sheriff Hiram Moore, a man in his late fifties, large, solid, graying on top, picked up the phone and pushed a button.

"Sheriff Moore...Hello Governor, how are you?...Well, I have a little touch of gout. Nothin' t' worry 'bout. What has you callin' on a foul night like this?...Oh, yeah, the one yesterday?...I heard about it...No, we haven't had any calls about it. 'Course," he hurried on, "half the lines in the county are down, too...You WHAT?...Blazes, man! It'll be most a day, mebbe more, after this blizzard quits afore we could get the airstrip open...What are you smokin'? We got people trapped in grocery stores what cain't git home, an you want me t' borrow a couple plows from highway maintenance t' go clear a runway?...Widda Barnes' house burned down this afternoon an' we couldn't git the fire department to her. Be sensible, man!"

He twisted angrily around in his squeaking chair. "Governor, if some dang'd airplane crashed in these parts, why hell, there ain't no survivors. I don't know 'bout the mountains out your way, but the one's we got go mostly up and down, and they're solid rock...What's the goldarn hurry to go a'findin' dead folks when the live ones cain't even get home?"

He took a deep breath and sighed, "Okay, the Feds asked you...Okay, we'll get some planes up soon's it clears enough t' see anything...Okay, I'll alert the CAP pilots. 'Course you know there ain't exactly an armada of them anymore...Two's 'bout all. Say, have you by any chance tried to lay this on Gunnison County yet?...Not too eager, huh? An' what about little counties like Hinsdale, Ouray, an'— Oh, Highway Patrol an' Forest Service, huh?...Okay," he sighed, "I guess— Okay, 'bye now."

He pushed the button off then slammed the phone onto its cradle. "Baker," he yelled, "git in here!" He stood up and walked to the window, muttering, "Dang'd if I ever heard'a somethin' s'foolish!" He turned to Lt. Baker as he walked in.

"Did you vote for that man for governor?"

Lt. Baker grinned a little sheepishly and nodded.

"Well, *your* governor wants us t'..."

* * *

Tania turned away from Jim as Penny stirred in her sleep. Penny was suddenly awake, and she started uncovering herself.

"What are you doing?" Tania whispered.

"I'm too hot," came the reply.

Tania was pleasantly warm for a change, but she was nowhere near hot. She reached out to Penny's forehead. It was hot with fever. Oh, God, she thought.

"Cover up," she commanded, still whispering.

"But I'm hot."

"You have a fever. Cover up, please."

"Shouldn't we tell Jim?"

"He's exhausted. We have to let him rest. There's nothing he can do about this anyhow. Just cover up and try to sleep."

"I hurt."

"Honey, I know you hurt. So do I. We have to tough it out for tonight. He's had it. I mean, he even left the flashlight on when he got in bed; he must rest. Please cover up."

"Okay," Penny sighed. She restored the blanket covering.

"Come on over to me and put your head on my shoulder. I know this isn't any fun. We'll somehow make it through this night together. Okay?"

Later, Penny had a nature call. Tania helped her find her boots, gave her the roll of toilet paper Jim had put out, and handed her the flashlight. Penny returned shivering violently. Once warmed at Tania's side, she slept the night through.

Tania had a fitful night. The wind howling in the tree tops and the tent rustling in the wind were unusual noises to her. But, because she was very tired, she also slept.

* * *

"Okay," Lori said, "Tomorrow, I'll pack some things and come over here and stay until things settle down."

"I really appreciate it," Jackie replied. "The worst part of this is the not knowing."

"Would you rather *know* he's dead?"

"Well, *NO!* It's, well—"

"Until we know different, he's alive. Don't ask me how or why he's alive, just believe in him. Okay?...God, you *have* to; he's your *husband.*"

"But the man from the airline said—"

"Shit on him. He doesn't know any more than we do. All he knows is their damned airplane hasn't been heard from."

"If they could only search for it."

"Look at it this way: Every day they can't is one more day he's alive. He isn't dead until they find his body."

78

"I just wish something was happening. That's all," Jackie said.

"How do you know it isn't? Jackie, dearest, have some faith!...Look, when Jimmy and I were living together, we had some heavy discussions about airline safety. He always sits in the back of the plane. He contended then, and I'm sure he still believes it, the back of the airplane is most likely to survive. I didn't believe him, but he proved it to me, first with analysis, and then with pictures of airplane crashes. We spent one Saturday in a library going through old newspapers and magazines, principally *Aviation Week*. He's right. He had some other theories, too. If there is any survivor of this plane, he's it. You can make book on that.

"I used to hate him when he'd make such an argument because he was always right," Lori said. "He didn't shout or try to overpower me with his brilliance. He'd just quietly and patiently explain the facts of the matter to me. Facts which, as an engineer, I couldn't refute. He never argued when he was wrong."

Lori got to her feet, turned, and offered her hands to Jackie. "Come on, let's go to bed. Nothing's going to change tonight." She pulled Jackie to her feet and hugged her. "I know, I don't feel all that convinced either, but we have to hope; that's all there is."

Jackie needed Lori. She needed the woman's natural positive outlook, yet she was put off at times when Lori discussed her cohabitation with Jim while they were in graduate school. Tonight she had gotten something to hang on to and something to irritate her, but Lori was a rock, and she needed a rock to lean on. Oh, why did she have to feel the irritation? Lori, her dearest friend, was here sharing her grief with her, supporting her, giving her hope. Could she ever be as strong?

8.

Tania rolled back toward Jim. She had felt Penny's forehead which was blazing. The confines of the tent made any movement likely to disturb one sleeper or the other. Reaching over her head, she pulled the flap aside. Wednesday's daylight was grudgingly displacing night, and it was still snowing hard. This was her first experience in a tent and she felt insecure. The only barrier to fear and panic was the confidence she had in the man next to her. She was warmer than the previous morning, almost comfortable. The pains in her leg and head had subsided. The seat cushions, though much softer than the cabin floor, left something to be desired for support and comfort.

When she tucked her arm under the covers, Jim whispered to her.

"How's she doing?"

"She's hot. I got her to take another tetracycline a little while ago."

"I hope she can hold it down. She walked too much yesterday."

"She was trying to ease your load."

"I know. She's some little trouper. Has she had a BM yet?"

Tania nodded grimly, "She nearly froze, poor kid. She said she found some blood and some black."

He winced at the news. "That damn belt! We've got to keep her quiet so her gut can heal. She gets only clear liquid for a few days. I'll put a few soft drinks in bed with us so they can thaw. She's bleeding in the intestinal tract as well as the bladder."

"Speaking of going—" Tania looked at him in a direct way.

"I have to build a latrine."

"Now. I need it."

"This isn't going to be heated, you know."

"Just protect it from the wind...and hurry."

He scrambled out from under the blankets, dressing quickly in his boots, overcoat, and rain suit. After chucking a couple of logs onto the smoldering fire, he passed three frozen soft drinks in to Tania, and headed out to search for suitable wood for the latrine. A little over a half hour later, he finished lashing selected pieces of wood into a crude seat attached to the trunk of a nearby tree. Using remnants of the torn blanket, he wrapped the two branches forming the seat to pad them. He draped a plastic rubbish bag over the seat and hung a blanket on a cord from an overhead limb. Tania watched, fascinated by his assured manner as he worked. She guessed he had done this duty before.

"All finished," he looked in her direction.

"None too soon. Could you carry me to it please?"

"Aren't you going to wait for the paint to dry?"

"Very funny." She reached her arms out to him.

He grinned as he bent to pick her up, "Remember, it's twenty-five cents a shot."

"Just slip me under the door. Mom used to have me and my sister crawl under the door in public pay toilets...Oh God," she suddenly gasped, "I wonder if Mom or Sis know about this?"

Jim's jaw was firmly set. "Bad news travels fast." He placed her on the seat, pulled the blanket around her, and turned away.

"Jim," she called plaintively from inside the blanket, "Help."

"What's the matter?" He turned back.

"I'm embarrassed; I can't get my panties down because of the splint."

He pulled the blanket aside. "Put your arms around my neck so I can lift you." He raised her up and started to work the offending undergarment around the ends of the splint.

"Hey! Your hands are freezing! Agh, you fiend!...Eeee!" she shrieked, "Jim, please!"

"What'd you think they'd be?" he laughed. "You watched me tying knots for the last half hour in my bare hands. The very least you could do is invite me to warm them up."

"Aren't you? You—"

He lowered her onto the seat again.

"Thank you," she said insincerely.

"The pleasure was all mine," he winked, closing the blanket around her.

"I'm sure it was...Damn!"

"Now what's the matter?"

"The shock of your cold hands was so much, now I don't have to go."

Jim's howls of laughter woke Penny. He apologized to her, then turned back to Tania.

"Do you want to stay there and freeze for a bit, or do you want to go through all this again?"

"Hand me the TP and shut up."

By the time breakfast was ready, Penny was asleep again. Jim handed Tania a cup of hot cereal.

"Ah, my favorite breakfast: brown gook."

Jim looked up from stirring his cup, "We'll have to give up breakfasts in a week."

"Is that good news or bad?" Hot oatmeal had never been her favorite.

"Maybe," he spoke slowly for emphasis, "this is not your favorite repast, but when you don't have *anything* for breakfast, this may just take on a certain charm."

She sighed, "I suppose." She ate a spoonful. "What are your plans?"

He swallowed before replying. "Firewood and food."

"Pretty basic."

"I sure hope you didn't expect TV, discotheque, and ice cream. We're down to basics, lady: food, shelter, warmth. Bare survival...period."

"Right now, ice cream is not on my list. No way! I was more interested in your longer term plans."

He took another spoonful of his cereal while looking at her. "Well, we need lots of wood for when the weather clears."

"Why?"

"We'll have to keep three signal fires going while they're searching for us. Let's hope, they find us and we won't have to plan beyond a few days. On the other hand, if they don't find us, our planning now must include conservation of all our resources. I feel we should operate as though we're not going to be found and let it be a nice surprise if it does happen."

She didn't want to think beyond the first nice day and being found and rescued. She wanted competent medical attention, she wanted safe, substantial housing, and she wanted a comfortable bed. The uncertainties here were more than she wanted to cope with. It was not that she found him lacking in his providing for their survival thus far. She could see he knew what he was doing.

She took another spoonful of cereal. "You've been camping like this before?"

"No, not really. I've been camping, but never in the winter in the snow. I've read about it, and I was going with others to do some of this, but that was going to be like a training exercise. Keeping dry is the big thing in winter camping."

"Like staying in the tent?"

"Well, yeah, but you're getting wet, even in the tent."

"I don't see how."

"Your sweat."

"I'm not sweating; I'm barely warm."

"You're not sweating like in the summer after running a couple of miles, but your body is putting moisture into your clothes anyhow. We'll have to get you out here in a little while and pull the coat off and let you steam out for a bit. You'll get a little chilled, but you'll be surprised how much more comfortable you'll be afterwards."

When he removed his coats, she could see the steam rising from his shirt. He shook his inner jacket to aerate it. After stuffing his coats into the tent, he removed his shirt, exposing his thermal underwear shirt to the wind. More steam rose from his body. He reached for her hands.

"Come on, let's dry you out some."

"No, I don't want to do that."

"If enough of your moisture accumulates, you'll become very cold as it turns to ice. I'm surprised we haven't had trouble up to now with all we did yesterday."

"No, I'll catch cold."

"You will not catch cold. A cold is a virus. If you've been exposed, you'll catch it. This will keep you warmer, honest." He seized her wrists to help her out of the tent. When he could, he bent and lifted her up.

"I am not getting undressed for you," she stated with firmness.

"Nobody said you were. We're just going to get you out of the fur for a while." He stood her near the fire on the cushion they had used yesterday, taking the fur from her and covering their heads with his rain jacket.

At first she didn't feel especially cold, and she could see the moisture leaving her clothing. The fire warmed one side of her. She steadied herself with a hand on his shoulder.

"That's not so bad is it?" he asked, holding the coat open to the fire.

"Did anyone ever mistake you for an archangel?" she asked, remembering her first sensations as she awoke after the crash.

"A *what?*"

"An archangel," she repeated, laughing at his bewildered expression.

"Well, my mom used to call me 'my little angel' when I was a baby they tell me, but I don't think I've ever been confused with an archangel—more probably with Satan. Where'd you get that?"

She laughed again, "When I was coming to after the crash, you apparently said something to me about was I all right or something like that. I was sure I was dead, and I thought you were an archangel greeting me at the gates of Heaven."

"I think you made a mistake there; this is *not* Heaven—at least not as I envision it."

84

"You got that right. So when did your mom stop calling you her little angel?"

"It depends on whose story you want to believe. My sister claims it was when I learned to crawl and get into things—"

"You have a sister? Any brothers?"

"Nope, just my sister. She's a couple of years older than me."

"What's the other story or stories?"

He blushed a little, "Well, Dad said it was when I cut my first tooth and bit Mom's nipple when I was nursing."

"Oooo," she winced at the imagined pain. "I think I'd go with your dad's story."

"Well, I don't know, but she stopped nursing right then!"

"I'll bet!...I'm getting cold."

"Okay, balance for a minute while I put the coat in the tent and we'll dry the backside a bit."

She put her hand on his shoulder again and stood, exchanging warm for cold on her body.

"We should do this again this evening, close to bedtime," he noted, "and at least once every day from now on."

As she cooled in front, he warmed the fur again by the fire and put it around her shoulders. He then began to warm his own clothing and put it back on. She then was deposited back into the tent and under the bedding where she noticed she was warmer than before.

"What about Penny?" she asked.

"I don't dare until her fever breaks. I don't want her moving any more than necessary."

For the next couple of hours Jim dragged wood into camp, propped one end of the larger pieces up on a rock, and broke them down by tossing a smaller rock onto the unsupported middle of the dead limbs. He stacked the broken pieces and covered them with the toboggan door and live limbs.

"Where are you finding dry wood?" Tania asked as she watched his tiring labor.

He stopped to pant for a bit. "I'm hauling dead limbs out of standing trees. One side might be wet, but, on the whole, the wood is dry." He looked around, "Let's see, latrine, fire, wood...I guess food's next."

"Why don't you rest for a while?"

Opening his pack, he took out the bolt to his rifle. He quickly covered the pack again. After brushing off the snow from his clothing, he crawled into the tent and lay down next to her.

"Good idea," he panted. He pulled his rifle case from along side him and took out the barrel and stock. Propped on his elbows, he carefully fitted them together.

"I hate guns," Tania commented, watching him. She saw his frown and hastily added, "I'm sorry, but—"

"No, that's all right. I can understand."

"It's that guns have done so much damage to people; wars, holdups, murders."

"I'm not denying that. But it's not guns per se; it's the people who use them for those purposes. If we didn't have guns, we'd use knives, bows and arrows, and clubs to do our dirty work. If someone wants to kill someone else, guns or no, he or she will find a way. To me, this is a tool."

She noted the slow measured care he used in fitting the telescopic sight to the rifle. It was the same care he had used in cutting into her leg. Nothing was forced, just eased gently into place and secured. He fitted the bolt into the breach and suddenly slammed it closed, startling her by the uncharacteristic quickness of his movement.

"From this moment on, this is a dangerous item," he announced.

"Why? There's no bullets in it."

"It looks just the same with or without a cartridge in the chamber. Treat it as though it were loaded."

She watched as he loaded a cartridge, then put the rifle to his shoulder, propped on his elbows, sighting through the scope at distant objects. There was nothing hurried about him, and she wondered why he had loaded the rifle at all. He seemed only to be idly peering through the sight. The sudden, angry crack as the rifle fired caused her to gasp; she had not expected him to shoot, nor could she see any movement in his hands or body when the rifle went off. He opened the chamber, ejecting the spent cartridge, laid the rifle down on top of its case, and crawled out of the tent to have a look at the tree he had aimed at.

When he returned she looked up at him, "You startled me. I wasn't expecting you to shoot at anything."

"I'm sorry. I had to check the sight. Looks good." He brought two pieces of wood to her. "If the fire begins to go out, pitch these on it." He pulled the rifle out of the tent and extracted two more cartridges from the box, placing them in a pocket. "Wish me luck," he smiled, still squatting at the tent opening.

She kissed her finger tips, then stretched to touch his stubble-covered cheek. The gloom of the continuing snow soon swallowed his tall form. The sound of the shot had penetrated Penny's fevered sleep, and she woke shortly after Jim left. Tania turned to her.

"Where's Jim?" Penny asked. "I heard something...a loud noise."

"He's out hunting. That was him testing his rifle," Tania replied quietly. "How are you feeling? Do you want something to drink?"

Penny nodded, still more asleep than awake. Tania pulled a soft drink can from under the blankets and opened it for her. Penny, a little delirious from the fever, said nothing, drank over half the can, and fell asleep.

Tania worried about what she had seen in Jim as he prepared the rifle. Her image of him was as a loving and sensitive man, but without a change in manner or tone of voice, he had discharged the rifle so callously. He seemed a man completely devoted to saving life, yet in a blink he could take one, apparently without any emotion. As she reflected on this, the distant sound of the rifle reached her; confirmation, she mused, of her thoughts. She wondered what had died.

Another side of her brain reminded her he was out in this terrible weather trying to provide food for her and Penny. He bore this responsibility, as he had that of keeping them from dying, without comment or complaint. It was a heavy responsibility, and she could see its effects on him as he loosened up only briefly. She wasn't sure she had seen him relax since the crash. Exhausted sleep didn't count. But then again, she didn't know him very well yet; maybe he was always a little up tight. A more distant report from the rifle reached her. He'd be back soon.

He appeared out of the gloom, his rifle slung over a shoulder, and carrying two rabbits by their ears. Holding them out to her, he grinned.

"Hasenpfeffer."

"I'm impressed," she replied. "How did you see them in this weather?" The rabbits were white.

"Tracks. Where the tracks ended, there was a rabbit crouching." He set the rabbits down, pulled the rifle from his shoulder, opened the bolt, and stowed it in the case, placing it alongside his bedding. Sitting on a rock near the fire, he began skinning the rabbits.

"I still hate this part of hunting," he observed. "The first animal I had to skin was a gopher."

"What?" She was incredulous. "Why?"

"Dad got me this air rifle, and I shot a gopher. So, as a training exercise, Dad said I had to skin it and dress it out like I was going to eat it. What a mess!"

"That would have cured me of shooting animals."

"Yeah, well— Then I got my first rabbit. 'Well, son, get to cleaning it out,' my dad said. 'No,' I said."

"I'll bet *that* went over big."

"You know," he said without looking up, pulling the fur off one rabbit, "I've never gotten used to eating rabbit with the fur on."

"You're kidding!"

He shook his head, "He cooked the damned thing up as it was and made me eat it. So," he chuckled at the recollection, "here I am, skinning rabbits. I'm a little stupid at times, but I learned...How's Penny?"

"She woke after you left, had some 7-up, and went to sleep again. She seems delirious."

"Probably. That's not uncommon with a high fever. She hasn't heaved?"

"I don't believe so."

He nodded, satisfied, "Hang in there, little lady," he said in Penny's direction. Finishing the second rabbit, he pulled another trash bag from their supplies, dropped the rabbits in, and buried them in the snow next to the tent. "Into the freezer."

"Jim, why don't you come in here and catch up on some rest?"

*   *   *

"...The investigation into the crash has turned up evidence the plane's engine systems have been improperly maintained. The NTSB inquiry will continue tomorrow with interviews of the two suspended mechanics. Interstate Airlines is working around the clock to get its planes re-inspected and the grounding order lifted. Crews and passengers are stranded in many cities as the planes clog air terminals.

"Meanwhile, no search for the missing airliner is possible as the snow continues to fall in Colorado..."

"Shit," Lillian said as she cut the TV news broadcast short with a slap at the on/off switch. "Sara, I may go fuckin' out of my mind, cooped up in this damned hotel room. If I'd known this was goin' to happen, I'd'a stayed home and puked some more."

"I wonder how long we'll be grounded." Sara, another flight attendant, walked impatiently around the room.

"I guess I'm glad I'm not flying at this moment, but I want to know what's happened to Tania."

"You two are pretty close?"

"Sara, do you know what love is? I mean real love? Do you know?"

"You love Tania?"

Lillian looked at her, unable to explain her feelings. She bit her lip, and, as tears began to flow again, she nodded. Yes, she loved Tania in ways nobody could understand. Her love could not match, in her mind, the love Tania had given her.

Sara watched Lillian for several moments, "You're not...ah...lovers are you?" She almost expected Lillian to strike her, but she wanted to know if there might be something about her she ought to know, sharing a room with her and all.

Lillian looked swiftly at her, crying. "N—no, but I wish we were. S—She wouldn't go f—for anything like that."

9.

When Tania awoke the next day, she wondered how she had slept so long. Bright rays of sunshine leaked through the tent opening. There was no sound of wind. Jim was not in the tent, but his shadow soon covered the tent flap. He pulled it open to greet her.

"Hi," he said cheerily, "you finally got a good sleep."

"I guess," she answered, bewildered. How had he gotten out of the tent without her feeling or hearing him? "What time is it? How long have you been up?"

"Oh, it's about eight-thirty," he answered, glancing at his watch. "A while."

He crouched and reached across her to grasp Penny's shoulder and give it a gentle shake. "Come on, honey, it's time to take another capsule."

Penny moaned, then slowly wakened. "Is this Wednesday?"

"No," he answered, "Thursday. Our third day. It's nice out; it stopped snowing. Come on, turn around so you can take your medicine." He held out a cup and the capsule to her. She took the capsule, put it in her mouth, and took the cup of water from him to wash it down. He felt her forehead.

"Still too warm."

"I'm sorry."

"You can't help it. You didn't ask for any of this. Just keep on resting until your fever breaks. How's your abdomen?"

"A little better. It doesn't hurt so much."

"That's real good, sweetheart. Cover up and keep on resting." He patted the back of her head, then turned his attention to Tania.

"Would you like to come out in the sun for a while? It's really very mild."

Heartened by Penny's improvement, she wanted to get out and stretch and rejoice in the improved weather. "Yes! This is not the most comfortable bed I've slept on."

He reached down to begin helping her out, "But the companionship—"

"You snore!"

He laughed as he lifted her up, "Jackie complains about that, too."

"Jackie?"

"My wife." He set her on a rock he had cleared of snow, then pulled the outdoor seat cushion under her feet.

She looked around while stretching her arms as far from her body as she could. Why was it, she mused, you get a little good news, like Penny improving and clear weather, and a little bad news, like Jim's married. She was really beginning to like him, to see him in her personal future. Danny had been fun, and the best lover she had ever had. But Jim, in just these few days, had made her start to compare him to Danny and had entered her dreams.

"You didn't tell me you were married."

"You didn't ask. It's no big secret. We had other things to talk about."

"I would have thought you might be concerned about her and how she is taking your disappearance."

"I am."

"Why didn't you say something?"

"Haven't you had enough to worry you? You don't need my problems, too."

True enough. There was the concern about her roommate she hadn't shared with him, and she was worried about her invalid mother and her sister. Her sister, one year her junior, was living with her mother and caring for her. They were both total optimists, but she wished there was some way of letting them know she was alive.

"I suppose you're right, but I feel you and I and Penny are very special. To survive, we have to share everything and support each other in every way possible."

"I agree with you." He came to her and took both of her hands in his. "I think there will always be a special kind of

closeness between you and me, and between each of us and
Penny. That's inevitable from sharing the kind of experience we
have in common. But face it, we have had too much going center
stage to be able to explore each other yet. I don't know, you
could be married, though you're not wearing a ring. Divorced?
Maybe you're living with someone. You could be supporting a
couple of kids on your own." He shook his head, "I don't know
who *you* really are, and at the moment it doesn't matter. All I
know is: I like the person I *do* know."

And she liked the person who was holding her hands,
married or not. It was true, she knew nothing about him except
what she had seen, and she hadn't told him anything about
herself. Did any of it really matter? Life at this moment
consisted of Jim and Penny; all else was irrelevant. She came
out to rejoice and be refreshed and somehow things had gotten
too heavy. She smiled up into his face.

"Let's stay with that. I like the person I know, too."

He released her hands and went about fixing her breakfast.
She looked around again. Her eyes, sick of gray and snow, of
wreckage and fire, drank it all in; evergreens with deep green
poking out from under the brilliant snow, an impossibly blue
sky, and twisting around, she saw the lake shimmering in the
sunlight.

"Oh, Jim! If we weren't in such a desperate condition, I'd
think this place was lovely. I don't think I've seen a bluer sky."

"We're not so desperate, and it is lovely. Don't lose your
perspective in judging Nature. Just because it might represent
a barrier to us at the moment doesn't detract from what it is.
So, enjoy. Our pleasures will be few enough."

"Did you see the rainbow colors in the snow blowing from the
ridges?"

He smiled, "Let me turn you around so you can enjoy the
lake." He picked up the splinted leg and helped her turn toward
the lake.

She took in the view. "Beautiful! It didn't look like much
when we came here in the blizzard. It's like a postcard."

"I hope it doesn't freeze over," he replied.

And then, looking down for the first time, she saw something else to excite her.

"Hey! Where'd these three fish come from? They're beauties!"

"I used a little rabbit for bait. They came out of the lake pre-frozen, I think. I'll clean them after breakfast."

"You have been busy—" she cut herself short as the sound of a light airplane began to fill the valley.

"Oop's, sounds like the first of the search planes," he said. "Time to light the other fires." Taking a burning brand from the fire, he ignited the two other mounds of wood, paper, and kindling. "Now, lady, is the time to do your praying thing. Pray *some* plane sees us."

* * *

The SR-71 reached the end of the runway at Beale AFB, turned and faced the long concrete strip. Long, black, sleek as no other, unique in its design, unmatched in performance, the Air Force's premier reconnaissance aircraft stood ready for its mission of mercy.

"Aspen 31 ready for takeoff."

"Roger, Aspen 31. Hold for civilian air traffic."

The engines whined as the flight waited. A dull roar echoed around the countryside.

"Aspen 31 cleared for takeoff. Have a good flight, Major."

The whine of the engines increased in pitch, and the dull roar increased to a thundering blast. A massive plume of dirty black smoke spread out to the rear of the plane. A sharp boom rolled across the farms as the afterburners ignited.

"Thank you," the pilot acknowledged. He let the brakes go and the plane gathered speed. "See you in a little over an hour. We'll find the lost bird."

The nose of the plane rose to a high angle, and then, trailing twin plumes of smoke, the plane lifted and began a slowly curving ascent. The noise shattered the early morning peace of nearby Marysville, California. A moment later the plane disappeared from view following a controlled ascent to allow the plane's skin and frame to grow in length with the increasing temperature as it gathered speed.

* * *

Deputy Sheriff Lt. Baker climbed into the right hand seat of the light airplane, strapped himself in, and put on his headphones. "When the plow gets out of the way, let's get going. Hiram's on a rampage; he's pissed for sure."

The pilot nodded, taking his microphone in hand, "Montrose control, this is Montrose County flight 57 ready for takeoff. Please advise."

"Montrose County 57, please hold."

The engine perked along, warming. Baker settled himself in and reflected on his boss's attitude toward this search. The blizzard had crippled the highways of the county and the equipment now clearing the runway was sorely needed elsewhere. He couldn't blame him for wanting to serve the community before going off looking for what most certainly had to be a fatal crash. The plow working the runway turned off to a taxiway.

"County 57 cleared for takeoff."

"County 57, roger." The pilot pulled the throttle knob out from the panel and the engine rev'd up. They moved down the narrow path and easily lifted into the air. Baker consulted his chart, reviewing the area they were to search.

* * *

The sudden boom rocked through the canyon, startling Tania.

"What was that?" she asked.

"Sonic boom," Jim replied, putting more wood on one of the three fires. "They're looking for the plane."

"It got me right in the pit of my stomach."

"It started another avalanche. See it?" He pointed to a cloud of snow plummeting down the ridge some distance from them. He waited for Tania to see it. "Only the military operate supersonic in the States. That guy is photo-reconnaissance."

"How do you know?"

"I don't *know*, but I'd be willing to bet it was an SR-71 from California."

She greeted the announcement with a look of doubt.

"Hey," he responded, "airplanes and everything to do with them have been my hobby since I was a small kid."

"And camping, and hunting, and whittling on people's legs—"

"That was the *first* time!" he objected.

She laughed. They had time while he was tied to tending the fires. There was something burning inside her she wanted to ask him.

"Why did what we did before the crash save my life?"

"Because the position you were instructing everyone to get into is almost guaranteed to kill."

"It's a federal regulation."

"I know. Is everything the government does correct or sacred?"

"No."

"Right. The various governmental agencies which regulate the airlines have been sticking their heads in the sand on this point for decades. The CAB, the FAA, and the NTSB have all ignored some of the work which has been done in passenger safety since shortly after World War II."

"Oh, come on! Flying is the safest way to travel."

"I'll give you that a lot of work has been done to *prevent* accidents, and it's been effective. I'm talking about what happens when you *do* have an accident. They're frequently fatal."

"And you think they needn't be?"

He nodded. "Some accidents will be fatal no matter what the aircraft configuration. When you go straight in, there aren't going to be any survivors. But *we* didn't go straight in. If they turned the seats around, something Cornell University championed for cars back in the late forties or early fifties, most of the people in the aft section of our plane would be standing around us right now—" he paused for emphasis, "uninjured!"

"Come on. I'm hurt."

"You wouldn't even have a headache if you'd been *sitting* in a rear facing seat, belted in. You bumped your head on the tray, and your leg was in an awkward position due to your haste while you were kneeling."

"But—"

"Why do you think astronauts reenter the atmosphere lying with their backs to the action?"

She shook her head.

"They can withstand higher 'g' forces. And if it's better for them, why isn't it better for airline passengers?"

"Nobody wants to travel facing the rear."

"Well, that's the argument people have used, but it's b.s.! Trains have rear facing seats, trolleys had them, stage coaches, Egyptian barges. People have been traveling facing the rear for centuries."

"The public won't buy it."

"If that's all you were offered, *and* it was explained you would be safer, that's the way you would fly. Many military transports have rear facing seats."

"Then why don't they make airliner seats face the rear?"

"Exactly! Why don't they?"

She looked into his eyes. He was dead serious, and he sounded like he was in his home territory.

"You said the position was deadly. They teach the position in flight school for all emergencies."

He nodded. "Given the forward facing seats, and most benign emergencies, it's probably okay. It keeps the passengers from flailing around. For our kind of accident, if the position doesn't get you, the seat belt will."

"Now wait a damn minute!" she complained. "Oh," she was deeply agitated, "you gotta explain that!"

He was unruffled, expecting her reaction. This was not the first person he had discussed this matter with. Instead, he had the patience of experience on his side. "With your head down on the pillow in your lap, your head is very near the seat in front of you. At impact, your abdomen gives under the seat belt and your head rams the seat in front, breaking your neck. Or, with the economy seat spacing in the aft sections, where we were, you have your arms crossed on the seat in front of you and your head on your arms. Your head bends back on impact with the same result. That's mostly what I found. If you're a shorter person, the seat belt will break your back."

"Damnit, Jim, the seat belt is a *safety* device!"

"You're doubled over," he continued quietly, "which puts a high strain on your lower spine, especially in older persons. At impact, the belt, in arresting your forward progress gives you up to a half a ton jerk in the abdomen and the pelvis, which can easily break a back."

She shook her head, "Oh, I can't believe—"

"If your head ramming into the seat in front is not stopping you, what is? Haven't you noticed seat belts in cars now include a shoulder strap, and manufacturers are now including shoulder straps for back seat passengers as well? Why do you think they're doing that?"

"Safer?" She shook her head slowly, realizing the truth of what he was saying.

"Right! The unaided seat belt will injure on impact!"

"Okay, Mr. Wise Guy, how'd Penny survive?"

"She's short, and young, and light. She didn't break her neck, but she took damage in her abdomen. She didn't break her back because the forces on her were less, and because her bones are more pliant and can better resist the stress. But it was my first concern with her: was her back broken?"

"You're sure about this?"

"I know a lady who was in the back seat of a car involved in a multiple vehicle accident. She was belted in and she got a broken back and severe abdominal injuries from the belt. I'm not saying she would have been uninjured had she not been wearing the belt, I'm only noting the damage the belt, without a shoulder strap, caused. If she had been in our plane, she probably would have died because we wouldn't have dared move her.

"So, to answer your original question, what we did was support our whole back against the seat in front of us to distribute the forces decelerating us. You have concussion because you let your head get away from the tray, instead of pressing hard against it."

She sighed, "How come you know about all this?"

He smiled. "The lecture I was to give yesterday in Boulder, to two hundred and ten engineering students, was an overview of aircraft escape systems. My department designs and builds ejection seats."

"I might have known—"

He checked the sky for aircraft and pitched wood on two of the fires.

* * *

"Mr. Melvin MacStrom?" the man inquired.

"Yes," Mel responded, somewhat sick as he watched the NTSB search of his warehouse and records continue.

The man handed him several documents, "I am Tadrick Kuffal of the U.S. Attorney's Regional Office. With this warrant, I am placing you under arrest for the specified criminal charges. You are to appear in the Federal Court, in San Francisco, to answer those charges. This will be a preliminary hearing. You must appear with your attorney. You are hereby subpoenaed to attend the NTSB hearings in the afternoon of the same day." He handed Mel another paper. "Be prepared to discuss in detail the specific maintenance of air vehicle N478639, Boeing airframe 6798, known as Interstate flight 238. In addition, you should be prepared to discuss the discrepancies concerning your inventory which the investigation team is uncovering. By the date of the hearings, there may be other specific airframes whose maintenance the committee may wish to discuss. My office will keep you informed of these additions which may be discussed at a later date."

Mel glanced at the folded documents. It had only been a matter of time, he reflected. He had expected this, and his lawyer was already notified of his problems.

When Mel did not answer, Mr. Kuffal continued, "You understand you are charged with certain criminal offenses?"

Mel nodded. "Yes."

"We will be taking you downtown to book you, and we will release you to your attorney after you post bail. Would you please direct me to the two mechanics, Mr. Cross and Mr. Plummer."

"They're not here. They're suspended pending the outcome of this investigation."

"Then your company suspects there was some wrongdoing?"

"I'm sorry. I cannot answer that question."

"Yes, I understand. I'm sorry, I shouldn't have asked it. Can you direct me to their homes?"

Silently, Mel turned to his desk and opened his Rolodex.

10.

The airplane traffic was disappointing over their location. There had been only the one small plane and the SR-71 sonic boom. They had heard others echo through the canyon, but none had appeared overhead. Tania decided to find out more about her companion, though she resolved to stay away from technical matters.

"Jim, you've been so calm except in the avalanche. How can you do it. I'm so tight with worry I could snap."

He smiled. "Okay, I'll confess. From before the crash until we got down here, I was very...let's say...taut—"

"It never showed!"

"Uptight! Big time! I tried not to show it. That's how come some of the sick jokes. I was trying to ease your tension while covering mine."

"I liked the jokes...But now that we're here—"

"I'm okay. I'm in an environment I can handle. The only big worry I have at the moment is Penny, and she seems to be recovering. I think you're doing okay, so I'm in some kind of control of the situation."

"What about being lost?"

"Well, yeah, it's a concern, but it's not an out-of-control panic...like the avalanche, the crash, or yours and Penny's injuries."

"But we're lost!"

"But we are also *alive*. Mother Nature has thrown some really bad weather at us, but we've survived. I'm finding food, Penny's healing, you're on the mend. Our situation is actually improving. We are *going* to survive. We can hope they'll find us. But if they don't, given some time we should be able to get out on our own." He hoped she would loosen up.

Well, that didn't go far. She sighed and began to relax.

"Look, Tania, instead of jumping at every little sound and worrying about our safety, I'd like you to concentrate on the beautiful things you've experienced since we got here. Those icicles in the stream, the wonderful taste of the water, the post-card pretty scene right in front of us, unspoiled by man. I'll bet you will find that when we finally leave, you won't want to. You will understand why people spend thousands of dollars trying to get away to a beautiful, peaceful place like this."

"Oh, come on—"

"No. You'll actually want to come back here."

She didn't want to believe the last part, but she already knew he was partly right. "You used several French expressions. Did you live in France?"

He began to rub her neck and shoulders to work out tension. "No, I took French in high school for college entrance requirements. It's kind of special to me."

French wasn't so special to her when she took it. "Oh? Why?"

He blushed as he answered, "I met my first love in class."

"Oh!" she exclaimed, delighted. "Would you mind telling me about it?"

"You'd rather talk about my love life than the beauties of nature?"

"Absolutely," she smiled warmly.

When she smiled like that, no way could he refuse her. "Well," he sighed, "we lived in this semi-rural town in the Middle West Bible belt. I was a freshman, and I hadn't really discovered girls yet. I have an older sister, as I told you. She was a junior, and she was a pain to me, so I wasn't interested in other girls. I was very shy, an introvert wrapped up in my model airplane hobby."

"So that's how you learned to use a knife."

"Yep."

"But shy? You shy?"

"Oh yeah! I had an industrial strength case of shy. Sis was the extrovert—and she was into boys for sure—or was it the other way around—"

"That's not too nice a thing to say about your sister."

"I happen to know she lost her virtue half way through her sophomore year...and liked it. Mom had her on the pill, but she never knew Sis was messing around."

"So, about your love—?"

"I was in this class of twenty-one girls and four boys. And my sister was one of the girls! This lady teaching the class—her thing was teaching us how to make love in French—"

"Oh, what a fun class!"

"Yeah, I guess, if you were into all that love stuff; I wasn't—at least I didn't *think* I was."

"But there was a complication?"

"Yeah. So everybody had to take turns going to someone of the opposite sex and saying you were madly in love with him or her."

"Lucky you. I'll bet you got more than your share of love declarations."

"Oh yes I did! My sister took great delight in picking on me, hamming it up, petting me and kissing me; I wanted to crawl under a desk. Several of her buddies used their turn to further humiliate me."

"That's cruel."

"Those were her troll days. But I kinda had my eyes on this absolutely beautiful, shy, Amerasian girl who sat across the room from me. We had exchanged some glances, but we were both too shy to get acquainted."

"I thought you said you weren't interested in girls."

"Not like the other kids were. You know, they were into kissing, and petting, and—"

"And you weren't?" She didn't want to go any further down that path.

"I hadn't had my first wet dream yet; girls were just a pain—"

"But you 'noticed' this little Asian cutie?"

"Uh huh. My big dream was to get to know her and sit and hold her in my arms—forever, I guess. At the time, I didn't know there was anything more to do."

Tania laughed. This was too funny. "So, it was love at first sight?"

"First touch."

"It gets juicier!"

"So Su Lin's turn—"

"Su Lin? Chinese?"

"Su Lin O'Leary. Chinese and Irish."

He checked the three fires, added some wood and sat on a log near her.

"...So she came across the room to me, and I thought, 'Oh, shit! She's going to do it, too.' "

Tania laughed, "So, did she?"

"She knelt down in front of me—the whole class was giggling—and she looked up at me with the biggest, clearest brown eyes I have ever seen. She reached up and touched my face, and said in a low, soft voice, 'Mon cheri, Jaime, je t'aime. Je t'aime beaucoup.' Which was what everybody else was saying, but she said it from her heart, with feeling, with tenderness."

"I thought Jacques was French for James."

"It is, but the guy next to me, his name was Jack, so he became Jacques. Jaime is Spanish for James."

"What did you do? How did you feel?"

He smiled, fondly recalling his reaction, "It was like suddenly there was only the two of us. We were kneeling in the grass in the shade of an old oak. The wind was soft and gentle...I don't remember kneeling with her, but I did, and I took her face in my hands—ever so gently—like I was holding my prize indoor free-flight model. I'll never forget the warm softness of her face or the sweet odor of her black hair...And I poured out my heart to her—"

"In French?"

"In French, as much as I knew. We went beyond the lesson for the day, struggling with the French, and then I gently kissed her. The class bell rang sometime during this, but we didn't come to our senses until the room was empty and the teacher put her hands on our shoulders and told us we'd be late to our next class."

"If you weren't interested in girls, why did she get to you so easily?"

"I'm just a dumb male," he shrugged, "How do I know?...I guess I had been so humiliated by the others in the class, and I did want to get acquainted with Su Lin—I was planning to use my turn with her—and she was so sweet and dead serious, and—" he threw up his hands in a helpless gesture. "I don't know. I do know I forgot what day of the week it was; I went to all the wrong classes; I forgot the combination to my locker." He chuckled, shaking his head, "Oh, I had it bad!"

Tania laughed like she hadn't in what seemed ages, now. "I wish I could affect men like that. How long did it last?"

"Almost four wonderful years."

"Did you make love to her?"

"Whoa, whoa, slow down. We were just freshmen in high school. Just walking with her or holding her hand was scary enough. I don't know how I got enough nerve to kiss her, but it changed everything in both our lives."

"Just one kiss? How could that change your whole life?"

He leaned toward her and gestured with his hands, "We were two kids with terminal cases of shy: we had no self-confidence with members of the opposite sex. To her, her mother had hatched the plan; she had rehearsed it with her dad, she had carried it out in front of that heartless class, and she succeeded beyond her wildest dreams."

"Her parents were in on this?"

"You bet. They were neat people. I still love them as much as I love her...To me...at first I didn't understand what had happened, but I realized for once I hadn't chickened out. I had seized opportunity when she came knocking."

"Jim, I don't believe what I'm hearing. It was your self-confidence which convinced me to kneel down next to you, your self-confidence which convinced me to let you work on my leg, to let you take us out of the plane."

He smiled, "I told you how 'confident' I was. But that kiss got it all going."

"Oh, come on!"

"Hey, I couldn't even kiss my mother on the cheek, but I kissed her!"

"So what happened after that?"

"Okay...well— I walked her home, nervous, excited, thrilled she wanted to be with me."

"Holding hands and carrying her books?"

"Heck no! I had already gone beyond my limits of familiarity. Just to walk with her was to risk ridicule. Shy kids are extremely sensitive to what others say about them. Her mother, a beautiful Hong Kong Chinese, warmly welcomed me into her home, sat us down at the dining table, brought some Chinese sweets, and got us to studying French while she called my mother. I was invited to stay for dinner so her father could meet me—"

"How nice!"

"Exactly! She and Mr. O'Leary were delighted Su Lin and I had become friends, and after dinner asked us to reenact what we had done in class. We did; it wasn't as magic; but they were ever so warm in their appreciation. Mr. O'Leary put his hand on my shoulder and thanked me for coming home with Su Lin, and told me I was welcome to come home with her and study anytime."

"What neat people. My folks were never enthusiastic about any boy I brought home. They figured sooner or later he'd want in my pants," she sighed, "which was more or less true."

He could understand. "Yeah, that was my parents with my sister. Anyhow, the three of them drove me home so they could meet my folks. The relationship got off to a cordial start, and it grew. We got over being shy with each other, and then with everybody else. We started holding hands when we walked together—"

"To a lot of heckling, I'll bet."

He raised his eyes, "Oh, yeah. By supporting each other, we learned to ignore it, and it stopped when the kids found out they couldn't get a rise out of us, and *our self-confidence grew!*"

His picture of high school brought back many memories to her as she listened—fond, carefree memories, a few not so nice. "Kids can be so cruel, but I think I'm beginning to see where you're coming from."

Reliving the past was no less pleasant to him; it was far preferable to the reality facing them.

"We were pals, buddies. We didn't know the meaning of love; we just liked each other, we were comfortable, and we were happy. We competed for top grades in all our classes—she generally won, but I was always close. We were both college prep; my A's were as important to her parents as hers. Their support made it work."

"And so you changed."

"And so we changed." He nodded agreement, "She burst into a new girl, happy, vibrant, energetic, and—"

"Confident?"

"Right on. It was contagious; I caught the same bug. But it took that first kiss."

"What broke it up?"

She had asked the question for which he had no satisfactory answer. He had a partial answer, but the real reason was hidden to him. "She and her family moved away. God, it about killed us to part."

"Oh, I'll bet. How did you say goodbye? Lots of tears?"

"Lots of tears," he nodded. "It was early summer. We went out to a favorite place to lie in the sun and say a slow farewell. I was caressing her arm and cheek when she took my hand and slipped it under her T-shirt and placed it on her bare breast."

"And you didn't make love?" She realized she might be asking too personal a question, but he seemed perfectly willing to talk about almost anything.

He sadly shook his head. "She told me she loved me, and I kept feeling this wonderful warm softness. I would have kissed

it, but she stopped me. So we cried awhile...and said goodbye—"
There were tears in his eyes.

"You still love her?"

"Yes."

"What would you do if you met Su Lin again?"

"I really don't know. I've asked myself, oh, at least a million times." It had driven him nearly wild with anxiety. "What was your first love like?"

"Nothing quite so touching or beautiful as yours. The peer pressure for sex was very heavy, and I didn't see the wrong of it until much later."

"Something like my sister's experiences, I guess. She was one of the more popular girls because she put out in the back seat or the forest preserves—until one of her buddies got mauled in a gang rape. That stopped her loose sex."

"I'll bet! I wasn't *that* popular, but I wasn't an angel either. I didn't learn how to say 'no' soon enough to stop the first couple of guys. Then I had a reputation to live down. You know?"

He nodded, then checked the fires and the sky. There was still plenty of smoke from each fire. The sound of a light plane became audible and grew louder. Shading his eyes, he searched the sky.

*   *   *

The plane was banking, turning to head down another leg of the search pattern. Lt. Baker leaned against the side window, looking for signs of the downed airliner. In the distance he could see the lake.

"Hey, Bert, there's a fire near the lake."

"Probably another of them Forest Service fires," the pilot replied.

Baker continued to look, turning back, as the plane continued its turn, to examine the fire he saw in the distance.

"I didn't know they were logging near the lake," he muttered as they turned.

"Me neither. But it's in Gunnison County. Well, we sure didn't find no plane; let's head for home." He leveled the plane on its new course, heading toward the approach to Montrose airport.

Lt. Baker checked the map on his lap and crossed off the last quadrant with a pencil.

"Okay, I guess," he sighed. "We've covered our territory. Hope Hiram's cooled down a mite."

* * *

"Damn!" Jim pounded his fist into the other hand, "They didn't see us."

"So what else is new. They're looking for the *plane,* Jim." she said with special emphasis. "That's why they told us to stay with the plane."

Jim paced around, upset. She was right on that, but he was also right; they could not have lived at the high altitude until this day.

Tania let him agonize for a time; she hadn't forgiven him for leaving the plane, but as his mood didn't improve, she felt it time to change the subject.

"How did Su Lin's parents handle your dating her?"

"There were some restrictions."

"Oh, I'll bet there were."

"Not like my parents tried to enforce with my sister; she just ignored them. We had an hour to be home, they wanted us to do any necking at home in the living room, but they encouraged us to show our affection openly."

"Oh, come on! Now you're b.s.ing me—"

"I am not! We'd watch TV movies on the couch with her parents, and we'd be cuddled up on one end, caressing and kissing, and they'd be on the other end doing the same thing. Is love and affection something you have to be ashamed of and only show in private? They treated our affair as a serious, sensitive thing. They wanted it to be a happy experience...and it was."

"I can't believe you didn't want to try sex with her."

"Hey, I didn't say we didn't want to try it; we did. Well...the first year, I didn't know what that thing in my pants was for, nor did she. But after sex education classes we sure did."

"But you didn't?"

He shook his head, "Her parents were real straight up with us. They set some limits, and they trusted us not to go beyond them. One night we had a real, straight-from-the-shoulder, very open and frank discussion with them about sex. We'd like to try it. Okay, they could understand our feelings. We were welcome to do it—"

"Hold on! Her parents said it was okay?"

He nodded as he continued, "But there were certain conditions. Any time we wanted to go ahead with it, okay, upstairs in her bed, her mother would coach us the first time—"

"I've never heard of such a thing!" She was incredulous; her parents would have died on a cross first.

"This is one of the things," he nodded, "which set her folks apart from all others. They knew they couldn't keep her from sex forever; they had a beautiful daughter, and sooner or later some guy would take her. They wanted to be sure she didn't get pregnant, and they wanted to help us do it right so it would be a wonderful experience. There was no question in their minds we loved each other."

"My parents would *never* have done that!"

"Nor mine! I about got my head taken off when I mentioned I wanted to have sex with Su Lin. They went to the 'NO' school of parenting. So, Sis and I didn't listen to them—like you, I'll bet."

Ruefully she agreed, "Right on."

"See, Su Lin's folks didn't cut off communications with their daughter or me, they didn't say no, and we both respected them."

"Would they really have—?"

"They offered to take us right upstairs. We wanted to think it over."

110

"Would they have been disappointed if you had taken them up on it?"

"I don't think so. Look at it from their point of view. If they couldn't keep her from sex, they'd rather she do it where they knew what was going on and with whom, and so she could end up feeling good about it; than to have her skulking around with someone they didn't know, getting into trouble, and feeling guilty about something which is supposed to be a beautiful part of love. Yeah, and they got this impossibly beautiful girl through high school a virgin and knowing what love really is...Go ahead, try to fault that."

Tania slowly shook her head in admiration.

"There *were* some drawbacks," he added.

"I can't see how. What could possibly be wrong with heaven?"

"Yeah? Try this out. After I lost touch with Su Lin—my letters were returned with no forwarding address—I was terribly alone and lost. I've spent a lot of my adult life trying to find someone like her. I had the perfect woman, loved the perfect love...too young."

"I haven't had that love yet." She envied him.

"I only hope," he added in a serious tone, "I can raise my daughter with the same kind of understanding."

"You have a daughter? How old is she?"

"Yeah," he said digging for his wallet, "She just turned four." He opened the wallet and held it out for her to see a picture. His wife was pretty, the daughter adorable.

"Hey!" Penny shouted from the tent, "I'm hungry!"

Jim looked up at Tania and grinned. "All right!" he shouted back. He hastily got up and started for the tent. "What would la petite mademoiselle desire? Might I suggest the 'chef's surprise?' Perhaps a little vin de ginger-ale?"

11.

Jim was in a good mood. He had Penny sitting on the log next to him, the bedding was airing on several strands of nylon parachute cord, and Tania and Penny were airing their clothes as well. The day continued mild, but the air traffic was still disappointing. Penny had ravenously devoured the food he had fixed for her; he had her on a very restricted diet and activity program. While she was feeling much better and wanted to move around, she felt a little weak, and she now understood his concerns about too much exercise. Jim's joy at her radically improved condition couldn't be contained; he hugged her from time to time. She, hungry for affection, stayed very close to him. Tania, although she understood, was jealous of the attention he showered on her.

"Why do you have three fires going, Jim?" Penny asked.

"There are several international signals of distress. The most famous is SOS used on radio. The Morse code for SOS is three dots, three dashes, and three dots again. Three lights, three whistle blasts, and three fires are lesser known, but accepted methods of signaling for help. I have the three fires, and this morning when I laid them out, I stamped the word 'HELP' in ten foot high letters in the snow upwind of the fires."

"Do you think anybody will see them?"

"I certainly hope so. But we haven't had a lot of air traffic overhead to see them. Maybe they found the plane early and didn't need to conduct a more thorough search. An Air Force plane went through earlier today. If he photographed us, sooner or later they'll come looking for us."

"How could they see our fires from the high altitude he must have been operating at?" Tania asked.

"With the camera systems they have on that bird, they can read newspaper headlines at 70,000 feet. They also blow up and post on bulletin boards their favorite sunbathers, *au naturelle*." He put his head down and looked up at Tania, smiling.

"Is that all men think about?" Tania asked, disgusted.

"I haven't met too many women who don't go at least somewhat out of their way with dress, makeup, and perfume to attract male attention. Then when they get it, they think men are *voyeurs,* which they are, and oversexed, which they may also be, but only with the total cooperation of the other gender."

"You're just like every other man!"

"Hey, wait a minute. What do women lie out in the sun in the raw for? It's actually bad for them, leading to skin cancer...They do it to get a glorious tan so they'll look great in a itty-bitty bikini. What do they want to look great in a itty-bitty bikini for? To attract men. Now, if women want men to look at them, why do they complain when they do?"

"You're disgusting!"

"I'm not saying men aren't every bit as vain as women. They are. They go out for muscle building, which is absolutely useless, unless this cute little chick is attracted to a lot of muscle. They tan themselves, they preen and primp, and dress up, all to attract the female. But they don't complain when they get looked over; they worked for the attention and they enjoy it. All I'm saying is when a looker gets a peek at something he isn't supposed to see, it's generally with the cooperation of the lookee, intended or not."

"Isn't there some privacy left in this world? Now I have to worry about some peeping-Tom camera at 70,000 feet."

"Look at it this way. You should feel some pride if your neat tush, or your equally nice front side is chosen to be displayed on some squadron bulletin board instead of Miss Blimpington's 350 stone bod who was sunbathing just down the line from you. They don't know you, and you don't know they have your picture, so what's the harm?"

"It's...it's the principle of the thing!"

"I hate to break up this fascinating discussion, but it's getting late in the day. I think we had better get your outer clothes back on, get Penny to put the bed back together, and get about a light supper. I just wish I had some way of knowing what the search turned up." He stood.

Penny looked up at him, then started to run to the tent.

"Walk!" he shouted after her.

"I'm sorry," she called over her shoulder, slowing. She crawled into the tent and started pawing through her handbag. "I just remembered, I have a little transistor radio."

* * *

Jackie and Lori sat watching the TV news.

"...search aircraft have been combing the southwest corner of Colorado for the downed airliner—"

Jackie rubbed her stomach area, trying to relieve tension which had been there since she first heard of the plane's disappearance.

"...Government sources announced a reconnaissance mission was flown and the wreckage has been located perched high on the slopes of rugged 14,309 foot Mount Uncompahgre—"

"Oh, God, Lori," Jackie gasped.

* * *

Lillian paced back and forth while Sara sat on the edge of the bed. They were watching the network news.

"...Local authorities are planning a closer look tomorrow, but are not optimistic of finding survivors. The weather has been severe in the area, and the temperature is expected to drop to thirty degrees below zero tonight, with wind-chill factors going below minus 100 at those elevations—"

Lillian winced and turned away from the TV.

"It doesn't look good, does it?"

"Impossible," Sara replied. "They rammed a mountain and now the temperature drops out of sight...Where's that leave you?"

"I don't want to think about it. I'll have to move. I can't carry the place by myself. I talked to personnel today, and they said they'd help me for a month or so until they know for certain what happened." She blinked back tears which were beginning to form. "It's not the goddamned apartment; it's Tania! She's— she's like my big sis—sister."

"I'm sorry, Lil. I know you were so close."

"I grew up in a fam—family where anger and vi—violence were a—a way of life," Lillian bawled. She suddenly pulled her blouse off to reveal several scars on her back. "Here, look at these. 'You have sinned in the eyes of the Lord!' my old man scr—screamed, 'Ten lashes!' Fu—fuck 'im! Fuck the gospel quotin' son-of-a-bitch!" Her fist waved in the air in defiance.

"I don't *have* a family other than T-T—Tania. Sh—she's the only one who's ever given a shit about me."

"I'm sorry. I didn't know—"

"Nobody knows!...I s-sp—split when I was sixteen and worked the streets for a living. I'm a pr—prostitute and an alcoholic. I—isn't that great?"

"And Tania—?"

"I was s—so out of it, I can't remember when or h—how I met her. Can you believe that? S-Sa—Saint Tania dried me out, got my head sc—screwed on straight, and got me into f-fl—flight school...I'm sorry, Sara...Oh, Go-o-od!" She flopped across her bed, unable to continue.

* * *

Penny's little radio sat on the log, tuned to a local radio station. Reception was scratchy due to the mountainous terrain between them and the station.

"...Also in the local news today, the Forest Service continued the burn of logging slash piles, sending many columns of smoke into the air. There were many calls to the fire department about these fires. The burning is expected to continue tomorrow—"

Jim pounded a fist into his other hand, "Damn! They thought our fires were part of those burns. Well, they'll be up looking at the wreckage tomorrow; we'll have to keep our fires going a little longer...and hope." He switched the radio off. "Let's save the batteries in this for news for the next several days." He handed the radio back to Penny. "Thank you." He set about preparing supper, the last of the airline dinners.

"What are slash piles?" Tania asked.

"When they cut trees, they trim off the limbs and root out the stumps at the site. They pile this stuff, called slash, until the first snows, then burn them when there's no danger of forest fires. Something must have delayed the burns."

"I guess it's going to be cold tonight," Tania said. "I'm getting chilled already."

"I'll move you into the tent, then." He came to her. "I'm sure glad we had a chance to dry the bedding and our clothes." He picked her up and carried her to the tent. "I'll rig my rain fly over the tent to cut our radiation losses."

* * *

Lt. Baker walked into Hiram's office, waited a few moments while Hiram finished scanning a report, then cleared his throat.

"Oh, hi, Warren, how'd it go?" He settled back in his chair. "Sit down."

"I don't know. That's why I'm here. We didn't see the plane, but I understand it's up on Uncompahgre in Hinsdale County's territory."

"That's right," Hiram said, lighting his pipe. "So, what's your problem?" He blew smoke toward the ceiling.

"Well," Baker hesitated, "while we were making a turn on our search pattern, I thought I saw smoke down by the lake."

"Like as not, you did. They's been a lot of calls about them Forest Service burns today."

Baker twisted uneasily in his chair. "There hasn't been any logging near the lake in the last ten years."

Hiram looked reflectively at him, exhaled a little smoke, and then ran his finger along a map under the glass on his desk. "Shoot, that's near eight, ten miles from the ridge they say the plane's stuck on."

"Yeah. That's why I don't know if I have something or not."

"The lake's in Gunnison County. Have you notified them yet?"

"Yeah, I talked to Gene over there. He seemed to think it was some camper. But, hell, Hiram, how could a camper get in there? The road's been closed for over two months. Damn big drifts."

"One fire or more?"

"From our angle, I couldn't tell. Could'a been two, but I can't be sure."

"Okay, supposin' it wasn't some camper, what do you think it was?"

"I been kind'a wondering if it could be survivors from the plane."

"Oh, come off it!" Hiram chided him, "How the hell could they git themselves down t' the lake? In this kind of weather? Hell, our local climbers don't want no part o' Uncompahgre right now. You been smokin' somethin', Warren?"

"I know it sounds a little touched, but I could swear I saw the smoke."

117

"Well, the whole dang'd thing is out of our hands now, so go home, get a nice warm bath, and get a good night's sleep."

"Okay, Hiram. Thanks for hearing me out." He got up to leave.

"No trouble, Warren. You handled the plow thing with Highways real fine. Good night."

* * *

Jim returned to the campsite from his early morning fishing empty handed. He'd been skunked before, but this was more serious since they needed the fish. The lake had partially frozen over during the night beyond where he could get his line, and the snow had covered all rocks he might find to throw into the lake to break the ice up. It was too thin yet to support his weight, so fishing was out for the time being. It either had to warm up enough to melt the ice, or stay cold enough to finish the freeze over to sufficient thickness for him to walk out and do ice fishing. He put his collapsible pole into his pack and headed out to gather wood for the day's fires.

Penny and Tania were still asleep when he returned, dragging a couple of large limbs behind him. He left for more and soon had a tangle of limbs requiring breaking up. When he began throwing the rock he had used before against them, the noise wakened the women.

"How do you get out of bed, put your boots on, and slip out of the tent without my hearing you?" Tania complained.

"Practice," he laughed.

"Practice?"

"I'm married, remember?"

"I can see you slipping out of the side of a bed, but we're so jammed in this tent, you don't have room to wiggle around, much less do what you do, without disturbing me."

He winked at her and heaved the rock again.

"How is it out there?"

"It's Kiki bird weather." He picked up a piece of limb and put it on his pile.

"Kiki bird? What's a Kiki bird?"

"It's a little bird who sits on a fence, shivering with his friends and sings, 'Kee-kee-keerist it's cold!'"

"Jim! You're impossible!" But he returned her broad smile and chuckled.

"It's damn for cold. You'd better stay in there for a while." He positioned the remainder of the limb for another break. "I'll fix breakfast as soon as I finish this limb. How are you two feeling?"

"My nose is cold, and I have two of the coldest feet in the world. I'm waiting for you to get back into bed," Tania said.

"No headache?"

"Not today," she responded, cheerily.

"Great. Penny?"

"I think my fever's back." Tania turned quickly to her.

"Aw, honey, that's too bad. Here, let me feel your forehead." She put a hand out to sense Penny's temperature. "You're just a little warm."

"She's still on the antibiotic," Jim said. "You just stay quiet, Penny." He heaved the rock down again.

* * *

Sara and Lillian pulled their luggage carts along to the departure gate. The walk along O'Hare's corridors seemed to never end.

"I'm glad to be getting out of this town," Lillian said. "I'm not made for being stuck in a hotel room for long."

Sara glanced at her. "I just hope the plane's okay. I don't trust anything since the mess over the maintenance popped up."

"Today is probably the best day; they've just been over everything with a microscope. Tomorrow, who knows?"

Sara was glad to be flying again, also. She had spent the most nervous two days she had ever had, cooped up with Lillian.

119

She liked Lillian, and she understood Lillian's uneasiness, but right now she preferred to have the company of her other crew members.

Lillian wanted to be working, working hard; she needed something to keep her mind from dwelling on Tania. At the same time, she was anxious to get to New York so she could find out what the day's news about the wreck was. The morning news had featured the sheriff of tiny Hinsdale County explaining he was sending a rescue crew by commercial helicopter to investigate, and, if possible, to put men on the mountain to ascertain the status of any survivors. An attempt to recover the plane's data recorders would also be made. He held out little hope for survivors because of the weather conditions.

A special bulletin from the company headquarters had notified all crew members not to discuss anything about the maintenance of Interstate aircraft. A company spokesperson had been designated to handle all public and media inquiries.

The National Transportation Safety Board investigation had spread to other airlines guilty of many of the same abuses which were uncovered at the Interstate maintenance facilities: the use of non-approved replacement parts, kickbacks from parts suppliers, paperwork cover-ups of maintenance problems, and failure to follow correct maintenance procedures. In the absence of data from the plane's recorders, the cause of the crash had been tentatively laid to these abuses.

Lawsuits against the airline were already being filed on behalf of families whose loved ones were aboard Flight 238. The morale of the Interstate flight crews was at a low ebb; their job security was threatened by a possible financial collapse.

A subdued flight crew greeted Sara and Lillian as they reached the boarding gate. All knew of Lillian's grief over Tania; they themselves were in mourning. Two of the crew put their arms around Lillian's shoulder and whispered a few sympathetic words. The jetway entrance was unlocked and the quiet group entered the plane to make it ready for the passengers.

Once inside, Lillian called her friends to stop what they were doing. "Okay, look, you guys. I know what all of you are trying to do for me...and thank you. But, somehow it makes it worse if you baby me. I want to work my ass off. If the cockpit needs coffee, let me take it. If some passenger needs something special, let me take care of it. I need to work. I need to talk about something else, *anything* else. And one more thing, Tania wasn't the only one on that flight. If we're going to pray for someone, let's pray for all of them. Okay?"

* * *

"This is Alicia Martinez reporting live from Lake City, Colorado. Hinsdale County Sheriff, Paul Sanford, just moments ago, announced he can only conclude from today's attempted exploration of the Interstate aircraft accident site, there were no survivors. The near loss of the rescue helicopter in treacherous winds has forced him to cancel plans to remove bodies and the vital data recorders until conditions improve on the mountain, which may mean later this Spring.

"This is what it looked like earlier today when the tail section of the aircraft was blown off the ridge and part way down the slope by winds gusting in excess of two hundred miles per hour. Watch the rescue helicopter at the right of your picture as it almost loses control—"

Lillian punched the TV off in dismay. "Shit!" She pounded the top of the TV. "I was hoping, Sara, hoping and praying. Two hundred mile-per-hour winds!" She shook her head in disbelief. "That tail section looked like a leaf as it tumbled over the ridge."

"Incredible," Sara said. "Nobody could survive that."

"Until then, it looked like someone could have survived in the back part, but that, and the cold—" She shook her head, "No way. I hope they hang those cheating bastards!" She pounded the TV again. Her anger suddenly turned to sorrow. She put her head down in her hands. "Oh God!" she cried in a small voice, "I don't want to face our apartment when we get home, knowing she won't be back."

"Why don't you come over to my place. Betty's out of town for a few days. You could sleep in her room."

"No, you don't want to watch me drink. I'm going to get so stoned, I won't know where the bathroom is."

Sara grabbed Lillian's wrist. "How do you think Tania would feel about your drinking?"

Lillian pulled herself free. "I can't help it. She was my rudder."

"So now you're going to pay her back! Just throw everything away? That's just stupid!" She grabbed Lillian's wrist again. "Come on, Lil. Think about what she did for you, for God's sake. Okay, it's going to be tough, but stand up, make her proud of you."

Lillian rubbed her stomach with her free hand. "It hurts, S— Sara," she wailed.

"Damn right it hurts! Do you think pouring alcohol in there is going to make it any better? The only way you will ever make that pain go away is to live up to what she expects of you. When you can feel good about yourself, you'll get over the pain. Rejoice because she entered your life!"

"I don't know if I'm strong enough."

"Every time you start to pick up a glass of booze, you *think* about her, *see* her, *listen* for her encouragement. I know if I were her spirit, I'd be damned pissed at you if you started drinking again." She suddenly released Lillian's wrist in disgust.

Lillian looked at her, then bit her lip tentatively.

* * *

Jackie's eyes flooded with tears. Weakly, she reached to turn the TV off. She stood, staring through the tears at the tube, shoulders drooping, defeated. At last, with great effort, she straightened and took a deep breath, and wiped the tears from her eyes with the back of her hand.

"I don't know how I'll do it, but I'll carry on, Jim. I know you would want me to. God be with you, darling." She broke down, weeping again, "Could you somehow h—help me tell An—Andrea?"

* * *

Jim thumbed the little radio off and looked at his silent companions. He rubbed his growing beard, a nervous tick he had developed in the last two days.

"Okay, they're not going to be looking for us. According to them, we're dead." He looked at Tania, "Did you hear him describe the tail section blowing off the ridge?"

"You were right. I'll give you that."

He nodded slightly. "Okay, gang, we know it's up to us. Nobody's going to be helping. One good thing; I've got two gritty women."

"Thanks," Tania said, "but we're depending on you."

"No, no. I almost got you killed a couple of times. I've only led projects where nobody's life was on the line. You guys are going to be party to all decisions from now on. It's a group effort."

12.

Hardly had the sirens stopped when there was a loud knock on the door.

"Paramedics," a voice shouted through the door.

Eric Jacobs shuffled as fast as he could toward the door. "I'm coming," he called. His arthritic legs and his feeble condition prevented him from making swift progress. He opened the door and stepped aside as two paramedics rushed in. "She's in the bedroom down the hall," he said. "Please hurry. I think it's her heart."

The paramedics rushed down the hall, peering into each opening. One carried two large black cases, the other dragged an oxygen bottle on a small cart behind him. They turned into the bedroom.

"Mr. Jacobs?" the fire captain asked, entering the tidy apartment.

"Yes?"

"I'm Captain Varley, station sixty-five, Chicago Fire Department." He glanced at his clipboard, "Your wife is Miriam?" Looking around the room, he waited for an answer. It was a modest apartment on the near North side of Chicago. The furniture was old but in good repair, covered with a fading floral print. The wallpaper was an old floral print also.

"Yes."

"How old is she?"

"Sixty-three."

He wrote the age on the form. "Has she ever had a heart attack before?"

"...Yes, about three years ago."

The captain wrote the information down. He was becoming concerned about the old man because his answers were becoming slower and fainter. "Did anything bring this attack on?"

"...I think...I think it was the news our d—daughter, Maude, and our granddaughter...ah...Penny, perished in the airplane crash four days ago. Sh—she had just watched the...news. When she saw the wreckage tumble down the mountain, she grabbed her chest and stumbled to...to bed."

Varley looked up from his writing, "How do you feel, sir?"

"N—not very well. Weak...It...it was a terrible thing..." his voice trailed off.

Varley dropped his clipboard and reached for the old man's arm, "Here, you sit down, please. I'll have the men check you out when they're finished with your wife." He bumped a Tiffany lamp on the table next to the chair, but caught it before it crashed to the floor. Watching Eric carefully, he picked up his clipboard.

"Your full name, please."

The voice was strained. "Eric Emmanuel Jacobs."

"How old are you, Mr. Jacobs?"

"...Sixty-five," he mumbled in a daze. "It was a terrible thing...All those people...and Maude...and dear, dear little Penny...s—so helpless...we're so...h—help—agh!" He grabbed at his chest.

"In here, Matt! Quick! The old man's having one, too."

* * *

Jackie was quite down when Lori got to the house after work. She told Lori what she had seen on the afternoon news report. Lori had heard most of it on the radio, but she had a driving urge to see the video report. She hastened to turn on the TV.

"Why do I have to watch it again?" Jackie complained.

Lori ignored her and set about getting the VCR ready to record the footage of the wreckage. She sat on the very edge of the couch, peering intently at the news broadcast, far from discouraged. Jackie watched again, hurting inside. When the broadcast ended, Lori grinned. She rewound the tape and brought up a frame showing the wreck before the wind blew the tail section away. She froze the frame on the screen.

Turning to Jackie, she smiled, "Our guy is alive!"

"How the hell can you say that?" She wanted to believe her.

"Okay, promise not to get pissed off because I'm talking about something he and I talked about while we were living together. This," she pointed to the TV, "shows what Jimmy and I had a big discussion about. You can't see too much of the front, but the mound of snow is very short ahead of the wings, meaning it crumpled up pretty badly."

"Yes, I guess so. Why is that important?"

"It's important because it shows the crushing *took energy* out of the plane's momentum during impact. That was one of Jimmy's big arguments: Don't sit up front because it is the first to crush. But, see, it *slowed* the rest of the plane while it folded. It and the center section probably burned because of fuel. You can see some of the burned cabin where the snow's been blown away."

"I still don't see—"

"Look at the tail section!" she waved her arm excitedly at the screen. "Aside from some local damage at the fuselage joint where it broke, it's almost like it came from the factory! That's the key point of Jimmy's theory. He noted if any part of a plane survives intact, it is most generally the tail." She looked into Jackie's unbelieving eyes.

"Hey, I know," she continued, "I didn't believe him either. That's why we spent a whole Saturday looking through photographs of airplane wrecks. Sometimes it was only the horizontal and vertical stabilizers, but not infrequently, the whole aft section, like this. Sometimes the whole thing burned, but just as often the tail didn't. But the important point: Your best *chance* of survival is as far back as you can get."

"But you saw it go over the side. How could he survive that?"

"I'm getting there. But first, you have to survive the impact in your seat. He had an answer, and I'll bet you he was prepared." She looked at Jackie intently. "The answer to your question is: he wasn't in the plane today!"

"How can you be certain?"

"He was going camping?" Jackie nodded. "He wasn't going to check his pack?"

"No. He said they would let him put it in a closet in the—" suddenly she began to see Lori's point, "...back."

"So just how long do you suppose he stayed way the hell up on that ridge? It wouldn't take him very long to figure it was too cold. If he wasn't seriously injured, he got his ass out of there, pronto."

"But, what if he was badly injured?"

"Jackie! For Christ's sake! I'm giving you something to hope for. Why the goddamn hell do you insist on hanging on to negatives? The guy is *alive*, DAMNIT!!...Have some faith! He's just down in the woods somewhere, lost, but he'll turn up sooner or later." Though elated at what she had seen, way back in her mind churned the same doubts plaguing Jackie's thinking. She pushed them as far back as she could. From this moment on, she would believe in Jimmy. Why the hell she had ever turned down his proposal of marriage she could not fathom. "Come on, let's get some supper. I suddenly have an appetite."

* * *

Tania rolled to face Jim the next morning. It was snowing out. He was weary, so she prevailed upon him to get some rest.

"What are your plans, Jim?"

"For today?"

"No, for getting us out of here."

"Well, I guess we have several options, and I don't like any of them."

"Now with Penny better, why don't you leave us here and hike out to get help?"

"That's the option I like the least. Penny can't take care of you because you're too big for her. We have only one set of bedding and shelter. What am I supposed to use while I'm hiking? Another thing, I remember reading about a light plane crash in the Sierra some time back where a relatively uninjured man left a badly injured man to hike out for help. The badly injured man's brother found the plane some time later, and apparently, from his brother's diary, just a few days after he died. They never found the body of the man who went for help.

"I think we should stick together," he concluded.

She remained silent for a few minutes while she thought over what he had said. "Okay, why don't we pack up and get out like we came in?"

"I've been mulling it over fairly seriously. What I'm not sure of is which way to go."

"How about following the stream?"

"It's tempting, but—"

"It'd be downhill."

"Maybe. This is mesa and canyon country. One of the deepest gorges in the country isn't too far from here, if I remember correctly; the Black Canyon of the Gunnison. We're fairly sure this is Gunnison County from the radio reports. This stream likely flows into the river which cut that canyon. If it gets out to fairly level country before joining the river, all well and good. But it could go into a minicanyon of its own, and we would have to climb up one of these two ridges.

"Hiking out might take many days, and the weather hasn't been constant enough for us to attempt it. We could get lost even worse."

"If you're lost, you're lost. How can you be lost worse? Right now, we're lost."

He chuckled, "Okay, you're right. What I'm kinda thinking about is staying here until your leg heals enough to walk on. By then the weather should be better, and we would have a better chance, no matter what terrain we encountered."

"I'm not too excited about that option."

"I didn't figure you would be. If you're portable, then we might get out in a couple of days. If I have to drag you out, it could be an exhausting week or more. And we would have to find suitable campsites each night we were on our way. I might have to hunt during the trek for food, too. If we're traveling, we'll need a lot of food."

"I need food, traveling or not."

"Well, yeah. But not like you need it for heavy exercise. This will be no picnic."

"How far do you think we'll have to go?"

"I don't know. I'd guess anywhere from twenty to forty miles."

"How much food do you think we ought to have before trying it?"

"I would guess at least four days worth. As long as the weather is like this, we're not going anywhere. If it gets bitter cold, we're better off here."

"Why?"

"Because we're not putting a lot of sweat into clothing we can't get out before bedtime, and because we're not increasing our food needs using more energy heating our bodies."

Why is it, she reflected, *engineers are always so damn logical? Jim, I want out of here. But*, she reminded herself with a sigh, *he hasn't been wrong yet.* She might not like his solution, but it was the lower risk path, providing they could maintain the food supply.

Jim could read the disappointment in her eyes. He gently stroked her cheek. "I know, you want to get out of here. It isn't very comfortable, it's boring, but I am determined to survive this thing, and bring you and Penny along with me."

She put her hand on his stroking her cheek to hold it there. It was the first real sign of affection he had shown her, affection she wanted more than getting out of this place.

Every hug he had freely given Penny was one she wanted. She looked at him with eyes which tried to convey feelings she wanted to express more openly, but dared not.

*   *   *

Mike Mitchelson, Jim's boss, dropped by on Saturday to offer Jackie his condolences and to offer any assistance he could. He was submitting the forms to the company's insurance group to get her paid the coverage the company carried on all traveling employees. He had expected to walk in to deep sorrow, and instead found a grudging optimism in Jackie.

When introduced to Lori, she dragged him to the TV and went through her pitch once again, with even more conviction than she had with Jackie. Knowing he was an engineer, she gave him a more technically oriented presentation. Far from disbelieving, he was impressed, and questioned her further, receiving completely competent engineering answers.

Mike spent almost two hours talking with Lori. The longer he stayed, the more he believed, and the more impressed he was with her. He made several decisions; he would not clean out Jim's desk, nor seek a replacement for him; he would move as quickly as possible to interest Lori in coming to work for his company. He needed someone with her drive and assurance and her technical savvy, especially in Jim's absence.

"What would it take to interest you in coming to work for us?" he finally asked.

"If you're talking about Jimmy's job, no way! No possible way!" Lori replied without hesitation. Anger was rising within her.

He held up his hand, "That position is not available; I'm talking about another group under me. We need someone like you to get it moving, and you could help move Jim's work until he returns. What do you say? Could I send you an application form?"

"I don't know," she was hesitant, "You'll have to give me time to think about it. I hadn't been looking for another job. And, I think you can understand, this is not really the time for considering my personal situation."

"No, I quite agree. Why don't I send you the form, and when you can get things together, fill it out and give me a call?" He stood.

Lori agreed to his sending the form. He took Jackie's hands in his as they stood in the doorway.

"As far as I'm concerned, Jim is still an employee. I am sending the insurance forms in, however. I wouldn't expect too much to happen until some more tangible proof of his death is forthcoming out of Colorado. The announcement made was not an official declaration of death. That sheriff or the county coroner may tie things up for quite a while. I will argue, if Jim is not officially declared dead, then he must be alive, which means he is still on our payroll since he disappeared on a company sponsored trip. One way or another, you will be getting money. Were I you, I'd hang on to Lori's version. I am." He kissed her cheek and left much happier than when he came.

Mike's acceptance of Lori's explanation, his interest and questioning, had bolstered Jackie considerably. Mike had mentioned cleaning out Jim's desk when he arrived, but before he left he said he would hold his job for him. It couldn't be bullshit if he had been so impressed with Lori to offer her a job. When she closed the door, she grabbed Lori and crushed her with an embrace. Tears ran down both faces.

Lori finally pulled back, "Let's wake Andrea and go shopping."

* * *

The days passed, dragged, Tania thought, and turned into weeks. Penny had recovered and was restless. They were both tired of reading the one copy of the in-flight magazine. Some days they had food if Jim was successful at hunting or fishing while other days they went hungry. The weather had been cold and snowy, and then mild and sunny, and the lake had frozen over completely. Jim had ventured out some distance and cut holes to fish. Penny accompanied him for wood gathering and fishing, leaving Tania alone in the tent or sitting by the fire on a log. Tania cursed her inability to contribute to the work of the camp. Jim was bearing too much of a burden; she wanted to help. Instead, she was his biggest burden. He had to carry her in and out of the tent, and she still was embarrassed at having him help her with her panties when Nature called. She had tried leaving the panties off, but found she needed them for warmth.

All three of them were beginning to stink. Bathing under these circumstances was unthinkable. Jim's beard was getting quite full now. Tania enjoyed running her hand over it when they were bedded down. It was much softer now with the hair longer. And, he was giving her more affection. Not as though he wanted to take her body, which was absurd to consider in their crowded quarters, but as though he genuinely cared about her. He always had.

Tania sat on the rock outside the tent while Penny worked at keeping the fire going. Jim was off hunting. *Why does he have to be married?* Tania asked herself. *He's such a complete man, such a great father to Penny. She adores him...Like I don't?* She clasped her hands in her lap. *Lord. Please grant Jim some good fortune so his burden will be lighter.*

Jim, as he walked through the forest looking for something to eat, thought long and hard about his feelings for Penny. *What a wonderful kid! Bright, helpful. I wish she were mine.* And Tania, whom he found himself more deeply involved with than was proper for a married man. *Come on, James, get a grip. So okay, maybe she is one hell of a woman, so what? It's Jackie and Andrea you should be thinking about. But she's been coming on to me. Because I'm helping her survive? God, I hope she isn't falling in love with me.* His own feelings toward her were out of control. Tania represented elements of all three women he loved, a combination he could not ignore.

She reminded him of Lori when she participated in the operation. *Lori would have said, "I'll control the blood; you do what you have to do."* Yeah, but Tania hung in there. *She's got guts when the chips are down. And she's no complainer, either.* The several redressings of the wound had been encouraging, with no sign of infection. *She's tough. I don't think Jackie would have held up as well.*

She reminded him of Su Lin in her natural beauty. Although Su Lin was by far the most beautiful, Tania exceeded either Lori or Jackie, and she had many of the warm qualities of both Jackie and Su Lin. She was concerned about Penny, deeply concerned, and both Jackie and Su Lin possessed the same quality.

Yet, she also reminded him of Jackie, and to a lesser extent, Su Lin. *She sure isn't at ease with camping out. 'Course, neither is Jackie...and I guess Su Lin might've been uneasy, too.*

Tania seemed restless in her forced inactivity, which brought Lori to mind again. *You can see Tania's itching to do something, but she just sits.* He chuckled to himself, *But Lori...shit, she'd be crawling all over, taking care of things and getting on my case as well.* Nothing stopped Lori for long.

It's not like you've got a choice, Jimbo. You're married, remember? And you love Jackie for a lot of reasons. He sighed, "Yeah, I guess."

He looked up from his walking, from a kind of stupor, trudging along without paying attention to where he was going, and gasped. There before him was a small, wooden cabin, shuttered for the winter, well below the lake as his hunting took him further and further from the camp. He hurried to it. An ordinary padlock secured the door. Breathlessly he walked around it, noting an outhouse and wires entering a locked fuse box. He could see, as he returned to the front, trees forming the boundaries of what might be a road. The snows had covered everything many feet deep, including blocking the entrance to the cabin. No matter, he could clear enough room to get the door open. To hell with hunting! He turned and started running back to camp.

"Hey, guys," he shouted, still many yards from camp, "I found a cabin down below the lake."

Tania almost fell from the rock she was sitting on. Penny screamed in excitement. She dropped the log she was about to pitch on the fire and ran to him. He grasped her hand and dragged her along back to Tania, where he stood, out of breath.

After several deep breaths, he panted, "It looks like there might be a dirt road leading up to it, but it's buried under a lot of snow. The...ah...cabin's locked, but I think I can break in." He panted some more. Holding Penny close, he continued, "Come on, let's get this place packed up!"

"Way to go!" Penny squealed, jumping in her enthusiasm.

"Anything is better than this tent," Tania added, smiling.

"This place isn't very big or fancy."

"Two weeks cooped up in this will make it seem palatial!"

"Hey," he looked a little hurt, "Don't knock it; you're still living."

"Jim, I didn't mean it that way. I guess, if I had to, I could live another month in it, but—"

Though Tania was ready to leave on the instant, Jim took his time to carefully pack everything. He remembered to unbury the items left in the "freezer," which would provide only the next meal. He finally came to Tania and lifted her up to place her on the toboggan. This time she had no misgivings.

At the cabin, Jim and Penny busied themselves clearing the entrance to the door. He went to his pack, took something out of a pocket, and returned to the door.

"I used to know how to do this," he commented as he started to pick the lock. Minutes flew by as he worked. To Tania, they were hours.

"Break it," she suggested with growing impatience.

"Ah, there it goes," he mumbled, removing the lock. He opened the door.

Penny bolted inside. "BEDS!" she screamed, "chairs, a table, a stove! CHECK IT OUT!"

Jim went to Tania, untied her from the toboggan, lifted her up, and carried her into the cabin. She looked around as they entered and her heart doubled its pace in excitement. Penny was bouncing on a youth sized cot. There was a double bed, four wooden chairs, a table, a wood-burning stove, a sink, and even an *electric* refrigerator. He set her in a chair.

"Voila Mademoiselle, la petite maison par la Seine. Tres chic! Tres cozy! One hundred and eighty francs a night."

She laughed and punched his arm playfully, "You're a nut! A big, beautiful, crazy nut!"

Jim and Penny went around opening the shutters. He tried the faucets in the sink, but nothing came out.

"Probably shut off to prevent freezing the pipes."

Penny opened a cupboard, "Hey, here's some canned stew! Some canned veggies!...Uuuuu ICK!" She removed some molded bread and, holding it at arms length, walked it to the door and threw it out.

Tania looked up and saw three bare electric bulbs mounted in porcelain sockets on the central beam of the cabin. She was overwhelmed with relief and emotion and began to cry.

Jim noticed her, "Aw, look, honey. I know it's not much, but it was all I could afford on this week's check."

"It's beautiful!" she bawled, "I'm so damned h—happy...Go on, f—finish moving in and get some wood for the stove."

Her tears continued to flow as she watched Jim and Penny go in and out bringing in all the blankets, cushions, pillows, and other belongings. Jim leaned his pack against a wall and placed the rifle, in its case, across the table. She still was uneasy about it.

"Come on, hot stuff," he said to Penny, "let's go back to the camp for the wood."

Penny bounded to the door. "Let me pull the toboggan."

"Do I get to ride?"

"You're too heavy," she giggled.

As they left, she grabbed him about the waist, affectionately. He put his arm down to press her to him. Happy tears trickled down Tania's face as she watched the door close. She heard Penny's high pitched giggle as they left for the camp. *Lord, I thank you for your many blessings.*

Some time later she heard Penny's happy screams approaching. She looked at the door expectantly. It burst open and Penny rushed in, covered with snow, turned, breathless, and threw a snowball out.

"I got you, you monster!" She slammed the door and leaned back against it, panting.

"Monster?"

"He washed my face in snow."

The door started to open in spite of Penny's frantic efforts to keep it closed.

"NO! " she screamed as her feet slid across the floor.

Jim entered with an arm load of wood. "Do I get any help unloading the wood?"

There was soon a fire in the stove, and a plentiful supply of wood stacked near it. Jim went to the table and picked up the rifle. He turned to Tania.

"I saw deer tracks. Keep Penny here."

"No, " Penny whined, "I want to go with you."

"NO!" Jim was unexpectedly firm. He looked hard at Penny, "I don't want any hunting accidents. You stay here."

She stared back at him for several tense seconds, then suddenly removed her coat and sat at the table. He went to the door.

"Good luck, Jim," Penny said in a soft voice.

"Thank you, honey." He left, closing the door.

Tania reached across the table to grasp Penny's hand, "Why don't you and I get busy while he's gone?"

Jim returned to the cabin to find Tania's and Penny's wet clothing hanging from a line stretched across the cabin near the stove. The women were seated at the table, wrapped in blankets. The cabin was warm.

"Hey," he smiled, "looking good! You've been busy."

"Three weeks in those clothes is too long," Tania said. "You're next; we saved the water...Have any luck?"

His smile hardened, "Yes and no...I had to shoot a doe."

"At least we'll eat for a while."

"That's the way I looked at it. I'll dress it out, now."   He leaned the rifle against the wall near the door and left.

It was dark, and the electric lights were on in the cabin; Jim had picked the lock on the fuse box. He sat at the table wrapped in a blanket; his clothes were dripping next to Tania's and Penny's.

"Okay," he looked at his companions, "I want these lights on at all times we are not sleeping. The refrigerator, too."

"Why?" Penny asked.

"We failed to get a message out to the civilized world with the fires and the notes in the plane, so we'll send out a slow message."

"A slow message?"

"Sure," he smiled. "There isn't a power meter here at the cabin, and you wouldn't expect one at a remote location like this, but there *is* one somewhere; no power company I know gives the power away. And someone has to pay for the power. That someone is not expecting a bill for the winter months he isn't using the cabin. Oh, there's some kind of minimum charge, I'm sure, but we're going to see he gets the biggest bill he's ever had on this place—"

"And he'll come out here to find out what's going on!" Tania concluded, grinning. "It's a 'slow message' because it may take a while before he gets the bill. Right?"

"Right on," he nodded, pouring from an airline miniature liquor bottle into a cup. He handed the cup to Penny.

"You're giving her Scotch?" Tania complained.

"Just half a bottle with water."

"Jim!""

He was annoyed, "This much won't hurt her. She's earned the right to celebrate with us." He rubbed the top of Penny's head, affectionately. "Curly top."

Penny grabbed at his growing beard. "Shrub face," she giggled.

Jim lifted his cup in a toast, "To our new home. May we be evicted soon."

"I'll drink to that," Tania said.

13.

The cabin lights were out, Penny was snoring lightly in her bed, snug in Jim's sleeping bag. Tania rolled under the many blankets to face Jim and jabbed him hard in the ribs.

"Ouch," he complained in a whisper. "What was that for?"

"Damn you! You gave her the whole bottle. You got her drunk!"

"Come on."

"She was drunk. Didn't you see her stagger going to bed?"

"It didn't hurt her."

"You shouldn't have given her any."

"I think it's best to train kids at an early age how to handle it. My folks started letting my sister and me have drinks with them before dinner when we were twelve or thirteen."

"*She* isn't twelve or thirteen," Tania insisted. "Have you ever dried out an alcoholic?...Huh? Have you?"

"No."

"My roommate, Lillian, is an alcoholic. I've been through some damned tough times with her...God, I hope she has the strength to stay sober through this."

"Okay, maybe she had some problems. I don't think Penny will become an alcoholic."

"Oh, good God, Jim! She's lost both her parents. She'll never be able to forget the wreck; her mother's body, the flames, the smells, and the other bodies. What more does she need for problems?"

"She gets one more when we break out of here. She deserves it. Okay?"

"No! Why does she have to have so much as another drop? Damnit, Jim, you don't understand the other side of this."

He wanted to get away from her attack. "How did you get an alcoholic for a roommate?"

"I went looking for one," she snapped.

"What the hell for?"

"Because an alcoholic driver killed my father and crippled my mother."

He groaned, "So why?—"

"Because I felt so goddamned helpless. I wanted to do something positive about alcoholics. I wanted to be personally involved...I really wanted to kill every drunk driver, but that wouldn't have done me much good."

"Not after they locked you away."

"It's not that, Jim. Hate and revenge never accomplish anything; they're self destructive. What I've been able to do with Lillian has really made me feel good about myself, and Mom is proud, too."

"How did you find her?"

"I went cruising through the bars in St. Louis where I was living. She was not only an alcoholic, but a prostitute as well, and she was just getting into drugs. I took her home—she doesn't remember anything about our first two days—and I dried her out."

"It doesn't sound like fun."

"She was worse than housebreaking a puppy; puking on the carpets, crapping wherever she was, and when I wasn't looking, getting another bottle. I've never been through such a disgusting time. I almost gave up on her several times, but I was committed to helping some drunk, and I figured I had her and she was going to be it."

"How'd you finally break her of it?"

"With love. I gave her the love she never had at home. I showered affection on her—and it is so hard to do when she's cursing you and puking all over you. I held her in my arms, and I told her I cared about her. I finally got through to her. But love was only the beginning. You have to *understand* what drove them into that state. That's the real fight."

"Why would that be so difficult?"

"A drunk frequently does not want to talk about the very thing they're trying to wash out of their memory. They don't *want* to recall the pain." The long and painful efforts she had

140

trying to get to know Lillian, trying to get some semblance of a reason for her behavior, flashed through her mind. She could vividly see the nights where she had pinned Lillian's arms above her head on the bed, kissed her again and again, telling her she loved her, and pleaded with her to share her problems so she might understand, so she might in some way be able to help her. Little by little she had cracked the shell, and it had all come out.

"She had a terrible family existence; little food, little money, lots of violence between family members, hatred. In spite of this she was a top student, but her family tore her down, so she left home. Broke, she went to St. Louis, discovered she could support herself by lying on her back in bed, but she couldn't stand what she was doing or what she had left behind, so she tried to wash it away with whiskey."

"Which, I suppose," he noted, "made her less desirable as a paid lover."

"Oh, yeah. She was on a downward spiral. But once I understood her, things became easier. Okay, she needed lots of love. I'm not much into kissing another woman, but I kiss her every day, and I hug her, and I caress her on some evenings when she's down, and I tell her I love her, which I do...now."

"You're not?—"

"No, but we're about this far from it." She held her hand up, silhouetted against the light from the moon on the snow, with the thumb and forefinger barely separated. "We are very close, and I don't mind admitting we're close; it's a special relationship. Very special."

"That was all it took?"

"No way. I conned her into going to AA with me, and I helped build a support group for her. We still go to AA from time to time. By sharing with others, she began to feel better about herself, because there were others who had similar experiences.

"Once I got her dried out, I helped her complete high school, and I got her enrolled in flight attendant school. I've done everything I can to build her self esteem. I've given her some kind of culture with music and art. We go to plays, to the museums, to concerts, to rock festivals, dates, housework, shopping, we share everything. She's a productive, useful, sensitive person, now. But I never drink when she's with me."

"I understand. Is she with Interstate?"

"Yes. She's turned out to be a damned good flight attendant. The passengers love her and the crews, too. And I love her, but nothing like she loves me. But we're straight; we both have men we're dating—" She stopped suddenly, realizing Danny was now past tense. She pulled her fist to her mouth, trying to stifle a sob, but it came out anyway.

"What's wrong," he asked quietly.

She tried to control herself, but it was still too soon after his death. After a minute of inner struggle, she wiped tears from her eyes and gave a quick twist to her head, trying to shake off her emotions.

"Danny, the g-guy I was dating...was our pilot."

"Your guy was largely responsible for our survival."

"I thought the position you had us in—"

"Without that last minute flair and stall, the position would have been academic; we'd have been crushed along with the others."

She looked at his moonlit face for several moments. "Thank you for saying that. It helps, knowing he had something to do with my living."

"I'm not just saying that. He had *everything* to do with all of us living."

She wiped her eyes again. "Anyway, there's the story about my roommate, and why I'm against alcohol."

"I'm sorry, I didn't know," he whispered.

"And you still don't know, if you ever meet her."

"Got it."

"Jim, I am so afraid for Lillian." She put her hand on his chest, grabbing at his shirt. He covered it with one of his.

"Because of this?"

"Yes. This just might push her over the edge."

"You and she have friends?"

"Yes."

"And AA support?"

"Yes."

"You'll just have to have some faith in others for now." He squeezed her hand and pulled her closer with the arm under her head and shoulders. "Hope her love for you is strong enough to sustain her."

"Speaking of love affairs, I think I see one going between you and Penny."

"Yeah, I'm afraid so. I really care about her."

"Do you care about me?"

*   *   *

Lillian dragged her luggage cart into the apartment, dropped the handle, and closed the door. She picked up the cart handle, placed a handful of mail and a brown paper sack on the dining table, and dragged her suitcase into her bedroom. Returning, she went to the kitchen, grabbed a glass out of a cupboard, and returned to the dining table. She sat and sloughed the paper sack covering a bottle of whiskey to the floor. A generous portion of the bottle soon filled the glass. As she started to raise the glass to her mouth, she stopped and stared at it. Tears ran down her cheeks. She tried again to get the glass to her mouth, but an inch away from taking a drink, she lowered the glass to the table.

"Oh, God, Tania," she cried in a weak voice, "Help me. Speak to me. I'm so goddamned weak. I need you."

She picked up the glass, walked into the living room, and stared at a picture of Tania on an end table, tears flooding her eyes. The phone rang. Setting the glass in front of the picture, she moved lethargically to answer it. Nothing seemed to matter anymore.

Her voice was weak as she answered, "Hello?...Oh, hi. I just got back...Tonight?" She suddenly felt relieved. "Yes, please.

Could you give me ten minutes to change?...Oh, thanks. You have no idea how much I appreciate you calling." Tears still ran down her cheeks. "Jan, I was about to take a drink...No, I need all you people in AA since Tania's gone." She listened, then pleaded, *"Please* help me...Thanks. I'll be ready. 'Bye"

She wiped her face with her hand and hurried to the bedroom.

* * *

Lt. Baker stared in fascination at the photo transparency he had received from Washington under the Freedom of Information act. It would take considerable magnification to see the wreck, but he could see without any aids that the photo did not contain the area he wanted. Using a magnifying glass to look closer, he could not believe the detail. Tomorrow he would take the photo to the high school where he could use a microscope. He had never seen a reconnaissance photo before, and this would prove an educational experience. Hiram had not been enthusiastic, but he hadn't said he couldn't use the sheriff's office and official business as a reason to obtain the photo.

The entire photo was white with the snow the region had received, but he had no trouble picking out the contours of Mt. Uncompahgre. The magnifying glass brought out the shadows cast by the tail of the airplane. There it was. Amazing. Here were the local roads. He picked out distinctive farms and other features he could recognize. But, the mountain was near the northern end of the photo, and his interest lay on the frame previous to this one.

He turned to the typewriter next to his desk and began to compose a letter; he needed another photo.

* * *

Mike Mitchelson held an after hours meeting with a few key members of his staff. They gathered as their people went home for the evening.

"I won't keep you long," he announced. "Tomorrow, I have a lady coming in to see me. I'm going to have her give the whole department a presentation she gave me a couple of weeks ago. She's a close friend of Jim Hoskins. I want you people to look her over very carefully. Ask her any question you can think of, technical or otherwise. I'm considering her for the head of the actuator group."

"What's her name?"

"I'm sorry," Mike apologized, "Lori Cranston."

"Does she have any qualifications for that slot?"

Mike smiled, "Do you think I would be considering her if she didn't? She has a Masters from Cal Tech in Aero engineering, which she got with Jim. She presently heads an actuator group at NorthAire Aviation. I'll be bringing her by after the meeting to talk to several of you, but don't be bashful in the meeting, speak up. That's all. Thanks for staying over."

* * *

Penny, Tania, and Jim were seated at the table, finishing a breakfast of venison. Their mood was light as they enjoyed their greater comfort.

"Okay, Jim," Tania was suddenly serious, "this is the last meal we have I don't fix. Now that we have a warm, dry place, the work in here is my," she tapped her chest, "domain. Please fix this damned splint so I can get around."

"I don't know if I can," he protested. "You mustn't put any weight on the break since both bones were broken."

"Anybody who can patch an artery can certainly solve this little problem."

"A splint can only work so long as you don't move anything. A cast—"

"I don't care," she waved her arm impatiently, "about splints or casts. You're the engineering genius; fix it! I'm going out of my tree not doing anything."

Jim scratched his head, perplexed.

"Look," she softened her voice, "it's not because I don't appreciate what you've been doing. I do. But I want to do my share of the work. Please?"

He turned to Penny, "Would you please get me those shorter pieces of cord I used to lash the latrine together. I have to measure her leg. We'll have to find something else to support the leg."

Penny hopped up from the table and went to his pack. She returned with cords assorted in length. Jim took one and stretched it the length of Tania's leg. He made a knot in it at the measurement. He took another and wrapped it around her leg near the top of her thigh, knotting it where it lapped itself. Soon, several cords representing dimensions of various parts of her leg lay beside her.

* * *

Jackie put her coffee down and reached to wipe Andrea's chin and face before Andrea slipped off her chair to go play. The TV was on, tuned to the morning news, and the commercial was just ending as Jackie put the napkin down.

"...Gunnison, Colorado. An Army helicopter carrying five persons has just crashed near the wreckage of Interstate 238 on Mt. Uncompahgre. Government officials, not satisfied with the local sheriffs' refusal to risk their men, tried to land and recover the plane's vital flight recorders. The crash killed all aboard—"

Jackie grimaced, then walked to the TV to turn it off. There were other matters she had to attend to; she didn't need more death on that hated peak. Sitting at her small desk, she shuffled through bills which had accumulated, trying to decide which she could afford to pay.

She shook her head slowly, "I don't know where the money is going to come from."

* * *

After about two hours, Jim and Penny returned to the cabin, dragging several long pieces of aspen bark in with them.

"I sure hated to skin that tree—" he started.

"Like you hated to shoot the doe. I feel my needs are greater than a tree," she stated firmly, leaving him no doubt about the firmness of her demand.

He set Penny to preparing a dishpan of hot water on the stove, while he picked Tania up and placed her on the bed, propping her up with pillows and folded blankets so she would be relatively comfortable and could watch what he was doing.

"Don't you dare move any part of this leg until I'm done," he cautioned as he started untying the many headrest cloths which held the splint to her leg.

"I want to wash it," she objected.

"*I'll* wash it. You stay put. I don't want to disturb any healing which has happened so far. Our stay here is dependent on when you can walk."

Carefully, he worked the splint and blanket wrap off her leg. The wound was healed, she noted. She was overcome with an urge to scratch the leg as it began to itch in the air. After a sharp reprimand from him, she sighed and leaned back, crossing her arms and tucking her hands under her armpits to keep them out of trouble. He took a rag they had been using for sponge baths and washed the leg for her, using great care around the break, but a satisfying vigor elsewhere, relieving some of her itching. The leg toweled dry, he continued rubbing with his hands, to stimulate circulation.

"You'll do anything to get your hands all over my body."

147

"Oui, Mademoiselle, j'aime frotter la jambe d'une très belle dame." (Yes Madam, I love to rub the leg of the beautiful lady.)

"Vous êtes un vieux homme sale." (You're a dirty old man,) she replied, struggling with her French.

"Moi? Oh, oui, oui," he grinned as he continued to rub her leg. "Umm, très gentille! Très jolie!" (Umm, very nice! Very pretty!)

"What are you two talking?" Penny asked. "I can't understand you."

"French, " Tania replied. "And it's a good thing you can't."

"I don't think that's fair."

"Right now, Jim's not being fair...Enough, Jim!" She slapped one of his hands, favoring him with a quick wink. Not that she wanted to stop him; she just didn't want Penny as a witness.

He set about fitting a bark cast to her leg, using the hot water to soften the bark and make it more pliable. Finally, turning the piece of blanket inside out, he rewrapped the leg in the blanket and fit the bark over it, tying it up with the cloth bandages. After removing the down boot she had been wearing, he replaced it with her shoe he had brought in his pack. She watched him fashion a bark overcovering to hold her foot perpendicular to her leg and tie it in place. Jim fitted a shorter piece of bark to reinforce the area immediately over the fracture, securing it in place with two bandages.

Finishing, he rubbed the bark, grinning, "I love what you've done with your Lady Schick. So smoooooth!"

She playfully slapped his face. "Fresh!"

While Tania watched, Jim took two forked branches he and Penny had brought in with the bark and carved all the rough bark and other protuberances off to produce a fairly smooth surface. He cut each leg of the fork to about six inches, then held one up to Tania's body to estimate length. Cutting the stouter ends took more time, but at last two crutches were ready.

"Okay, Stumpy, let's try it."

He held out his hands to her, waited while she laid the two crutches to one side, and helped her to her feet. She stood, keeping her weight off her injured leg and, using him for support, leaned to pick up the crutches. Tucking one under each arm, she tried a few awkward steps. Having never used crutches before, she had trouble coordinating her movements of the crutches with her feet. She rested a few moments then made a transit around the tiny cabin, stopping in front of Jim.

"I think I need pads on the crutches. It's hurting under my arms...At least I can stand."

"Yes, you probably do need pads." He accepted the crutches.

With an airline pillow tied around the fork of each crutch, he demonstrated to her how to use the crutches by keeping her elbows straight to avoid bruising her armpits. She soon was able to navigate fairly well and asked for her other shoe. A couple more tours around the cabin and she smiled.

"I guess it'll take some getting used to, but at least I can get around." She drew herself to her full height. "Okay," she asserted, "from now on, straightening beds, sweeping the floor, washing dishes, washing clothes, and cooking are my duties." She pointed at Jim, "You're the outdoor person. You carry me to the little house out back, you hunt, and you and Penny gather wood and fish. Penny brings in the snow to melt for water. When you're hunting, Penny can help me. Got it?" She looked at him and Penny. When they nodded their assent, she smiled.

"Okay, I've got things in hand, here. Out!" She pointed to the door.

"Oh," Jim complained, "I wanted to stay and watch you root around." He ducked as she swung a crutch at him.

Now, Jim thought, *I'm seeing the real Tania.* He liked her spunk. He was still concerned about the leg; he didn't trust the rigidity of the bark and hoped she would be careful not to stress it too heavily, but he knew she had been getting increasingly restive, and this would improve her attitude greatly. He and Penny put on their jackets and coats and bundled up against the snow which was falling again. Penny closed the door behind them.

"She's sure got spunk; I'll say that for her," Jim commented as they made their way toward the lake. He had his collapsible pole in hand.

"She's super nice. Do you like her?"

"Honey, I like both of you. You're both super." He looked down at her. "What'd'ya say we see if 'Old Mushmouth' is still nibbling the bait off our hook?" He liked Tania more than he wanted to tell Penny, more than he wanted to admit to himself.

* * *

Tania crashed to the floor, the crutches slid away in different directions. There had been a twinge of pain in her broken leg which had caused her to twist away, off balance, and now she was sprawled on the floor as she tried to protect her leg. Her elbow and forehead reminded her of the foolishness of what she had attempted. For the moment, she was too scared to move or think. Her heart pounded wildly in her chest, and breathing was difficult.

Slowly she took inventory. First, the leg. Was it okay? Well...no new pains. So far so good. The elbow. She rubbed it cautiously. There was a bruise. She flexed it a little bit, then more as there were no negative reports of sharp pain. Okay. With conscious effort, she controlled her taut breathing, forcing a deeper, more relaxed mode.

After several deep breaths, she began to put her mind to how to regain her standing position. With effort, she was able to scooch nearer to one of the crutches. She grasped it and used it to draw the other nearer to her. Then, using a series of sit-ups and roll-overs, she was able to herd her crutches and herself to the bed. She drew herself up onto the bed and sat, nearly exhausted.

Thank God, she thought, *Jim wasn't here to see this!*

* * *

Lori fidgeted while Mike went through an unnecessarily long introduction. He explained he had met her at Jim's house, and she was a close friend of his. She looked around while the introduction droned on. Every person in the department was crammed into the conference room; engineers, draftsmen, secretaries, and support people. She was not at all nervous. She knew what she had to say, she believed in it, and nothing could intimidate her. These were the people Jim worked with. By God, she'd give them something to hang on to. When the introduction ended, she stepped up on the small platform Mike had arranged in deference to her diminutive stature.

"Hi," she said with characteristic enthusiasm, "I'm here to tell you Jim Hoskins is alive, and just why I know that..."

An hour and fifteen minutes later, there wasn't a doubter left. Mike was pleased. His people had questioned her at length, but nothing had shaken her. She had maintained her poise, answered every question directly and with conviction.

He took her to the actuator group, had a drawing of their latest design spread out on a drafting table, and asked her to give her comments on it. She looked it over carefully.

"Well," she said after several minutes, "it's too expensive, it will fail in vibration and fatigue testing, and it's too hard to mount and service."

She had everyone's attention. Some were upset, but others had more than a casual interest in her comments. All watched in fascination as she described how she thought it would fail, and estimated the number of cycles in fatigue. She marked up the print with her estimate of the line of fracture. Shocked faces stared at her. How could she know? One of the engineers left the group to go to his desk, returning with a copy of the actuator which had failed as she had predicted. Her estimates of when it failed were only a few percent off.

What would she do to redesign it? She spent the next hour outlining how it should be changed and giving her reasons for the changes. Red pencil lines flowed across the print, with some hastily scrawled notes here and there.

"If you changed the mounting to something like this, it'd be easier and cheaper to machine, it'd have better fatigue strength, and the whole thing would be easier to get out for servicing." She looked up at the many faces staring at her. "Look, guys, the airlines don't want something they have to spend all day getting out with special tools. They want something they can pop out *muy pronto* and put another in its place. Airplanes don't pay for themselves when they're not flying. If you don't believe that, then get out to some flight line and talk to the mechanics."

Mike stood behind the group and grinned the whole time. He watched thousands of dollars of cost melt away under her red pencil. When he pulled her away, there were still some skeptics, but they were in the minority. She had established herself as technically competent, and had gained many admirers. After lunch, Mike dropped her off at her truck. There wasn't a dissenting vote in his two-o-clock staff meeting.

"Then it's settled," he concluded. "All that's left is to negotiate a price." He had listened to one enthusiastic comment after another. "And," he continued, "I hope there's no question in anybody's mind why I'm holding Jim's position open?" He smiled at the shaking heads. "Okay, let's get on with the status of our projects. Roger, you're up."

14.

Tania hummed a bit of a happy tune. She found it hard to believe the change in her morale which had occurred in the last 30 hours. Though tired from her day's labors, she was pleased. She had cleaned and dusted and fussed around the cabin, completely independent of Jim. There was a real roof over her head, and she no longer doubted she would survive. Impatience was replacing uncertainty, assertiveness replaced forced docility. True, she still depended on Jim for food and fire, but she had some control over her own destiny, some control over her day-to-day existence. She was an independent woman, and her forced inactivity and her utter dependence on Jim were upsetting factors.

She sat in a chair, humming and tapping a hand on the table, waiting for Jim's and Penny's return. Rubbing her bruised elbow, she thought about the last few weeks. It wasn't because Jim was domineering; she didn't resent his treatment of her in any way. Simply, he had made the best of every situation he had faced, and she was unable, until now, to contribute. Maybe this contribution didn't really advance their cause toward returning to civilization, but she felt she was part of the team now, not the burden she had been.

The change in living quarters had not, she realized, fundamentally changed their situation. They had survived extreme cold and heavy blizzard in the cramped confines of Jim's tent. Their sources of food and the attendant uncertainties remained unchanged. Only their comfort changed; the bed was far more comfortable. And she was warm, and that counted for a lot.

Her thoughts turned to Lillian. She hoped—prayed—Lillian would have enough strength to endure what must be a very trying time for her. Here she was, her immediate future seeming to be relatively secure, and Lillian was facing the collapse of her world. She prayed yet again for strength and help for her roommate, for support from their mutual acquaintances. Her relationship to Lil was a very precious thing, and she felt closer than she ever had, if only because she couldn't be with her to comfort her, to—to love her.

At this moment, Jim and Penny came in the door, covered with snow. Jim carried two good-sized fish on a cord.

"Those are mine!" Penny informed her with pride.

"Hold it, you two," Tania butted in, "Take your coats and boots off by the door. Don't go tracking up this place after I just cleaned it." It felt good to watch them obey. Respect. They respected her, and she could indulge in a little self-esteem. She smiled at Penny.

"They look very nice. Are you cold?"

Penny was too excited to consider whether she was cold or not; those were her first two fish. She proceeded to tell Tania all about the great event, talking rapidly in a high pitched voice. Tania tried to share her excitement. She was beginning to feel as close to the girl as Jim evidently did.

"Okay," Jim said as Penny wound down, "how's the wooden leg?"

"Fine. It's aching a little, but I feel pretty good."

"I thought," he stroked his chin, "it looked a little at-tree-phied."

Tania shot him a pained look.

"It'll probably attract every dog in town," he continued.

"If it'll point the way to town, I'll let 'em at it."

"Just so they don't bark all night," Penny joined in.

Tania stared at her, "I think I'll leaf that alone."

A merry group sat for supper. Tania led them in a short prayer of thanks for the good fortune they had in the last two days. She had used one of the two cans of vegetables found in the cupboards to supplement their diet of meat. It was a welcome treat. After dinner, she and Penny washed the dishes. The two dish pans they found in the cabin simplified the chore. Their problem was an acute shortage of soap, which they hoarded for occasional washing of clothes. The dishes were merely rubbed and scrubbed in hot water, then rinsed in cleaner water.

Jim and Penny played Gin after the chores were done. Tania kibitzed Penny and helped from time to time.

"Could I see those pictures of your wife and daughter again?" she asked Jim while Penny was dealing.

He went to his pack, pulled out his wallet, and handed it to her.

She looked more carefully at the pictures she had seen briefly, studying Jackie and falling in love with Andrea. The pictures were only two of several in the wallet. One showed a woman other than Jackie, holding Andrea, both absorbed in something out of the picture. A very touching, sensitive photo. Another showed the same woman with Jim. He towered over her.

"Who's this?" she held the wallet out to him.

He discarded a card. "Lori."

"Your sister?"

"No, a close friend. Later?"

Tania looked at Penny's hand, pulled a discard for her, resorted the hand and said, "Gin. Go on, honey, put 'em down."

Jim started counting his points. Tania looked at the pictures again.

"I adore your daughter. She's very cute." She showed the pictures to Penny. "It looks like this Lori loves her, too."

He smiled, "She does. Andrea calls her 'Aunt Lori.'"

She turned over another picture and gasped, "Is this Su Lin?" He nodded as he sorted his hand. "She's *gorgeous!*"

"Now you know why I was crushed when they moved away. That was taken Junior Prom night. She was the Queen of the dance." He looked at Penny, "Okay, you little rascal, it's time I paid some attention to this game to teach you some respect." He threw out his first discard.

Penny snatched it up, put another face down. "Two," she said gleefully.

It was not to be Jim's evening. Penny finally went to bed, having won almost every hand.

"That's what I get for teaching her this game," he lamented.

"You showed her the game, I *taught* her," Tania corrected.

"I hoped we'd get to the root of the matter."

"Am I going to be the butt of tree jokes from now on?"

"I wooden be surprised."

"All right, Shrub-face, I'll get you."

"Of course," he rapped his knuckles on the bark, grinning, "we could do knock-knock jokes if you prefer." He helped her stand, then took her hands in his. "You are beautiful tonight," he said softly, looking into her eyes.

"Not like Su Lin."

"Don't compare. You are beautiful in your own way."

"What about me makes you say that?"

"It's true; don't knock it."

"I'm not knocking it, Jim," she replied, her voice very low. "I just want to know why you think so."

"First, you're happy, putting special lights in your eyes, lights which enhance your entire face. Your hair is as nice as I've seen it."

"I spent a whole hour combing it out. It helps to have a nice big mirror."

"Okay, the next thing I was going to mention is that you're more comfortable here. So you're relaxed and confident, which adds another glow. And finally, you're assertive, you're yourself for a change. I like this self."

"Thank you." Glowing in his compliments, she hoped the evening would become more intimate. She took her hands from his and put them on his shoulders. "A woman enjoys being her best for a good man." She reached up and kissed him.

"I intend to remain a *good* man," he said softly. "Please."

Tania tried not to show her disappointment. "Let's go to bed and get the lights out for poor Penny," she said.

He supported her arm as she hobbled to bed, and removed her one shoe after she sat on the bed.

After tending the fire, he turned out the lights and removed his boots. Tania held the blankets up while he slipped into bed beside her. A half hour later, she was still wide awake, but Penny was asleep.

"Jim?" she whispered.

"Umm?" He was half asleep.

"Would you tell me about Lori?"

"Oh." He rolled to face her.

"Is she your wife's friend?"

"Her best friend. God, I hope she's holding Jackie up through this."

"Then you met her after you met Jackie?"

"No, no, you have it all wrong. I knew her long before I met Jackie. I asked her to marry me."

"Maybe you had better start from wherever the beginning is."

"I had a tough time after I lost track of Su Lin. I was looking for a relationship like I had with her."

"That shouldn't have been too hard."

"Think back, Tania. When I was going to UCLA, the nation was in the midst of the feminist and the sexual revolutions. Now I'm not saying all the women on campus were like what I found, but for sure the ones I took a fancy to were. They seemed to put their sexual desires ahead of forming any kind of meaningful relationship."

"And you, I suppose, did not take advantage of this?"

"I make no claims of purity. All I'm saying is the women I dated—some longer than others—were ready and willing to go to bed with me, but didn't want to get heavily involved in a relationship."

"I've known a number of men like that. They like the good times but they don't want responsibility."

"Nobody wants responsibility! If you can get something you want without responsibility, you go for it. It's a human character weakness. How about yourself? You said you indulged and never had what I had with Su Lin."

"I was pressured into most of it."

"Come on, that's a cop-out and you know it. You like sex as much as anybody else and, if you'll be honest with yourself, you wanted most of it."

She sighed. It was true, she had to admit. "Okay, I don't want to go into all of that. A lot of it was...ah...disappointing."

He nodded, "Same here. I was offered sex, and I took it, and I liked some of it, but I *wanted* the relationship. Can you buy that?"

"Yes, because I've been there."

"Okay, so I graduated without being seriously involved with any woman and went on to Cal Tech to get my Masters. I rented an apartment near the campus for more than I could afford, so I advertised for a roommate with the school housing office. Lori showed up."

"The picture showed her as being rather short."

"Don't ever call her short...Ah...diminutive. Lori's a perfectly proportioned five-feet-two, one hundred-and-twelve pound package of go-go-go. She's independent, confident, aggressive, assertive, energetic, and damned intelligent...And she's also attractive."

"I was wondering when you'd get to that. Probably the first thing you noticed."

"Not really. She showed up in Air Force fatigues; all I could tell was she was short—"

"Diminutive?"

"Yeah, okay...Oh, and she had a pretty face, though her hair was somewhat of a mess."

Tania admired Lori's tactic of hiding her attractiveness while out apartment hunting. "So?"

"So, I started showing her around; the bedroom, bath, kitchen and so on, and she says, 'You're not just looking for some hot snatch to keep you warm at night, are you?' I answered, 'No. I'm looking for a student to share this apartment and the expenses.'

" 'Nice kitchen. You're not gay, are you?'

" 'No. I'm straight. What difference does it make if I'm not looking for someone to cover my mattress?'

" 'Plenty.' She liked the bedroom I showed her. It turned out we were taking the same degree. She asked how I determined the price, which was half the rent and half the utilities. And she really wanted confirmation that we truly shared costs, cleanup work, and so on. By this time, I had shown her the whole place. I told her about the new laundry facilities the place had, and about the guard service the owner had employed to protect the cars and the households."

"That doesn't sound too unusual," Tania commented.

"Wait till you hear this. She said, 'I like the place, and I think I could like you. But before I would settle anything, I want a blood test on you.' "

"What?"

"That's what I said. So she explained the last guy she shared a place with turned up with AIDS. In her words, 'It scared the shit out of me. I don't want to move in with anybody who's gay, or who has that disease. I want to know the person I'm living with is healthy and has healthy habits.' I really couldn't blame her."

"Well, yeah, I can see her point."

"So, I said, 'Well, gee—' and she said, 'I'm not asking anything I won't do. We'll go down and get a premarital physical. I'll give you my report, you give me yours. That's fair isn't it?' She has always been absolutely fair with me."

"Still it seems to me she was very forward in making such a request. Why didn't you look for someone else? I would have."

"She is. Nothing intimidates her. I happened to like her for that. She also had other qualifications I liked—"

"Like two boobs and a nice tight butt?"

"Aw come on! I had no chance to observe her body. No, I sensed she was being absolutely straight with me. She had insisted we would share everything 50-50, but most importantly, she was taking the same degree I was.

"I did learn about her bod the day she moved in."

"No fatigues?"

"I had agreed to help her move her stuff. She showed up at my place wanting me to drive her to a truck rental place. She was wearing the very tightest and briefest pair of DaisyMaes you have ever seen. Her tube top was barely three inches wide, and nearly transparent. 'Go on,' she said as I stared at her, 'look me over. Get it over with so we can get on with the moving.' So I did—"

"You men are all alike."

"Come off it. You mean you women don't look the guys over pretty carefully? Like hell you don't! You like a nice big bulge in the front of a guy's pants with a tight tushy in the rear—"

With a start, she remembered what she and Cherise were talking about before the crash. "Oh, God!" she gasped.

"What's the matter?" He put his hand to her face.

"Cherise. Sh-she thought you were pretty cute, and...and we commented on your...ah...'build.'" Tears moistened her eyes.

"I'm sorry, I didn't mean to remind you of her." He stroked her cheek and discovered the moisture. "There's nothing we can do for her, Tania."

"How did she die?" she cried, "Please tell me how she died."

"No. She died instantly. Don't ask for more. She died doing her job, like your friend in the cockpit...From what little I knew of her, she and Lori had a lot in common; very up, very cheerful, a hard worker, positive."

"You won't tell me any more about Cherise?"

"No."

She sniffled and dried her eyes. "So, you were looking Lori over—"

"Oh, yeah. Next she tells me it's hot outside, why don't I change into some shorts and be comfortable; I was in jeans and a tee shirt. So, 80 percent naked, we went off and got a truck, which she drove, and we moved her in. And she worked like any man I've ever known."

"She didn't have some other guys, friends, helping?"

160

"Nope, she was, and still is, pretty much of a loner. The next morning she got me up at some ridiculous hour, and we go out running in a park. And two afternoons a week, she's dragging me to a gym to push machines around. She has a magnificent body, and she works like hell to keep it in great shape. She changed my diet, too."

"What were you, some kind of wimp?"

He chuckled, "Well, maybe, but I don't think you quite realize what I was up against—"

"Like what?"

"We were in the park, running. She's maybe a half a block ahead of me. This big guy jumps out of some bushes at her with a knife; he wants to rape her."

"You went to her rescue?"

He shook his head, "It was over in two seconds. She hoisted him up and slammed him down like a professional wrestler, then drove the hand holding the knife so he severed both organs of his manhood."

"Good! I think I'm beginning to like your Lori. Was she scared?"

He laughed softly. "Scared? Two policemen, who were cruising by, came rushing over. She's running in place while they're cuffing this bastard. He's squirming and bleeding and she says, 'Bet that's the last time you get the urge for nooky.' Then she tells the cops, 'I've got two more laps to do. Here's my car keys.' She took the string off her neck and pointed to her car. 'When you're done with him, I'll meet you there.' And she was off again, like nothing had happened. I stopped and stayed with them."

"Weren't the police upset because she ran off?"

"They were so flabbergasted, they didn't know how to handle her. So, one guy ran to the middle of the park and watched her, and the other called on the radio for an ambulance. When she was finished, she pulled up to her car, took her keys back, got out the towels and a sweat shirt, and started cooling out and stretching while these guys were taking down her name and

161

address and her statement. They had nothing but admiration for her. She pressed charges, along with several other women victims, and he went to prison for a long time."

"I guess you were impressed?"

"I was definitely impressed! And I was even more impressed by the kind of student she was. Cal Tech is one of the toughest schools anywhere, and the premier one in aeronautics. She and I competed for top grades in all our classes, pulling straight A's. There was no time in our schedule, beyond the exercise, for social activity. I had expected she would be dating some guy, but it wasn't the case. We formed a very congenial relationship, and we truly shared all the work around the place, all the studying, and a mutual respect for each other."

"But you didn't fool around with her?"

He shook his head, "Anything personal with her was by invitation only. I expected we would remain just friends—oh, good friends to be sure—until we graduated."

"But, you said you asked her to marry you. Something must have changed."

"It did," he nodded, "Our life was nothing but study, school, exercise, and shopping for food. One Friday, along about Thanksgiving, she slammed a book down on the dining table where we were studying and said, 'I'm not having any fun!' I agreed it had been a tough grind. 'And I'm horny as hell,' she continued."

"She doesn't sound much like a lady."

"I never said she was...She *can* be very ladylike, but that's not her general style. So, I said something like, 'Yeah, *tell* me about it!' So she kind of looks me up and down and says, 'Well, why don't we do something about it?' Always slow on the uptake, I asked what she had in mind."

"You *must* be slow!" Tania laughed quietly. "Don't tell me; let me guess. She said, 'Sex, dummy!' Right?"

"Close enough."

"So, did you?"

"We became lovers that night, and fell in love a couple of weeks later."

"I thought sex for sex's sake turned you off."

"This was different because we already had a strong relationship in place. It wasn't love the first night, but it was pretty close. Afterwards, our Friday and Saturday nights were reserved for our love."

"What about the other nights in the week?"

"Much too busy studying. But we did, on some bad rainy mornings, get our aerobic exercise lying down.

"We went an extra half year beyond our requirements to pick up some other courses we were interested in. The summer in between, we had a chance to find out what each was really like."

"I would have thought you would have known each other fairly well by then."

"Yeah, but we discovered we both liked camping, hiking, fishing, country music, and a host of other things. We had time to ourselves on the evenings and weekends, and we expanded our knowledge of each other. Each had a job for the summer in different companies, but we commuted some distance just so we could hang on to the apartment. We got season tickets to the Greek Theater. We *lived* that summer. It was as wonderful as when I was with Su Lin. Maybe better."

"You asked her to marry you. What happened?"

"The day we graduated, I took her in my arms and asked her to become my wife. She kissed me and pushed away from me. It was the only time I've ever seen her cry. 'Jimmy,' she said—she always calls me Jimmy—'I'm sorry, I can't.'

" 'Why not?'

" 'I still don't know who I am, what I want, where I want to be. I can't tie myself to you. I can't be forever competing with you. If I'm going to be your wife, then I have to be your wife first, and whatever I want to be second. I can't do that. I love you, Jimmy. God, I love you. Can we still be friends?' "

"You don't seem to have a lot of luck with your romances."

"No, I didn't. I blubbered that we could still be friends, and we are. We love each other just as much as we ever did. We just aren't lovers anymore."

"How did she become Jackie's best friend. I would have thought Jackie would have made you give up seeing Lori."

"Under ordinary circumstances, I guess that might have been Jackie's position."

"It wasn't?"

"No." He shook his head, "You still don't understand. Lori is different. She and I would see each other for lunch quite frequently, and we would compare notes on how the jobs were going, and so on. She knew when I met Jackie at a friend's party, and she knew when I decided to ask Jackie to marry me. At that point, she asked me to introduce her to Jackie."

"You must be some kind of fool! I can't conceive of a more potentially explosive situation. Uuh!" she shuddered.

"When you love someone, the very core of that relationship is trust. I trusted Lori, and I trusted Jackie. Now, Jackie was very shy, and she is still very nervous when I'm in the presence of some other woman, especially if she's attractive."

"So here you are bringing your former lover to meet her?" Tania shook her head in disbelief.

"Well, simply put, Lori just bowled Jackie over. She told it like it was, leaving nothing of importance out, and she concluded the dumbest thing she ever did was to turn down my proposal of marriage. She wanted to meet Jackie and tell her not to be a jackass and turn me down, also."

"If I were Jackie, I wouldn't have accepted that. I'd have told her to get out."

"Jackie isn't you. And you haven't dealt with Lori face-to-face. Lori said we still loved each other, but we weren't lovers, and we would not be again. When she told me no, she severed all claims to me, and she couldn't blame me for finding someone else. She said she, Jackie, had to be the luckiest woman on earth, and she, Lori, wanted to help her, to be her friend. 'Now,' she concluded, 'how can I help you with your wedding, with

164

Jimmy, with anything?' Jackie bought it, and she's never been sorry."

"I still would have asked her to leave. What help could she possibly be?"

"Well, she kept Jackie from coming unglued as the wedding approached. Jackie was a virgin. What was the wedding night supposed to be like? Lori gave her some very intimate advice, and Jackie and I had a great time on the whole honeymoon. When we got back, Lori began teaching her more about sex. And, I tell you, she is like a second mother to Andrea. She and Jackie have become very close friends. Maybe something like you and...ah...Lillian. They're not into the kissing bit—I don't think. That's special to your situation. But they share everything, every little detail. They go shopping together. They're really sisters, if you ask me, two women who never had a sister, who have found each other. And Jackie is much stronger from Lori's influence."

"I guess you don't have too much to complain about. Do you think Lori's been able to help Jackie in this crisis?"

"I'm sure of it. It's what keeps me from worrying too much about it. I want to get home, but I can take a longer view of our situation and not pull some stupid stunt which might get us all killed in a mad effort to get out of here."

Now she understood his patience; Lori would keep the home front from falling apart. It was up to her to match him with patience. She put a hand on his cheek and rubbed his beard. She wished she could see him.

"Thank you. I'll try not to be so nosy after this."

He gently ran the back of a finger over her cheek. "And you're still beautiful."

15.

Jackie sounded a little panicked when she called Lori at her office. There was something she wanted to discuss, but not over the phone. Lori checked her watch; she would be off in an hour. She told Jackie she would go home, pick up some clothes, and stay with her the whole weekend. Jackie seemed cheered. It was over a month since Jim's plane had gone down, and her belief in his survival was eroding more with each passing day. Lori had to admit, to herself only, she too was beginning to have her doubts. She needed to do something to break the situation open. But what could she do?

She had little enough time to consider the problem; this was her last day at NorthAire. Members of the department had taken her out for a long lunch, typical, she supposed, of all aerospace industry going-away lunches. She was the only sober one there, but she appreciated their attention to her and the many nice presents she received, presents from individuals beyond the group donation gift. The room had been hot and crowded with more than forty in attendance. And she had tears in her eyes as she made the rounds saying good-bye to some dear friends. Now, she had to take her personal belongings down to Personnel to check out and have her security debriefing.

It was raining when she pulled up to Jim's house, parked and locked her truck, and carried a small suitcase to the front door. Jackie was relieved to see her, embracing her after she entered and set her suitcase down.

"Okay, what's got you bugged?" she asked, taking her raincoat off.

Jackie didn't want to discuss it with Andrea up. Lori bent to receive Andrea's rush to her. Her little smiling face did as much for her as it did for Jim. She scooped Andrea up and hugged her. "Hi!" she said happily.

"Hi, Aunt Lori. You gonna stay?"

"For the weekend, honey. Have you been a good girl this week?" She nuzzled her nose into Andrea's chest, causing the child to giggle, squeal, and finally laugh.

Jackie left them to continue fixing dinner. Andrea and Lori would play together until supper. And while they played, Lori forgot all her sadness at leaving her job, all her worries about Jim, and her concern about Jackie and her deteriorating morale. She held Andrea on her lap while being shown many drawings Andrea had made since she was last there. "These are all very beautiful, honey."

"Aunt Lori, when's Daddy coming home? Mommy won't tell me."

Lori closed her eyes, unable to answer. She held her close and rocked slowly back and forth. What could she say?

"He isn't coming home, is he?" Andrea cut Lori's heart.

"Whoa, whoa, whoa. He *is* coming home. But your mommy and I don't know when—"

"He's not, he's not, he's not," Andrea screamed, and pounded her little fists on Lori.

Lori looked Jackie's way, "Is this what you—?"

Jackie shook her head. "She's been doing that all day, but that's not why I called you."

Lori tucked her head down in Andrea's hair, next to her ear. "Honey, have I ever lied to you? Have I ever, *ever* lied to you?"

"No," the little voice answered.

"I'm not lying to you now. I don't know when your daddy will come home. Your mommy doesn't know, but God does. What I do know is: he *is* coming home. And right now, sweetheart, that's all your mommy or I have to go on. I know it's hard on you; you want him home. But it's also hard on your mommy, and it's hard on me. We want him home, too. Please, Andrea, this is all we know. We have to be brave."

"He doesn't love me anymore."

"Oh, honey, that is so wrong. There is no one who loves you more than your daddy. Don't *ever* say that. Oh, God," she moaned. She pulled Andrea as close as she could without hurting her. Where was the happiness she had felt just minutes ago?

There really was no good way to explain the situation to Andrea; she didn't understand lost, accident, or death, nor did Lori want to attempt to get any of those concepts through to her. Yet, as she held her, she realized sooner or later, she or Jackie would have to explain *something* to her. Although she and Jackie could grasp the fairly complicated reasoning she had gone through to conclude Jim was probably alive, in no way was Andrea going to understand. She would have to be told something simple...like her father is lost.

"Tommy says Daddy's dead. What is dead?"

Lori had an urge to strangle the little boy next door. Yet, he couldn't know any more than his parents had told him. The newspapers had published a list of the casualties, and Jim's name had been among them. The neighbors had come to the house to offer their sympathy and support to Jackie, but this was before the pictures of the wreck had been available.

At this moment, Jackie was glad Lori was the one holding Andrea; she certainly had no explanation she wanted to try with her child.

"First of all, sweetheart," Lori began, struggling for inspiration, "your mommy and I believe your daddy is alive. We believe he will be coming home soon, and we want you to believe that, too. Do you know what alive is?"

"No."

This concept wouldn't be easy either, but she'd rather be explaining alive than dead.

"Okay. You, and I, and Mommy, and Tommy, and Tommy's dog are all alive. Take a nice deep breath." Andrea looked puzzled. "Go on, take a nice deep breath."

Andrea took a deep breath, held it, and let it out noisily.

"That's it. When you can do that, you are alive. Close your eyes." The child's eyes closed. "Can you see anything?"

"No."

"Okay, open them. Can you see me?"

"Yes."

"Touch my face. Feel how warm it is?" Andrea nodded. "Touch yours. Is it warm?

"When you can see things, when you can feel things, when your face is warm, you are alive. Raise your hand." She waited. "You're alive when you can raise your hand. All the things you can do mean you are alive. And that is what your daddy is. It's just he's not here where you can see him."

"What is dead?" Andrea persisted.

Lori took a deep breath and exhaled. She looked helplessly at Jackie, who returned her look just as hopelessly. Lori turned her attention back to Andrea.

"Okay," she sighed, "Do you remember the kitty next door?"

"Yes."

"Do you remember what happened when the car hit the kitty?"

"Yes, it was squished."

"That's right. Did you see it move again?"

"No."

"Was it breathing?"

"I don't know," the little voice informed her. "It just got stiff."

"The kitty was dead. It couldn't move, it couldn't breathe, it couldn't do any of the things it used to do when it was alive. That's what dead is."

Jackie came to Lori's rescue, "I think it's time to wash up for dinner."

"Is my daddy stiff and squished?"

Lori pulled Andrea to her tightly. "No, honey. He's alive, just like you and me. Let's go get cleaned up for dinner." *Okay,* she admitted to herself, *I'm chicken.*

Andrea was in bed, and Lori was exhausted. Andrea's questions, and the seemingly futile efforts she had made to explain things to her left her with little cheer. She and Jackie sat in chairs in the living room.

"Okay, " she sighed, "what is it you wanted to talk about?"

"I'm pregnant." The expression on Jackie's face was not happiness.

"Are you sure?"

"Dr. Stone told me this afternoon."

"Gee, that's great. You've been wanting another; now you'll have it."

"I talked to him about an abortion."

"For God sakes why?"

"If Jim's dead, I don't want to have it. I won't be able to handle Andrea, much less a tiny baby. I'll have to go back to work."

"Well, yeah, *if* Jimmy's dead. But don't be in a big hurry. Give the guy a chance to get home. Oh, Jackie, honey, this is wonderful news!"

"You keep saying he's alive. If he is, where is he?"

"That's what I'm trying to figure. I'm missing something. Damn, I wish I could just...just somehow *see* the situation there." It had been an increasing frustration to her. "But, look, you have to keep faith. You have to carry that baby."

"Another thing, I'm beginning to hurt for money. His company—your company as of next week—is dragging its feet sending me his paychecks."

"I thought Mike was carrying the ball for you."

"He is, and he's getting fed up with them. They won't admit he's dead and send me his insurance, and at the same time, they won't say he's alive and send me his paycheck."

"That's the bureaucracy of a big company. Nobody wants to take responsibility for a situation which is not in their manuals. Do they have an ombudsman?"

"I don't know."

"I'll check on it when I sign in next week. Are you okay for now?"

"For another week or so."

"Holler if you need help; I've got some stashed away."

"I couldn't ask that of you—"

"Like hell you can't! Don't you *dare* go to some damned money lender. You come to me. Damn, don't you know what you and Andrea mean to me? You're family!"

"I know," Jackie sighed, "I love you like a sister. And that's why I can't possibly let you do that—"

"BULLSHIT!! If I ever find out you went out to some financial institution instead of coming to me, I won't be your sister any more!" She made a mental note to herself to see to it she paid for the groceries for this weekend.

She sat glowering at Jackie. Slowly her temper cooled, and her inner mind reminded her Jackie was under considerable stress and might not be completely rational in her thinking. Finally, she smiled, got out of her chair and went to Jackie, squatting in front of her.

"Please excuse my outburst. I know you have a lot on your mind. All I'm asking is to let me help you."

Jackie knew she needed Lori, and she was grateful for every minute of companionship Lori could give her. She felt uneasy about accepting money from a friend, fearing it might eventually lead to misunderstandings and a bitter end to the friendship. She grasped Lori's hands and squeezed.

"Look," Lori continued, "you have a little while before you have to consider an abortion. I would prefer you not have it, period. As for work, yeah, I can see you might have to do that, but with Mike and me pushing on the company, something should break loose soon for money. I want to give you some money to tide you over. I'll set no interest or payment schedule because I know you'll pay me back when you can, and at whatever rate you can afford. I know what's going on here; some rotten bank does not. Okay?"

Reluctantly, Jackie agreed to wait things out, and to let Lori help her financially. Lori wrote her a check for one thousand dollars from her checking account, and another for nine thousand from her savings, which she expected would take time to clear.

"Now," Lori concluded, "that should relieve some of the stress. Let's get some sleep."

* * *

Lillian, Sara, and a dozen other flight attendants, dressed in their uniforms and flanked by twenty or thirty pilots and second officers stormed up the steps of the San Francisco Federal court house. Their way was blocked by a line of policemen. Lillian led her group up to the officers, then turned to face her followers and the crowds behind them. Her sorrow at Tania's death had turned to flaming hatred of the men whose greed had caused the crash, so, urged on by Sara and her other crew members, she had organized an industry-wide protest. Flights all over the country were grounded this day for lack of crews. Some of the men responsible for the phony parts scam were being arraigned and the media was on hand in force.

Lillian held up her hands. "We stop here. Nobody goes to jail for protestin' what these men done," she yelled. Her eyes swept the scene with satisfaction. Signs were everywhere and waving for the cameras, signs with slogans, signs with pictures of every crew member.

"We're here to demonstrate our concern about flying in airplanes that have been sabotaged by the greedy bastards inside. We want the public to know we're in this with them. Our lives are on the line too, and we're not getting back into planes that aren't safe. But we're professionals, not some mob, so we stop peacefully.

"What we ask is simple enough: We want JUSTICE!" She was interrupted with cheering. "We want the men who killed our friends and your relatives by using phony parts charged with MURDER!" This brought a bigger cheer. "We want," she paused as emotion overtook her, "to know where the FAA inspectors was while this was going on! Are they in on this too?" The roar increased. "We want to know where the payoffs start and end." Tears filled her eyes. "They killed my ROOMMATE!"

172

she screamed, waving her fist high in the air. "The bastards deserve to die—"

*   *   *

As the days wore on, the weather at the lake turned warmer, and the winter snows turned to cold spring rains. The hunting became sporadic, and the fishing treacherous as the ice on the lake became untrustworthy. As a result, there were many days at the cabin where there was no food. Jim took a leaflet from his pack and suggested that Tania get familiar with hypothermia, afraid either he or Penny would go through the weakening ice and require quick and effective treatment for severe exposure. He was close to giving up fishing, starvation or no, because he feared the consequences of falling in the cold lake more. Many packets of sugar and several soft drinks they had taken from the plane, he had reserved for quick energy in the event of such an emergency. He spent some time instructing Penny on what she should do if she should fall in.

The moderate weather had also sent the stream which flowed out of the lake over its banks. The water crept closer to the cabin daily. They had run out of toilet paper some time ago and were using handfuls of snow for their sanitary purposes, a practice which required considerable fortitude. But Jim remained proud of his little family. They held up to the hardships well with only minimal bickering. He lavished affectionate treatment on each, and praised their stubborn refusal to be conquered by their circumstances. Tania had to use his sewing kit to take up skirts and his pants to keep them from falling off their dwindling bodies.

Jim was concerned that their weight loss also equated to a loss in strength, strength they would need on the walk out. That day, he hoped, was soon approaching. One evening, returning from hunting, he found Tania and Penny waiting at the opened cabin door. He followed them in and stood the rifle against the wall near the door. He held out his hand, opened it, palm up, to reveal two cartridges and one fish hook.

"That's all we have left," he announced.

Tania sighed, "I knew it couldn't last."

"I guess we had better get that splint off before you begin to leaf out like the other trees."

"Another month of tree jokes and I'd cheerfully kill both of you."

Penny laughed, "Her bark is worse than her—"

"Penny!" Tania glared at her.

A few minutes later, Jim removed the last of the hated splint from her leg. She began to scratch.

"At least there's no termites," Jim giggled, ducking Tania's wild swing at his face.

"Don't let him bug you," Penny added.

Tania favored her with a sharp look of disapproval, then flexed her leg several times. There was pain. Plenty of pain, but she was determined to stand. She reached for Jim's hands.

"Want the crutches?" he asked, pulling her to her feet.

"No. You help me."

He went to her left side and placed an arm around her waist. She put her arm around his shoulders and tried a quick, jerky step, then another.

"I'll be glad," she said, "when I don't have to ask your help in going to the little house out back. I'm embarrassed every time I have to ask."

"Why? You've asked me to do something far more intimate than that. What's so embarrassing about having to go potty? We all have to do it."

"I'm...I'm embarrassed about it with...with you. I guess I wouldn't be so embarrassed if you were family, or we were married—"

"That's just the point, Tania. You're *not* married to me, but I *am* married." His irritation began to overflow.

She was surprised at his reaction. She spoke quietly, "Jim don't—"

"How would you feel," his voice was louder, "if you were married to me, and some other woman was asking me to make love with her?"

She was suddenly hurt and angry. "I thought I detected a desire in you."

"Oh," he boiled, "I have desire, lady. I have plenty of it where you're concerned. And it's not that I don't care about you; I care a *lot* about you—"

"You," she was just as hot, "have a funny way of showing it—"

"STOP!" Penny screamed, upset and crying, "Stop it, both of you!" She ran to the door, flung it open, and ran into the night.

Jim and Tania exchanged shocked looks as he quickly sat her back at the table. He ran after Penny. She hadn't gone far before he caught up to her. His hand on her shoulder stopped her flight. Crying, she angrily pulled from his grasp, but did not attempt to run.

He knelt by her, "Please, Penny, I'm sorry."

"Yo-you're the only t-two people who care about me, an-and I don't want you t-to fight."

"I'm sorry," he said softly, "It's just that—"

"Don'tcha see?"

"See what?"

"She loves you...And I love you."

"How do you know that about her?"

"We talk while you're out hunting. It hurts me to see you fighting."

He put an arm around her shoulders. "Sometimes a fight is good; it clears the air."

"No, it isn't!" she insisted. "Dad was killed after he had this big fight with Mom. He was so mad, he ran from the house, jumped into the car, and backed into the path of a bus."

16.

Tania practiced walking the following day, going outside for the first time without being carried. Jim accompanied her, but let her limp along at her own rate.

"I want you to remember that your leg is still very delicate. With both bones broken it should have had another month to heal," he cautioned. "Do any hard work with your right leg."

"Okay," she nodded, still in considerable pain. "It's sending me constant reminders."

She went into the outhouse, closed the door, and lowered her panties without any difficulty. This gave her unexpected satisfaction since it was another symbol of her increasing independence from Jim.

"What are we going to do about my period?" she asked through the door. It was late, so late it had been worrying her for some time; could she be carrying Danny's child? But the relief that it was finally happening was dampened because it brought a fresh problem.

"I'd suggest you go ahead and have it," he replied.

"No, damn you, that's not what I'm asking. We don't have any sanitary napkins."

"Oh."

"Well?"

"Well what?"

"Jim, I can't sit here all day. I need something now."

"Oh, okay. Keep your pants on."

"They're down at the moment," she retorted, but he had left for the cabin.

He returned with the headrest bandages he had used to hold the bark in place and the floor mop bucket with some water in it.

"Open the door," he called. He passed the items in to her. The door closed again. "Make a pad or something. You can put the used ones in the bucket, and we'll clean them out to use again."

176

"What do I use to mop the floor then?"

"Don't mop the floor while you're having your period."

"Jim, that will not do."

"Okay, mop the floor then."

She stepped out of the outhouse. "What's gotten into you? You used to be quite helpful."

"The only thing I'm interested in now is getting you walking well enough to get out of here. Secondarily, I'm hoping the stream will quit flooding."

"I can buy into that," she smiled, reaching for his arm.

Wanting to see what the stream had done to the road, he guided her down the road, testing her ability to walk. Penny joined them as they went past the cabin door. It was slow progress. Jim did not expect much, but he hoped she'd surprise him with a strong performance because of her exercise around the cabin. She sat on a rock, some distance from the cabin, realizing her period was robbing her of strength.

Jim left her with Penny and went on down the road. He had hunted portions of this area. The road had several low places that were under water, which he worked his way around, pressing on further. *Damn!* he thought. The road forded the stream, something he didn't dare wade with his two charges since he couldn't judge the depth or the force of the water. He began checking the hillside adjacent to the road for ways of getting past the rock outcrop which forced the road to cross the stream. Looking for likely places to climb the ridge, he worked his way back to the women. There was still plenty of snow covering the ground; it was going to be tough on Tania.

"What do you look so down about?" Tania asked as he returned. "Didn't my walking satisfy you?"

"No, it's not that at all. You did fine, providing you can make it back to the cabin. The road fords the stream down a little further. We can't follow it the way it is now." He helped her stand, and they made their way slowly back to the cabin. The leg felt a little better; her abdomen felt worse.

* * *

Wilma McCreedy sat at the old upright desk, opening bills and paying them by writing checks. Her husband, Walter, sat in a reclining chair half asleep. It was a rare day he wasn't being interrupted by the phone summoning him to one of his patient's homes. He had been a doctor in Montrose for thirty-five years, and he was well respected as a member of the community. Wilma was still active in youth organizations, primarily in 4-H, but she also served other groups as well. Their daughter, Marylou, had grown, gone to college, and married. They had a big, old home on a quiet street just off the small park near the center of town. Wilma's brother, Hiram, was expected for dinner. Both the McCreedy and the Moore families had long histories in this part of the state.

She opened another bill and took a quick second look at it. Unable to believe it, she looked through her collection of past bills and pulled another from the pile.

"Walter?"

He wakened suddenly, "Umf...ah, what, dear?"

"Come look at this bill here. I can't believe it."

Slowly he lowered the footrest to the floor, got out of his chair, and ambled to her side.

"Here," she thrust the offending bill into his hands, "what do you make of that?"

He blinked at it, then looked more closely. "What is this for?"

"It's the 'lectric for the cabin. We've never had such a bill."

"How do you mean?"

"Well, look, " she handed him another bill, "this was the last one. It has just the minimum charges on it."

"So?" The bill still was only a few dollars. He couldn't get too excited.

"Walter! We haven't been to the cabin in months. Where's the power goin'? Even when we've been there, we never got such a bill as this."

"Tarnation, maybe someone's broken into the cabin again. I've been getting a hankerin' to go fishing, anyhow. I'll just cancel my Friday patients and we'll go up this weekend to see what's going on." He searched for his pipe. He had given up smoking years ago, but he kept several smelly old pipes to suck on. He was rarely seen without one between his teeth.

* * *

Lori took Jackie and Andrea shopping. They browsed through a book store in the Century City Mall. Jackie became interested in a large atlas. Idly she pawed through the pages. Lori came by just as Jackie turned up the map of Colorado. She put her hand on Jackie's to prevent her turning the page, then ran a finger around until she had located Gunnison and Montrose, then Mt. Uncompahgre. The detail on the map was sparse, but for Lori things suddenly came together.

"That's it!" she exclaimed to a startled Jackie. "Oh shit, have I been stupid!"

"Wha—"

"Maps!" Lori continued.

"These are maps."

"Not the right kind. We need a topographic map of that damned mountain. Oh, why didn't I think of it before this?"

"I don't see—"

"Where the hell is your husband? If he's alive, he went someplace he thought he'd have a better chance to stay alive. From *these* maps, you can't tell what the terrain is like, but from a *topographic* map, you can see every detail of an area." She banged the side of her head in frustration. "For most of two months my mind has been all screwed up wondering what happened to him. Jesus, what a *dummy!!*"

* * *

In the hotel room Lillian stared at the TV, fascinated by what she saw. Sara, no longer afraid of Lillian, sat next to her on the bed as absorbed as Lillian in the broadcast.

"Mr. MacStrom, did you order the uncertified engine controllers to be used in the repair Flight 238's engines?" the NTSB attorney asked the witness.

"Yes, I ordered my mechanics to use them, but I was only following orders," Mel MacStrom answered.

"I see. Will you please tell the Board who instructed you to use the uncertified parts to repair Flight 238's engines,"

"The orders came from the main office in Dallas," Mel answered. "None of my people ordered the parts. They were sent from our central warehouse." Although he answered easily, having made up his mind to tell all, Mel squirmed uncomfortably in his chair and sweat showed on his face.

"From who specifically?"

"A fax from the Maintenance office, initialed by the head of Maintenance, Mr. Perkins...'Course it might not have been his idea, any more than it was mine."

"Mr. Perkins, huh? Henry Perkins?" Mel nodded his response. "Okay, we'll check that out. Do you have the fax?"

"No, it was destroyed."

"How did you get by using those parts with the local FAA inspector, Stewart Monroe, looking over your shoulder?"

"We've been paying him, like the other airlines have, to look the other way."...

Lillian slapped her knee. "Yesss! I told you there was more than our local guys! We got more picketin' to do. The Dallas office—you had to know, *and* the FAA. Get 'em!" she shook her fist at the TV, "Get 'em all!"

180

"You gonna take that union position they offered?" Sara asked.

"Me?" Lillian scoffed, "I'm no leader. No, I just want to see these bastards creamed, that's all. But while I'm involved with this, it's helpin' me with my feelings about Tania. I'm doin' something positive. That's what she'd want. But I don't need all the other grief I might get into on that job."

"I think you're a born leader. So do most of the rest of the attendants. The pilots are behind you. You ought to think some more about it."

"Aw Sara, I just couldn't—"

"Who says? You have. You've done it. You've kept the heat on. You've messed up that PR bitch from Dallas like she doesn't know which way to turn, now. So don't say you can't do it."

"With her, I think it's more like a draw."

"No, you won because she didn't get this thing to go away quietly."

"Well, maybe." Lillian sighed. Suddenly she jabbed Sara lightly with her elbow, "But wouldn't you just about give your left tit to look like she does?"

"Or that soft voice. I wonder how many men she's got groveling at her feet...Come on, Lil, it doesn't make a damn what you look like. It's what you're doing that counts."

* * *

For the past several days, Tania had tried to get out and walk to strengthen her leg, but her cramps and bleeding plus a severe headache had confined her pretty much to bed. Jim went out hunting or fishing every morning in an attempt to alleviate their hunger, and finally brought in one large and two lesser fish, caught through a gap in the ice as it drifted from the upper end of the lake. These, however would be the last fish since he lost his last hook trying to better his catch. He saved them for the evening meal since Tania felt better later in the day. He was down to two cartridges for the rifle.

That night, they sat around the table and talked about what they would like to eat when they might get out.

"I want the biggest, most humongous cheeseburger and a thick chocolate malt," Penny proclaimed. "...And fries with lot's of ketchup."

"I want— I want to bankrupt an all-you-can-eat place with a salad and fruit bar," Tania said. "Jim?"

"I was thinking of things like a thick vegetable soup and pot roast with gravy...and dumplings," he sniffed as though he could smell the steaming kitchen, "Maybe some hot apple pie with a rum sauce."

"Listen to us! No steaks or lobster? No wine?" Tania asked.

"Maybe later. I can only picture a down-home meal right now."

For breakfast, they came close to agreement. Fruit or fruit juice, eggs, bacon or steak, coffee for the adults, milk for Penny, and sweet rolls of some kind.

Tania covered Jim's hand with hers, "At this point, I would even go for a breakfast of dark brown gook and light brown gook."

"See," he grinned, "I told you it would take on a certain charm."

"But look what we've had to go through to make it a choice I would consider."

"Boy, you'd make a fine ad for the cereal company, 'Folks, if you've been starving to death for the last two months, then belly up to a steaming bowl of Light Brown Gook brand of instant oatmeal. It sticks to your ribs when your clothes won't.' "

"It'll bloat in your stomach giving you that full feeling for days," Tania added, laughing. She pretended to dump a bowl upside down on Penny's head, "See, Penny likes it."

"BRACK!!" Penny added, making a sour face and pretending to vomit.

They went from one silliness to another, mocking many of the TV commercials they had seen, and laughing. Jim had never heard them so goofy. He realized, that, in a way, this was their form of griping, of letting out their frustrations. Far better this way, he thought, than nagging and complaining; far better than he and Tania airing their differences as they had a few nights before.

He hoped Tania would be ready soon since her period had subsided. His ability to provide food was near an end. One way or another, their ordeal had to end in a few days.

After Penny was asleep, Tania rolled toward Jim. Nights were becoming more and more unbearable, sleeping next to him yet unable to freely express feelings that had become quite intense within her. Worse, she was sure he was wracked with the same feelings toward her. Because of the milder weather and the fire in the stove, they no longer wore their coats to bed. On some nights she had "accidentally" discovered, in adjusting her sleeping position, a full erection. This excited her into fantasy thoughts and kept her awake, increasing her frustration. Oh, why did he have to be married? Why couldn't he bring himself to accept what she so freely offered? It was wrong; she knew it was wrong, but everything about this man was so right. Right or wrong, she ached to participate in a passionate lovemaking session with him.

Though she couldn't get him to join her in making love, she kept close to him, kissed him goodnight lovingly, and snuggled down with her head on his chest to go to sleep. It wasn't just that he had saved her life. Oh, sure, she admitted, that was a big part of it, but it was the way he treated her and Penny on a daily basis, always calm, always concerned for their comfort and well-being, and never one to shirk the work required to sustain them. But, she also had to admit, it was his dogged refusal to break his wedding vows.

He, equally frustrated, allowed her kisses, even returned them in a guarded fashion, and kept an arm around her as they started to sleep. His feelings for her, in spite of his efforts to prevent them, had grown quite without bounds, and temptation kept him holding on to her, while reason kept him from acting.

The tension had kept him awake many a night. He was aware of Tania's discovery, and, in one sense, he had hoped she would take him beyond the point he could refuse her, yet he was at the same time grateful she hadn't. Their closeness in bed, which had started as pure necessity for mutual warmth and survival, he realized was now unnecessary but maintained by each, hoping the other would seize the opportunity to initiate what neither wanted to be responsible for. And thinking about it, thinking about Jackie and Andrea, thinking about his growing love for Penny made it all the worse.

As she rolled toward him, her hand landed where it had "accidentally" landed before, but this was no accident. She gripped him through his pants, put a leg over his, and pulled herself up to whisper in his ear, "Please."

Because she asked, he refused. But had she instead covered his mouth with a kiss...

* * *

The weather turned cold again and Jim and Penny went foraging for wood one morning after one of Tania's exercise sessions. They were hungry again. He had killed a rabbit the day before, but it didn't provide much food for three persons. There was only one cartridge left.

A lot of snow remained, but in large patches isolated by soggy ground. The method Jim had devised to pull down drier dead wood out of trees was to heave the weighted end of his nylon parachute cord over a limb, and he and Penny would pull until the limb broke and fell. They were some distance from the cabin as their continued need for wood drove them further in search of trees they hadn't already stripped. Jim heaved the line over a likely limb and he and Penny started pulling. As the limb broke and crashed down, he stepped back and fell awkwardly. He clutched his leg near the ankle. Penny rushed to his side.

"Are you hurt?"

" 'Fraid so," he groaned, "Please get me some snow from that bank."

She hurried to the snow and gathered up as much as her hands would hold as he gingerly removed his boot and sock. He applied the snow to the outside of his leg.

"I want you to *carefully* go back to the cabin and find a roller bandage and some tape in the lower left pocket of my pack. Don't run and trip on something. Okay?...And bring Tania's crutches, too." He looked into her distressed face.

She started to leave, but heard a low growl from nearby. Turning back toward Jim, she saw a coyote moving slowly toward him. He began to back himself up against a tree, picking up a branch that had broken from the limb they had felled. Glancing her way, he saw her standing, frozen in fear.

"I can hold him off," he assured her, "You get out of here quick!"

Hurrying, she rushed into the cabin a few minutes later, out of breath.

"Jim's hurt, and some wild animal is attacking him," she blurted out, rushing to his pack. She dumped the contents of the side pocket on the floor and grabbed up the roller bandage and tape. Tania hastened to the rifle and pocketed the remaining cartridge. Penny seized the crutches and ran out the door. Tania limped after her.

"Penny, wait for me."

Penny slowed, but continued to lead impatiently, as Tania struggled painfully through the underbrush.

Jim's problems multiplied as two other coyotes joined in the attack. He left the tree and hobbled to a large rock which he backed against, trying to keep the coyotes at bay and in front of him. He snatched up a large stone with his free hand. The coyotes, sensing he was injured, moved in closer. The hunting had been bad for them, too, and they were desperate for a meal. Jim swiped at them with the branch, driving them back a few feet. One charged him on the side away from the branch. He swung the rock down on its head, stunning it. It lay but a foot from his feet. The others became angered, and moved in closer.

Penny pulled up, horrified at what she saw, and gasped. Tania, struggling to keep up, finally arrived next to her, panting.

"Oh, God!" she gasped. She stared for a moment before she remembered the rifle in her hands. In panic, she tried to load it, but she had not watched Jim very carefully. She struggled to get the bolt open to insert a cartridge.

"Hurry!" Penny breathed.

While the struggle to load the rifle was going on, the stunned coyote recovered, slipped away from Jim's wild effort to hit it again, and joined the others circling for an attack.

Tania finally succeeded in opening the chamber to load the rifle. She closed it, then knelt to aim. Her out-of-breath condition, plus her inexperience with a rifle caused the crosshairs to wander wildly about the scene in front of her. Jim appeared in the sights several times.

Suddenly, the three animals charged at him at once. The loud crack of the rifle startled him, unaware that Penny and Tania were close by. One coyote dropped on his feet. The others turned and fled into the forest. He stepped aside from the dead coyote as Tania rushed to him. Suddenly realizing she still held the rifle and that she had killed something with it, she screamed in revulsion and dropped it on top of the dead coyote, covering her eyes with the heels of her hands. Then, remembering Jim, she flung her arms around his neck.

"Nice shooting," he said, encircling her body with his arms, "and timely, too."

"I never held a rifle before," she chattered, completely unraveled, "I-I was so nervous, I closed my eyes when I pulled the trigger. I-I was afraid I'd shot you...Oh God, are you all right?"

He held her tightly. "I haven't had a chance to find out. The leg hurts plenty." He hugged her before releasing her.

Sitting, he pulled his pants leg up. Tania looked at the leg.

"What happened to it?"

"I stepped in a hole of some kind. Could be a sprain or a break...Penny, get some more snow, please."

It was a subdued little group returning to the cabin. Tania carried the rifle in one hand and towed a tree limb in the other. Penny also dragged a limb. Jim carried the coyote over a shoulder and hobbled along on the crutches. He and Penny tied the coyote's legs and hauled it high into a tree after slitting its throat. Then, with the women's cooperation, he heaved the rock he used to break up the wood, while they positioned the limbs for the next throw. Penny brought him his knife, and he skinned and cleaned the coyote. That done, he struggled through the door and sat on a chair. Penny filled a pan with more snow to pack on his leg.

Tania got some of the meat cooking and put the rest in the refrigerator.

"That was the last shell," she commented as she sat next to him.

"I know. At least you got something we can eat."

"I'm not sure I want to eat it."

"Don't be too fussy; we don't know where the next meal is coming from."

Penny stood near him, "We were going to start walking out tomorrow. What will we do now?"

"I don't know, honey. I can't go far on it right now. We'll have to give it some rest." He looked at two disappointed faces.

"My butt is raw from using snow for toilet paper," Tania groaned.

"So's mine," he agreed, sighing, "I want to get out of here as much as you do...Look, guys, you were both something special this morning. Give me a chance to rest this thing, and we'll pull out as soon as possible. I want to take advantage of the cold weather since the stream is receding."

It was late at night when Penny screamed in her sleep. She woke, still screaming in full terror. Tania hurried out of bed and to her side. Putting her hand on Penny's wildly thrashing shoulder, she gripped it tightly and spoke to her calmly.

"What's the matter, honey?"

"Jim's dead! The coyotes killed him!" she screamed, beginning to cry.

"No he isn't," Tania soothed. "He's in bed. You had a nightmare."

"No," Penny bawled, "he's *dead!* I saw them kill him."

Tania started to get Penny up, lifting her shoulders. "Come on. Get up. Come to bed with me."

Penny sat up and swung her legs to the floor. Tania put an arm around her shoulders and guided her to the larger bed. As Penny climbed up on the bed, Jim put his arms out to her and drew her to him, startling her.

"See, I'm alive. It was just a nightmare," he soothed, pulling her head down on his shoulder.

Tania climbed back in bed and pulled the covers over Penny and herself.

"We have to get her out of here," he told Tania. "She needs a better feeling of security."

"I can buy into that," she replied, rolling toward Penny, putting an arm over her. Jim stroked Penny's head with his free hand, and she was soon asleep.

* * *

Lori called Mike to tell him she would be in late. She briefly explained that she needed a topographic map. After completing the call, she headed out the door to UCLA. The map library in the Geography building was in the basement. She stumbled going down the stairs in her rush. A few minutes later she stood staring at the map before her on a table.

"Christ! A lake!"

The nearer roads did not excite her. She reasoned that if he could have seen one of them, he'd have been home long before this. But the lake could explain a lot. She purchased two adjacent quadrangles and hurried back to her truck.

At home, she called the Montrose airport control tower to determine if the weather had broken in the days following the crash such that Jim might have had a chance to look around and see the lake. It had. Her excitement mounted. She called her father in Washington, chatted for awhile, then asked who was in command of the reconnaissance squadron at Beale AFB.

* * *

It was a cool morning in Marysville, California. A sergeant picked up the ringing phone, "Forty-twenty-ninth Recce Squadron, Beale AFB, Sgt. Able Thurston speaking...Why yes ma'am." There was a sexy sounding female on the line. He wanted to talk to her for a while. "Well, ma'am—" She didn't like being called "ma'am." "Yes, Ms. Cranston. What can I do for you?...Do we have a Col. Higgins here? Yes, we do." He wrote her name on a pad; not wanting to forget this babe's name. "Well, that depends. Which Col. Higgins do you want?...Bernie Higgins. Yes, we have a Col. Bernie Higgins here." He only knew one Col. Higgins, but this voice was something else; very sweet, getting sweeter as they talked, and with a trace of a Southern accent. "How long is my hitch? Two more years."

"Sgt. Thurston, would y'all like to spend the rest of that hitch at the South pole?" Lori asked, furious. "Well, your little old General reports to my daddy's staff meeting every week. My daddy will do just about anything for little old me. If ah ask him real sweet, he'll transfer yo ass to the South pole. Now Sergeant, ah'd like t' suggest thet yo get Bernie on the li-yun *now!*"

He walked to the Colonel's office door, "Sir, there's a Ms. Lori Cranston on the line for you. Shall I tell her you're busy?"

Col. Bernie Higgins paled considerably, "Good God! What's *she* want with me?"

"Shall I tell her you're out?"

"Don't you dare! Man, do you know who she is?"

"No sir."

"That's General Cranston's daughter, his only and very *favorite* daughter."

He picked up the phone, "Hello, Lori. It's been a long time— Able?...I'm sorry, he didn't know who you are...Yes, I'll speak to him. Now, where are you? What are you doing?" He listened as she briefly caught him up on eight years of time. "So, you're making it on your own. That's great!...What can I do for you, sweetheart?...Yeah, that takes me back, too. Lori, those were good days, great days— The plane crash?...Oh, yes, we flew the mission...Uh huh...We declassified the photo of the mountain. It's available through the Freedom of Information Act— Oh, you want a different one. Which one?...Uh huh...Look, I can do it, but it'll be weeks before it gets through channels."

"Bernie, could you get that photo and look in the region of the lake?...Oh, yeah? Who?" She scribbled on the phone directory. "A Lt. Warren Baker?...Montrose County Sheriff?...Yeah, okay, I'll call him...Thanks, Bernie...Yeah, and straighten that sergeant out...Okay, thanks...No, I'll call you if I need something more. 'Bye" She hung up.

"Sgt. Thurston, would you please come in here for a minute?" Col. Higgins called.

"You wanted to see me, sir?" he asked, entering the office.

"Did you give her the run-around?"

The sergeant shuffled his feet nervously, "Well, kinda."

"Did she mention anything about a transfer?"

"Yes, sir. But she can't do anything."

Bernie Higgins grabbed his head in pain. "Did she talk to you in a very sweet, southern voice?"

"Yes, sir!"

"Oh boy, are you in a heap of trouble. She never uses that voice unless she is pissed. Where did she mention for a transfer?"

"...The South Pole."

Col. Higgins stared at the sergeant. "If she calls again, you will be all courteous business. You will get me on the line with her as rapidly as possible, and you will not screw around with that dame again. If you do, you can count on spending the rest of your hitch in the most intemperate climate on earth. Why the hell did you do that?"

"She sounded so sexy, sir."

"She is that for sure...You could use her on your stupid basketball team."

"Yeah? She's tall?"

"Five feet two inches, and all trouble."

"Hell, that's small."

"I've seen her on a base down in Texas take on men six-two or six-three in one-on-one and beat them by thirty points. She plays a good foot taller than she is."

"She's so small she just ducks around them?"

"No, she likes to go straight up over them. And is that ever frustrating when you can't stop her, or she blocks your shots."

"Jesus!"

"...And," Higgins continued, "there isn't anything her 'daddy' wouldn't do for her. So, be very polite and efficient the next time she calls."

"Yes, sir! She's an Air Force brat?"

"You could say that. Just don't upset her again. That's all, sergeant."

* * *

"Montrose County Sheriff, Sgt. Stiles speaking. May I help you?...A Lt. Baker? I'm sorry, he's out for lunch. Could I or anyone else help you?...Yes, ma'am, I'll leave a message for him." He copied her name and phone number. "...ah...California. Miss Cranston?...May I tell him what this concerns?...The plane crash?...Yes, I'll tell him." He put the phone down slowly. What could she know about the lieutenant's obsession over that crash?

A half hour later, Lt. Baker walked to his desk, read the message, then dialed the number given. It rang with no answer. Checking his watch, he guessed that this person was out to lunch. He would call an hour later, but it was two hours before he could get free to call.

"Miss Cranston?...This is Lt. Baker of the Montrose County Sheriff's office. You wanted to speak to me?"

Lori explained her interest, her source of information that he too had an interest, and asked why he had requested the photo. He explained his sighting of the fire or fires at the lake and his feeling that there was something more that should be looked at. He also explained that technically the lake was out of his jurisdiction. Lori excitedly explained why she felt there was at least one survivor, and his news made her even more certain. She could hardly contain herself. Had he received his print of the photo yet? No? Okay, she would work it from the Air Force end. She thanked him, promising to call again if she learned anything.

Warren Baker sat at his desk and played the recorded conversation back again. He wished he had been more tenacious in following up on his feelings. She made a lot of sense.

He didn't have much time to contemplate. The sheriff called him into his office to inform him he was selected along with two others to help the Gunnison and Hinsdale sheriffs go to the crash site and begin removing bodies and recover the data recorders. He told Hiram of Lori's call.

Hiram looked at Baker as he thought. He liked his deputy, and now there was a more tangible reason to investigate further. "You get them t' swing by the lake on the way up. Look things over a mite. My brother-in-law said he wuz plannin' t' go up there, too. Says somethin' fishy's goin' on."

Baker smiled. "Okay, I'll do'er...Friday at seven-thirty AM, right?"

Hiram nodded. They didn't use the mold Baker came from too often. He was a solid man. This at least would put his obsession with this case to rest.

17.

Tania looked back over the valley as she and Jim rested. The going was very tough as they slowly climbed the ridge behind the cabin. It was with mixed feelings that she surveyed the scene, the lake in the distance, the peak beyond, and the little cabin almost invisible in the trees. She was glad to be leaving for civilization, apprehensive about their ability to surmount the task ahead of them, yet sad to be leaving their cozy little home. It wasn't much of a home. In it she had developed titanium-tough bonds to Jim and Penny. These bonds caused her anguish as she watched Jim gamely struggle along under his pack with his wrapped and splinted leg and one of the crutches he had made for her. He had fashioned bed rolls of blankets for Penny and herself by rolling the blankets lengthwise and tying the ends together to form a sort of horse collar to wear over one shoulder and across their chests. Nothing could protect him from the pain in his leg. To lighten his pack, the rifle and several other items had been left in the cabin with a note.

She was wearing a thermal vest from Jim's pack. The fur coat was secured under the top flap of the pack. Penny's coat was part of her bedroll. Though the air was chilly as they rested, all were streaming sweat as they labored uphill.

Penny was leading the way, looking for easy routes for Tania and Jim. He had talked with her before they started and cautioned her to stay within sight of him and Tania. Though enthusiastic as always, Penny realized the importance of obeying him and was a model of helpfulness. *This is no eleven-year-old,* Tania marveled to herself as she observed Penny's behavior. *Eleven going on sixteen, maybe.*

Rest periods were always too brief, and then they were off again. At long last, they reached the top of the ridge and a snow bank. Jim unwrapped his leg to apply snow to the injured area. Penny was allowed to take his whistle and explore along the ridge toward the place where the road forded the stream. She was to blow the whistle periodically and listen for a shouted return. If no return, turn back. A little timid about being alone and possibly lost, she stayed well within range.

"You were right, Jim," Tania said as she watched him tend his leg, "It is a beautiful valley, and I'd love to come back."

He paused in his labors to smile and nod. "Me too. See, Nature is not the enemy. She just provides the beauties and the challenges, and we have to be strong enough to prevail and wise enough to appreciate."

Penny came crashing back through some underbrush as Jim put the finishing touches on the leg-supporting wrap. She and Tania helped him shoulder his pack and they were off down the long slope of the ridge where Penny had explored.

Tania found downhill almost as tough as uphill because there was a tendency to pound her foot down, and she had to use partially healed muscles to hold herself back. Every step was agony for Jim, but he tried to keep the others from knowing how much pain he felt.

He kept them bearing northward as they descended because that was the general direction of the road and the canyon. They came to a clearing and a viewpoint. He gazed around, picked out the stream in the distance, and the road beyond. He took bearings on a place ahead where the road and stream were near each other, then scanned the nearby terrain for ways to get there. They were in forest cover, but they would lose it to scrub growth part way down. Far, far in the distance, over another hill, he caught a tiny flash of light, then another. Smiling for the first time since they left the cabin, he excitedly pointed to the place.

"Look, guys, that's where we have to get to."

After a few moments both Tania and Penny saw the flashes also.

"What is it, Jim?"

"Traffic on a highway!" He took a bearing with his compass.

"How far?" Tania wanted to know.

His smile evaporated to solemn. "That's our goal, but it could be five to twenty miles from here."

The happy expectant looks disappeared.

"But," he continued, "it's there. We can see it. It exists. We don't have to wonder anymore. So, let's see if we can't get closer to it before this day ends."

The scrub growth proved more difficult than the forest. At times there were almost impenetrable thickets blocking their way. Although most of their path was downhill, they made slow progress through the brush. Jim instructed Penny to look for animal trails they might follow with greater ease. Late in the afternoon they reached the stream, Jim's private goal for the day. They needed water to survive.

Tania was exhausted and her leg ached, though she knew Jim's must feel ten times worse. She tried to help Penny with pitching the tent to spare Jim any further effort. After spreading the blankets as she had on their first night in the tent, Penny scrambled down to the stream several times to refill their water bottles using a small microfilter from Jim's pack. All of them felt better after they had relieved the dehydration that had occurred as they had walked.

Jim cleared a fire pit and soon had outer garments drying on a line he strung over the fire between two sturdy shrubs. He insisted on reboiling the coyote meat before they ate to prevent sickness, using his gasoline stove for that duty. When he offered Tania one of the three remaining Tylenol and codeine tablets, she refused though hurting.

"Do you have some aspirin in your pack?"

He nodded.

"I'll take two of those. You use the codeine."

For one of the few times since the crash, he didn't argue. If he was to get any sleep, he needed the codeine.

* * *

Lori, excited by what she had learned from Lt. Baker the night before, dialed the airbase.

Able Thurston answered the phone and suddenly snapped to attention. "Yes, Ms. Cranston, will you please hold. Col. Higgins just left the office, but I think I can find him."

He pushed the hold button and ran out the door, flagging the colonel down just before he drove out of the squadron parking lot. The Colonel beat him back to the office; he had never seen Higgins in such a hurry. That dame must be something else.

"Yes, Lori," Higgins answered, a little out of breath. "I have something else I must attend to today, but I'll get it tomorrow and look at it for you. What am I looking for?" He jotted some notes as he listened.

"You're looking for one or more fires near the south end of the lake. I'll bet you'll find three in a line. Check for a tent, a domed tent, somewhere close by. And then look around the lake area for some more sheltered place he might stay. Okay?" She gave him her daytime phone number.

With the pressing business out of the way, she chatted with her friend and former lover for several minutes, complimenting him on straightening out the sergeant, and talking about old times in Texas. Finally, he had to leave for his appointment.

"...Listen," she said, "I can't thank you enough...Now, Bernie, you're married, so that's definitely out...No, not even for old times sake. I hate to bring you down, but the guy you're helping me look for is five times better than you ever were...Yeah, don't remind me. I blew it. 'Bye."

Why was it, she mused, that all he could ever think about was her ass?

* * *

Penny awoke first, hearing the hated growl of the coyotes. At first she believed she was dreaming again, but she realized, as the sounds recurred, that there were animals near the tent. She prodded Jim in the ribs until he wakened.

"What's the matter?" he asked groggily.

"There's animals near us. It sounds like coyotes."

Jim pushed the tent flap open and listened. Hearing the sounds, he charged out of the tent on his knees and picked up a smoldering branch from the waning fire. Screaming, he waved the red embers around in the darkness. Hearing the sounds of hasty retreat crackling through the brush surrounding them, he built the fire up to a full blaze with the remainder of the wood they had collected from the scrub before retiring.

Tania was now awake and frightened, having wakened to Jim's wild screaming.

"What's going on?" she asked, betraying her fright.

"Animals," Penny said, "maybe coyotes."

"Jim, are you all right?" Tania queried.

"For the moment," came the reply.

He pulled his heavy jacket from the pack and settled down with his back against a rock across the fire from the tent.

"Are you coming back to bed?" Tania asked.

"Not right away. Go on back to sleep. I'll be along shortly."

Fifteen minutes later he heard the soft crunch of dried leaves under the brush as an animal approached. He held perfectly still, feigning sleep. As the animal emerged from the brush, slinking past him for the pack, he suddenly jabbed the burning stick into its face. The coyote ran off into the brush yelping in pain. Jim crawled back to the tent.

"I don't think they'll be back tonight," he announced quietly as he entered the tent and lay down between his two companions. "I think the word will get around that we're not friendly."

He wrapped an arm around each as they put their heads on his shoulders, kissed each again as he had earlier, and tried to go back to sleep.

* * *

Tania felt better the next morning. The ache in her leg had subsided with rest. Restless and uncomfortable on the hard ground, she had wakened at dawn. She prayed for help to shorten their ordeal, asking mercy for Jim and his leg and a short path to the highway and help.

The day came on, crisp and cold. Penny and Jim wakened as light began to stream into the tent. The three of them lay watching the sun creep down on the walls. They weren't comfortable, but they knew the walking was worse. Jim hugged each and kissed their foreheads before getting them up to break camp and prepare for another day. He reboiled the last of the coyote meat, fearing it wouldn't keep another day. They ate it slowly, realizing they had no more food.

Penny refilled water bottles and they were off, following the stream and heading toward the next hill and the highway somewhere beyond. Tania had initial stiffness in her leg but it eased as she walked. Jim's leg started out sore and got worse. He was noticeably slower than the day before, his face pinched with pain, and as the day wore on he became uncharacteristically irritable.

By noon they had topped the distant rise where they again saw sunlight glints from moving traffic in the distance. Penny and Tania were disappointed that their goal appeared no closer than before. Jim, however, saw something that raised his spirits in spite of the pain: the dirt road again forded the stream and returned to their side. To get there was his goal for this day.

Late afternoon found them at the ford. Jim called a halt, unwrapped his leg, and spent the next hour soaking it in the stream as Tania and Penny set up camp on the road. Remembering the previous night, the two women foraged for a large pile of wood to support a campfire. Jim suggested that they take the opportunity to bathe in the stream, that they might feel less sticky for sleep.

199

* * *

Late that same afternoon Lt. Baker and Sheriff Moore huddled over a photographic print on Hiram's desk. Baker was excited as he watched Hiram run the magnifying glass around.

"See? It's just like that Cranston woman figured: three fires in a row and a domed tent. Looks like two people." Baker pointed with a pencil. "Bet they're holed up in Doc McCreedy's cabin by now...unless they're dead."

"Could be. Wilma said they got a big 'lectric bill for the cabin this month...What's that in the snow in front of the fires?" He looked closer.

"I couldn't make it out. White on white. Could be writing, I suppose."

Hiram nodded, satisfied. "It appears like you're right, Warren. I'll make arrangements with Bert to fly you up there— not enough light left t'day—tomorrah so's you kin look around."

"What about the Gunnison troops?"

"Now they's had nigh on to two months to check on this an' they let it drop. There'll be a mite of good publicity for the people that finds 'em, and I think that should be yours. So you go up there, look around, and act on whatever you find. I'll get you out'a goin' up for bodies. Don't tell nobody what you're up to. While Gunnison's doin' their duty on top of the mountain, you'll just sort of snatch the prize, if there is any, from under their noses." He took Baker's arm in his hand and winked at his deputy. "Mighty fine work. I'm glad you stuck with it."

* * *

Wilma carried a box out to the old, battered four-wheel drive camper. Walter took it from her and pushed it into the back. He picked up the fishing poles standing against the camper side and loaded them in on top of the other duffle, then closed the tailgate and the rear window. It was early Friday morning, and the good doctor fervently hoped Wilma would run out of things to bring to the truck; they were only staying two nights for Heaven's sake.

She went back into the house. Walter sucked on his empty pipe, hoping all she was doing was getting her purse and locking up. Another box preceded her down the stairs. He sighed and opened the rear window and tailgate for the third time. This time there was hope because she had stopped to lock the front door before leaving the porch. Her purse was swinging from one of her hands. Maybe, he mused, he should have set her in motion the night before.

"You done?" he asked, pushing the box in and securing the rear door again. He walked with her and helped her up into the high-slung truck cab.

"If you'd ever fix that place up, maybe I wouldn't have to tote all this baggage," she snapped back.

He went around to the driver's side of the truck, put one foot up on the step, and hopped on the other twice before exerting the extra effort to make it into the cab. With the engine started, he backed out of the drive, pulling an old railroad watch out of his pocket; seven-thirty AM. Good enough for going to the office, but on fishing days, one should leave before sunrise. Oh well, she was an otherwise worthy woman, and late starts were the price for her other talents. He sucked on his pipe.

"It's going to feel good to get away for a few days. The winter's been too long and too cold."

"I'd like it better," she snapped, "if I didn't have t' cook on thet dang'd wood stove. Why can't you get rid of it and put in an electric?"

"Maybe this summer. I'll put in a septic tank, too, and add a bathroom and shower."

She glanced quickly in his direction. She was pleased, but she'd lived with him too many years to make the mistake of counting on anything he said. "I'm goin' t' hold you t' that, you old goat."

"Now just be patient. We've only had the cabin a few years. It takes time to fix it up proper."

She had heard that speech before. It hadn't set well when he used it to procrastinate on the electricity. She would not tolerate it now. "Fifteen...fifteen years, Walter McCreedy, an' it's still 'It takes time t' fix it up, Wilma, dear!'" she mimicked in a high pitched voice. "It doesn't take fifteen years. I'm goin' t' call Charley Finney when we get back an' get him t' git up there an' give us an estimate. Tarnation, you won't put me off another day!"

* * *

Jim carefully stuffed things into his pack while Penny rolled the blankets into two rolls. Tania drowned the fire. The weather looked threatening to the west. A strong cold wind was blowing. As they started off with the easiest hiking they had encountered, Jim let Penny range on ahead. She was to remain on the road and wait at any junctions. The long rest and cold soaking in the stream had improved his leg temporarily, but a mile or so later he was in misery again.

"I can't go on," he groaned, sitting in the road.

"You have to," Tania pleaded, "The road can't be far away now."

"This pain is terrible."

"I know, honey, I know. Just rest a bit and try again. Please, Jim."

Though irked at the slow pace because she could almost smell the highway, Tania refused to leave his side and tried to be sympathetic. She had recent enough experience with the same pain. There was no doubt in her mind his leg was broken.

The wind picked up and turned colder. Penny came running back to them, shivering. "I'm cold," she said.

Jim helped her retrieve her snow outfit and get into it, securing the hood tightly around her face. He traded Tania for the down vest, putting her into the fur coat. Finally, he put the vest on over his other clothing and put his rain suit over everything to break the wind. But the wind was kicking up clouds of dust, blowing particles into their eyes and making breathing difficult.

Reluctantly, Jim decided they must seek cover until the wind abated. He removed the ties holding the ground cloth to his pack, got Tania and Penny to each hold a corner down, then rolled out several blankets on top. He lay down in the middle with his back to the wind. Tania was instructed to lie on her side in front of him, and finally, Penny was told to lie in front of Tania. Jim reached behind him and pulled the ground cloth and blankets over all of them, somewhat like a taco shell, and passed the ends to Penny to hold down tight. Down low, protected from the wind by the scrub shrubbery and the ground cloth, each was able to warm up enough to be comfortable.

"We'll wait the wind out here," Jim said.

"I saw a house down the road," Penny said when her teeth stopped chattering.

"What?" Tania and Jim chorused. "Where?" Jim followed up.

"I could barely see it. It was pretty far away. I was too cold to go that far."

"That's okay, sweetheart. We understand," Jim soothed, thinking furiously. "How far were you from us when you saw it?"

"I don't know. Not very far."

"Okay, guys, let me out," Jim requested, "I'm going for help."

"But you can't walk," Tania protested in amazement.

"I'm going to crawl. I have the warmest clothing, I have gloves and mittens, and I'll make some knee pads from some blanket and headrest ties. I'll leave the pack here."

Minutes later, two anxious faces peeked out from under the blue plastic ground cloth and watched him crawl out of sight in the swirling dirt clouds. "I hope," Tania said, "that when you are looking for a man to marry, you'll pass up the bright, flashy, handsome men and look for someone like him. He has more guts than most of the guys I've dated put together."

"I wish he was my father," Penny said with feeling. Tania pulled her close, after they sealed up the shelter.

* * *

The helicopter circled the lake slowly, then went to hover over the cabin. Baker had his face glued to the side window as he searched for any sign of life. Finally, he signaled Bert to find a place to land. He jumped from the chopper as the rotors spun down. Bert was close behind him. They trotted down the quarter mile of dirt road to the cabin, but before they reached it, Baker noted reasonably fresh footprints in the soft, moist soil.

"They're here, or they've recently been here," he said, squatting to look at the tracks.

They reached the door of the cabin and found it locked, but a note was stuck into the crack at the jamb. Baker retrieved the note and quickly read it.

"They left two days ago. There's three of them. Damn!" he swore. "Come on, Bert, let's see if we can find which direction they went."

The print left by the aluminum splint on Jim's leg was distinctive so they followed it to the base of the ridge. The signs of the struggle up the ridge were plain.

Baker turned back and began to jog. "Come on, let's get in the chopper and go look for them."

* * *

Walter turned the truck off the highway onto the dirt road. Wilma gritted her teeth as the old truck bounced harshly on the winter roughened road. They bounced along without speaking for a mile or so, the road twisting and turning while climbing the gentle incline leading up to the lake. He turned on his emergency radio scanner to check on the progress of the helicopter search.

"That's a darn cold wind, Wilma. Fishing might be a tad chilly."

"Well, I didn't figger we was goin' there t' fish anyway."

*　*　*

Jim stopped crawling and painfully stood to look for the house. Though he was clad in almost all the clothes he had, the wind had chilled him and he had little fuel in his body to generate heat. He saw the house, still a mile or more distant. Shivering, he went down on his knees again. "Gotta keep going. I gotta keep going." He recognized the early symptoms of hypothermia. He pushed himself onward. "They're depending on me," he said, slurring his speech. Each movement was getting harder to make. "I got...keep g—goin'."

Suddenly it began to rain and hail. The hail, a bit larger than moth balls, battered against Jim's head, covered only by a thin hood. The rest of him was fairly well padded, but the crawling was becoming ugly.

*　*　*

Ethyl Moore, sister-in-law of Hiram, was a sturdy, plain woman. She lived on a small, remote farm by herself, having been widowed by a farm accident. The wind had prevented her from hanging laundry out, and was prompting her to tend to chores indoors. She heard a noise on her front porch and went to the living room window to investigate.

"Mercy sakes!" she exclaimed, drawing her fist to her mouth, as she saw the muddy, yellow clad figure of a man groveling and shaking violently on the steps of the porch. She hurried to the door. Reaching the man, she put two strong arms under his and hauled him into the house, closing the door after she let him slump to the floor.

"What happened to you?" she asked rolling him face up. "Why, you're nigh frozen t' death."

"T—two women—" Jim coughed.

"What about two women?" Ethyl asked, rapidly undoing his rain jacket.

"T—two women...under...b—blue t—tarp..."

"Yes, yes. Two women under a blue tarp. Where?"

"R—r—road..." Jim swung his arm to point roughly in the direction he had come from.

"You just lie there. Don't go to sleep. I'll get something warm." She hustled out to the propane stove in her kitchen and turned on a burner under a teapot. Next she flipped a switch on her radio telephone.

"This is radiophone forty-seven dash four-two-three calling nine-one-one. Over."

"That you, Ethyl?" a voice came back.

"Yeah. Now listen up, Shirley. I got a man in deep hypothermia here. I need a doctor, soon's he kin get here. He's mumbling somethin' about two women under a blue tarp up the road a piece. I need someone t' search fer them. If ya can, get Hiram on it, an' tell him to move his fat butt. Over."

"This is Doc McCreedy. I have been reading the mail, and I'm pulling into Ethyl's place right now. Cancel the doctor."

* * *

The helicopter made a slow turn as Baker and Bert searched for the survivors.

The storm came on and the visibility went to near zero.

"I gotta put her down, Warren. I'll try for the road. Hang on."

The helicopter made a rough landing, and Bert killed the engines, fearing hail damage to the rotors.

"I saw something blue in the blur of the water on the windshield just before we landed," Baker said. "I'll get out and run down there and check it out."

"Okay, pardner. I'll call in to base and let 'em know we're grounded for a spell."

"Did you hear a helicopter?" Tania asked Penny.

"I think so, but I don't hear it now."

"Neither do I. Listen to that hail, will you."

"I'm having a hard time holding this tarp down; it's like something's pulling on it," Penny complained.

"I *am* pulling on it," a male voice said. "I'm Lieutenant Warren Baker of the Montrose County Sheriff's Department," he announced as Penny raised a corner of the tarp. "Well, would you ladies like a seat in a nice dry helicopter and a ride into town?" He grinned, knowing his search was over.

Baker picked up his microphone from the dash. "Montrose helicopter three to base. Come in please."

"Montrose three, this is base. Go ahead."

"Three. We have a pair of ladies with us we just picked up off the dirt road to the lake. They are our survivors. They tell us there's a man somewhere further down who crawled away looking for help. Have you heard anything? Over."

"Montrose three. Good work! Yes, we have an emergency call. Proceed to the Ethyl Moore house when you can fly and pick up the man. Transport to Montrose hospital. Hypothermia and a broken leg. Doc McCreedy is in attendance."

Baker twisted around to Tania and Penny. "That answer your questions? Relax now, he's in the best hands in the county: two strong women and a solid old country doctor...Now, how about some Snickers bars and some hot coffee or tea while we wait out this squall?"

"Lieutenant," Tania said as Baker busied himself in pouring drinks and digging out the candy bars from his food bag, "Not that I'm complaining, but why were you out looking for us?"

Baker paused to look back at her, "Well, it's a long story, but I thought I saw more than one fire at the lake while we were searching for the plane, and a Ms. Lori Cranston—"

"Lori?" Tania gasped.

"Yeah, from California. You know her?"

"No, but Jim told me about her."

"She sounded very intelligent, and she is one pushy woman."

"That's the way Jim described her."

"Anyhow, she told me why she was sure there was more than one fire, and why Hoskins could have survived. She urged me to look into it further and gave me what I needed to convince my boss to let us come looking for you. We stopped at the cabin first..."

Jim's right! Tania thought, smiling, *I haven't dealt with her face-to-face. I don't know her, but I am sure going to hug the stuffings out of her when I do.* "...and found his note, and came looking for us. Right?" Tania finished.

18.

Jackie turned on the television and went back to her ironing board. Andrea was happily playing on the floor with a Lego set Lori had given her last Christmas. It was near noon.

"This is newsbreak. Gunnison and Hinsdale, Colorado, authorities started the grim task of recovering bodies and flight recorders from the ill-fated Interstate Airlines plane which crashed there two months ago. They were surprised to find notes which indicate there were three survivors..."

Jackie stopped ironing and sucked in her breath. She watched and listened intently.

"...The notes indicated they would try to reach a lake some seven or eight miles distant. Neither county sheriff holds much hope, noting the severe winter the region has suffered— One moment, please."

The announcer was interrupted by a note being handed to her from off camera. Jackie pulled her fists to her chest as tension and hope began to build. The announcer scanned the note, then smiled.

"This is *good* news!—Dateline: Montrose, Colorado. Sheriff Hiram Moore has just announced the three survivors have been found alive. They have been taken to Montrose Hospital to be treated for exposure, dehydration, and some injuries...Oh, this is so great!...I repeat—"

The phone rang. Jackie was upset at this interruption and strained to follow the announcer as she fumbled to pick up the phone.

"Hello?...JIM!" she screamed in delight. Tears flooded her eyes as she sank back into a chair, tightly gripping the phone to her ear. "Oh, thank God!" She listened to her husband. "You are going to be all right, though?" She quickly wiped at her tears as she listened. "Oh good!...Just a minute, honey, let me get Andrea." She took the phone from her ear. "Andrea, come here quickly. It's Daddy." She held the phone out to Andrea as she came to her. "Say 'hello' to Daddy."

* * *

Walter hung several X-rays on the light box on the examining room wall. Tania listened to the phone ring for the eleventh time and put it back in the cradle.

"I guess Lillian is out or off on a flight. Mom cried and Sis cheered. I'll call the company next. They'll take care of us once they know we're here."

"Why don't you wait a spell. I have your X-rays here," Walter replied.

She jotted a number on a pad, "Could we have Jim in here for this? I'm sure he's anxious about these."

Walter smiled, "Of course."

Tania left the room and returned pushing Jim in a wheelchair. She pushed him up close to the light box.

The doctor turned to him, "First off, you have a hairline fracture of the *fibula*. Pity you had to walk out on it. We'll fix you up with one of those new-fangled lightweight plastic braces you can take off at night." He smiled at Jim, then turned to the light box.

"Well, here," he tapped with a pen, "we have Miss Richard's leg—"

"Tania, please, Doctor," she said.

"That's the way you want it, it's Walter, then." He paused to glance at her over his glasses. "The *tibia*," he indicated the larger bone with his pen, "is set about as good as it could be. Maybe a millimeter off, but quite good—remarkable when you consider the conditions under which it was set. Nice and straight, too." He moved his pen to the smaller bone.

"The *fibula*," he tapped the photo with the pen, "is several millimeters off. You might consider having it cut and reset— and soon if you're going to do it. It's okay, but not as strong were it better aligned."

"I'm sorry about that—" Jim began.

"Tarnation!" Walter exploded. "Don't you go apologizing for *anything* you did to her leg! I've seen professionals do worse than this. It's goldarn tricky to set both bones at the same time. And—," he sputtered "and she's *walking* on it!"

"He told me at the time it was only temporary until we got out to competent medical help," Tania noted.

"Temporary? Temporary, my foot! Competent? It couldn't get much better. Hmmmph!" He stared at Jim. Turning back to the light box, he continued, "Now, that piece of soda straw shows on this picture where we injected the dye. It's restricting the artery a bit, and it should come out. There's no need to hurry."

He turned to Tania, "You could have the bone reset and have that ugly scar removed at the same time you get the artery done."

"Would you believe," Tania smiled, "I don't want to get rid of that scar? I'm proud of it."

"I'd say most women as young and attractive as you would be just dying to be rid of it."

"Thank you," she acknowledged the compliment, "If I had gotten it any other way, so would I."

Walter went to Jim, "Son—you don't mind if I call you 'son' do you? I have a daughter a little older than you. In fact she'll be here shortly. I'd be right proud to shake your hand." He grinned and extended his hand to Jim.

Tania felt a tug on her heart as she watched the two men grasp each other. While her pride in Jim continued to grow, she had one more concern.

"What about Penny?"

"I couldn't tell too much. She has some scar tissue. I can't tell the extent of it. Most likely they'll take you folks to Denver in the morning. I'll go along and request an extensive scanner examination.

"She seems fine for the moment, but that sort of thing is likely to cause trouble down the line...It's a shame about her mother and father; she's such a bright, energetic girl—" The intercom interrupted him.

He moved to a desk and pushed a button, "Yes?"

"Hiram is back with the Judge. I put them in your office. I'll take the girl in to them, now."

"Fine," he answered, "We'll be in when needed. Now, Winona, you don't know anything about these folks 'til after the press meets them tomorrow. Understand?—"

"You're a little late. Hiram blabbed it to the news media. They are here at the hospital."

"Dang!" He turned to Jim, "Well...we'll see they don't find you at our place, anyway."

"What's all that about a judge?" Jim asked.

"Preliminary hearing to get her assigned a guardian and foster home," the doctor smiled.

"This'll scare her half to death."

"Nothing to fret over. See," he winked at them, "the juvenile judge is my daughter, and Hiram's my brother-in-law. They'll treat her just fine...She seems kinda stuck on you, Jim."

"I'm kinda stuck on her, too," he chuckled.

* * *

Walter's daughter smiled at Penny when Winona brought her into the office. Penny was like any number of other kids she had dealt with, nervous, uncertain, and scared. All she could offer was unbounded compassion she had learned from her father and mother. She was only thirty-six, young for a judge of this nature, and she was dressed in jeans and a stenciled tee-shirt. She sat behind her father's desk, a privilege he had granted only recently when she needed a place to interview another youngster. Hiram sat at one end, and a male court stenographer sat at the other with his machine.

"Okay, Penny, please relax," she began, "I'm Judge Marylou Jenkins. You may call me Marylou if it will make you feel more at ease."

Penny twisted nervously in her chair, a large old overstuffed, leather-covered monstrosity Walter loved for short naps. "Yes, ma'am," she answered timidly, nodding.

"That's okay, too. You know the sheriff, Hiram, and this other gentleman is Mitchel Conrad, my court stenographer. I want you to understand our concern is for your safety and welfare."

Penny nodded, still very nervous. She wished Jim was with her.

"Look, Penny, this is not a trial. You have done nothing wrong. This is just a hearing—a chat—to get acquainted and help me decide what to do for your temporary care."

"Why can't I stay with Tania and Jim?"

Marylou smiled, "Because I represent the State of Colorado. It is my legal duty to protect all wards of the state in my jurisdiction. A ward of the state means the state is your caretaker—it's responsible for you, something like a parent. You are an orphan, and therefore a ward of the state—"

"But I want to stay with Jim. I want him to adopt me. Tania said he might want to do that," Penny declared, deeply agitated.

"Whoa, slow down. I'm not saying that can't happen. I just don't know your Jim well enough to entrust your life and happiness to him yet. I have to find out if there is someone in your family who has prior rights to you, a grandparent, for instance."

"Oh," a small, subdued voice responded.

"Have you talked to Jim about staying with him?"

"No."

"Maybe he doesn't want to do that. I'll have to find that out, too. See? I promise you we will be good buddies and friends before this is over, but I have certain things I must do. If you'll help me, it'll all go much faster...Okay?"

After Penny nodded her assent, Marylou obtained her full name, her mother's and father's full names, and other facts concerning why she was on the plane.

"Do you know if your mother made a will?"

Penny was suddenly very excited, "She did! She did! The lawyer who helped after my father died sat with her at the dining table and made her make one."

Marylou beamed at her, "Good. Very good. Do you have any grandparents?"

"Yes," she responded, digging into her handbag. She handed the letter to Marylou, "This has their name and address. We were going there. I don't know much about my father's parents."

"Very good!" Marylou smiled broadly, "You and I will call them a little later. Okay?" She paused to read from the letter. "Eric and...?" She looked up at Penny.

"Miriam."

"...and Miriam Jacobs. May I keep this?" After Penny nodded, she put the letter in a folder, "Thank you. This will be a big help." Turning her attention once more to Penny, she asked, "Why don't you tell me about what happened on the plane and afterwards?"

* * *

Jim was in the chair in front of Walter's desk. Marylou smiled at him, but her manner was more formal than she had been with Penny.

"Mr. Hoskins, are you aware Penny wants you to adopt her?"

"I wasn't, but it doesn't surprise me. It's something I'd very much like to do, but I'd have to discuss this with my wife first."

"Oh, of course. But, assuming her relatives cannot take her, which, from my conversation with her, seems likely, may I assume you would be interested?"

"Yes, I would be very interested. I love Penny, and I don't want her to end up in some stranger's home."

"To that end, then, I'd like to learn more about you, your wife, and Miss Richards. I need to determine your fitness to be an adoptive parent."

"Ask away. Nothing is too personal."

Marylou contemplated him for several moments. "Okay," she said at last, "Why don't I start with the biggie and work my way back to more mundane things as seems appropriate? Just exactly what are your feelings and what is your relationship with respect to Miss Richards?"

Jim was a little surprised she would start with Tania, but he had also expected she would sooner or later get to asking about his feelings for her. "Tania and I have formed a very close relationship. I would have to say I love her—"

"Enough to leave your wife?"

"No. Not at all."

"Have you been...ah...physically involved with her?"

* * *

Tania settled herself into the old leather chair and looked expectantly at Marylou.

"Well," Marylou began, "this has been a very interesting afternoon. I've heard a lot about what's happened, but I'd like to hear your views on a number of issues...First, how do you feel about Mr. Hoskins?"

"I love the man," Tania replied without hesitation.

"He's married, you know."

"I know that. I love him. What else can I say? If he'd done for you what he's done for me, and you'd watched him with Penny, you'd feel the same way. Believe me you would."

"Then, I take it, you feel he would make a good father for Penny?"

"Absolutely! Best possible thing that could happen to her. She loves him, too, you know."

Marylou smiled, "Yes, she made it very clear. Have you been intimate with Mr. Hoskins?"

Tania slowly shook her head, "No, but I wish I could say yes."

* * *

Tania left the office, smiling, and Marylou beckoned to Penny to come back in. "Come on, Penny. It's time to make the call to your grandparents."

As Penny left Walter's side, where he had been entertaining her with humorous readings from some old magazines, Walter looked up at his daughter, "You're making long distance calls on my phone?"

"Aw come on, Dad. Just send the bill over to my office and I'll get it paid."

"So you say, but when'll I see the money? This year?"

Marylou glared at her father, then closed the door behind Penny. Several minutes later, the phone was ringing at the other end.

"Hello, Mr. Jacobs?" Marylou asked. "This is Judge Marylou Jenkins in Montrose, Colorado...Montrose...Yes...Judge...Yes, that's right. I have someone here whom I'm sure you want to talk to." She handed the phone to Penny.

Penny took the phone. "Hi, Grandpa. This is Penny," she squealed in high excitement.

"Penny? Penny Ferguson?" Eric Jacobs asked, surprised and confused.

"Yeah, Grandpa. I'm alive. We just got out today."

Tears flooded the old man's eyes. There was no mistaking her happy voice. "Oh, there *is* a merciful God! P-Penny, how did you survive? I-Is your mother there?"

Now Penny's eyes began to water. "Sh-she died, Grandpa. It was just Jim an' Tania an' me."

"Oh," his voice trailed off, "Are you all right? Are you in some kind of trouble?"

"Trouble? I don't think so. I was hurt in the crash but I'm okay now," she perked. "What kind of trouble?"

Marylou understood the question he had apparently asked and reached for the phone. "Grandpa, I'll let Marylou tell you whatever it is." She handed the phone to Marylou.

"Mr. Jacobs, I'm the juvenile judge handling your granddaughter's case. Let me assure you she is in no trouble." Marylou smiled at Penny as Eric began to understand. "I will be making arrangements for her care so don't you worry. I must ask you some questions—...Yes, this is a very happy thing...I'm very pleased she survived. I'm—...She seems in fine health, a little underweight, but that's to be expected. My father, who is her physician, says she has some internal injuries—...No, no. Interstate Airlines has already authorized payment for whatever she needs, and Dad will see to it she gets the best...Oh, yes. They should be calling you soon to arrange to bring you to her." Marylou sighed as she listened to Eric in his excitement rattle on and on. She motioned to Penny to leave the room.

"Mr. Jacobs, I'm sorry to have to interrupt, and I know you are thrilled, but did your daughter send you a copy of her will?...Oh, fine! Would you send me a copy with the lawyer's name and address?...Thank you, that will be a great help—"

*   *   *

Marylou entered the waiting room and smiled at Tania, Jim, Penny, and Walter and walked to stand in front of Penny.

"Your grandfather was very excited, but also a big help. I explained to you I have to assign you to a foster home while we settle all the legal issues?"

Penny nodded expectantly.

"I make you the ward of someone I know will take good, loving care of you. I assign you to my parents, Dr. and Wilma McCreedy. How's that?"

Penny exploded in joyous emotion. First she hugged the old doctor, then she stood to grasp Marylou. Marylou looked over Penny's shoulder to Jim, looking for his approval while returning the impetuous hug with her arm.

Jim smiled and nodded his satisfaction. Walter closed the magazine he and Penny were looking through and began to stand.

"I'd say it was time we got these folks over to the house. I expect they'd like to use a shower or tub for a spell."

"I'll *kill* anyone who gets in my way," Tania threatened.

Walter chuckled, "Wilma will take care of you two ladies' hair; she used to be a beautician. My barber will fix Jim up at the house."

Jim scratched his beard, "I'm itching to be rid of this."

"Ohhh," Tania moaned, "if it was trimmed, I think it would look nice."

Walter looked at his daughter, "You and Paul be by about seven for dinner?"

Marylou nodded, smiled, and waved goodbye as she left.

"On second thought," Tania mused, helping Jim to his feet, "Jim and Penny can go first; I want to *soak!*"

* * *

Mike looked over the assembled department. The conference room was crowded. He took the answering machine and plugged it into a power socket under the conference table. Holding his hands up, he waited for quiet. Lori stood impatiently, hoping she wasn't going to miss a call from Bernie Higgins.

"I want you to hear a call which came in while we were all out to lunch, today. Please be very quiet, this machine is limited in loudness." He pushed the playback button.

218

"Beep...Hello, Mike. This is Jim Hoskins. I'm in Montrose, Colorado. My two companions and I were found this morning. There's lots of loose ends we have to tie up, so I don't think I'll be able to come back to work until a week from Monday. Please say hello to everybody for me. We'll be holding a news conference tomorrow morning. Look us up. You can reach me at—"

Mike pushed the stop button. The room was dead silent for a few moments, then Lori, tears streaming down her happy face, crouched and drove a fist forward. "Yesss!" she hissed. "Oh yes, yes, YES!" Her fists pumped back and forth. "Way to go, Jimmy!" she screamed. "All right!" She leapt into the air, reaching for the ceiling and almost touching it.

She was joined in her celebration by most of the others in the room and pandemonium reigned for several minutes. Mike held his hands up, quietly waiting for order to be restored.

"I wish," he said at last, "every Friday could bring news as good. First, I think we should all bow our heads and offer a prayer of thanks." He continued to hold his hands up as they prayed.

"Next," he said, his voice rising in excitement, "we need a committee to organize the biggest, happiest 'Welcome home, Jim' party for Monday!" he shouted, shoving a fist toward the ceiling. "Mary, take down their names, please."

Lori stood to one side as people crowded around the secretary. Tears rolled down her face, held high with pride. Mike went to her and put his arm around her shoulders.

"I know this is a special moment for you. Take the recorder into my office and get the phone number and give him a call for all of us. You were the one who believed in him all the way." He squeezed her briefly, then dropped his arm. "When you're done, go to Jackie."

* * *

The phone rang in the elegantly furnished apartment in suburban Dallas. She reached languidly for the receiver, hardly missing a sentence in the magazine she was reading.

"Hello," she said in a deep, soft feminine voice.

"I'm sorry to disturb you at this time of night, my pet," he said, "but something has come up which requires your special public relations services. We received a call from one of the flight attendants on Flight 238; there were three survivors." He waited while she responded. He loved to hear her voice; warm, smoky. If he sent her to Alaska, she'd melt all the snow.

"I want you to take the Learjet tonight to Montrose, Colorado. Get with those people, shepherd them through a press conference tomorrow, and keep any fresh disasters from happening."

"I didn't create the other disasters, lover boy; you did. I think I've put most of the nasty publicity to bed, unless that Bromley gal has some other thing she wants to go around on, so don't go springing some surprise on me. You say there are three?...A man, our flight attendant, and a girl. Sounds easy enough," she purred.

"I want you to treat them as though they were visiting royalty," he said. "Nothing is too good for them. The finest restaurants, top medical services, first rate hotels; the whole number. We're making arrangements to fly family and friends to meet them in Denver Sunday."

"Every word you say is making it a piece of cake," she said.

"It isn't as easy as you think. The man is an engineer, and he's going to testify to the NTSB on Saturday on how they survived. I'm a little afraid of what he might say. So, you keep everybody looking at you, and they'll soon forget our Mr. Hero—"

"Hero? What hero?"

"What?...Oh, didn't I tell you? Miss Richards—that's our flight attendant—says he's some kind of hero. Oh, and this is really going to make your day: Miss Richards is that Bromley gal's roommate!"

"So her roommate *isn't* dead!"

"Figured you might get a kick out of that," he chuckled, "Okay, pet. You pull this off nice, and you can have the Los Angeles office—"

"I'll believe *that* when I see it," she twitted him. It was not the first time he had held out that carrot.

"No, I promise. Get packing. Greg says he'll want to get moving in three hours. God, I'm going to miss you." In answer to her question, he told her how to find her charges in Montrose.

* * *

Lillian entered the dimly lit cockpit. The instrument panel glowed in soft red-lighted dials and legends. She could see the regular flash of the running lights against the windows as she moved up behind the flight engineer.

"You wanted to see me, Abe?" she asked the captain.

"Yes," he answered firmly. "I have a very important call for you; headquarters is patching it through. I think you'd better pull the jump seat down and sit before you take this." He handed her his headset.

His crisp manner made her apprehensive. She cautiously put the headset to her ear.

"This is Lillian Bromley...TANIA?" she screamed, "Is that really you?"

"Of course it's me. We were just found this morning. I've been trying to get you all afternoon and evening," Tania said.

"Oh God!" There was a sudden tension and throbbing in her diaphragm as her emotions welled up making it difficult to breathe or speak. She felt weak.

"Are you okay?"

"No, I'm not. I-I'm bawlin' my eyes out. I t-thought you were dead. The authorities—"

"Yeah, *tell* me about it! We heard them give up on us on a radio. Where are you?"

"Hell, I don't know where we are. I'm working an evening flight to New York," she sniffled. "We get in very late. Where the hell are you?"

"Montrose, Colorado. I think we're going to Denver tomorrow for a few days. Are we still roommates?"

"Goddamn right we're still roommates! How did you ever survive? Were there others?" She listened while Tania briefly explained. "...Uh huh— Oh, shit, I'd've died!...Oooo God!...And then—?...Look, I don't know when I can get there, but I'll get there if I have to take an all night bus...Tania?...I-I love you— Okay, 'bye."

Limp, she handed the headset back to Abe. She was crying, but deliriously happy. She sat for some time with her face in her hands. When Abe handed her a handkerchief, she wiped her eyes, then dropped to her knees to give thanks to a God she never thought she could believe in.

* * *

It was mid evening at the McCreedy house. Dinner was over, and everybody had repaired to the living room. It was a large room, comfortably appointed with several stuffed chairs, an aging sofa, and a large reclining chair. An upright piano stood in one corner, long unused and out of tune. Penny was picking out simple tunes on it. Jim, relaxing in the reclining chair, tilted back to raise his leg high. Tania was holding court, talking about their months in the wilderness. Penny tired of the piano and went to Jim's side.

"Could I have my private place?" she asked quietly.

He smiled at her and lowered the chair to help her climb onto his lap. She grasped his hand and pulled his arm around her, snuggling her head down on his chest. He leaned back until he was more or less horizontal.

Marylou had been watching Penny and Jim the entire evening. She observed this event with interest and inquired what the business with his hand and arm meant. He briefly explained what he had told Penny about making a private place Penny could retreat to their first night together. The bit with the arm was closing the "door" to this "room." While he was talking, Penny, her tummy full, comfortable and secure on Jim's lap, went to sleep. Tania had never heard anything Jim had discussed with Penny that night, and she was as impressed as Marylou. More, because this was the first time in their two months together Penny had availed herself of this privilege. Wilma wondered, more to herself than anyone in the room, why Penny, with a room of her own upstairs, had chosen Jim's chest for solitude.

"Well," Jim replied quietly, "I think the room upstairs is strange to her, she's still uncomfortable about our separation coming up, and she really didn't want to go off by herself." He tenderly stroked her head with his free hand, then wrapped the arm around her body.

Tania asked why the McCreedys were on their way to the cabin. Wilma told her of the unusual electric bill.

"The slow message!" Tania exclaimed.

Tania happily gave an explanation, during which Jim nodded off to sleep. The conversation continued on for some time until Marylou noticed the two sleepers. She nudged her husband.

"I think we had better go home and let these folks get to bed. It looks like *they* didn't wait for us to leave." She glanced at Jim and Penny.

Tania, sitting next to her, placed a hand on Marylou's. "Do you see what I was talking about this afternoon? About the two of them?" Marylou nodded affirmation. "And this is the first time I've seen him fully relaxed since the plane crashed. He's taken the responsibility of our lives very seriously."

After the guests departed, Tania prevented Wilma from waking Jim and Penny, "Let's just put a blanket over them."

19.

It was early morning as her plane cut power to descend into Montrose airport. Gazing out the window at the rugged, snow-covered mountains nearby, she yawned. She had not slept well; her anger at the man she worked for and sometimes slept with kept her mind in a turmoil. Once she got herself set up in Los Angeles, she vowed she would cut him out of her life. He was using her, she knew, for his personal pleasures. But, she in turn was using him, trading her self-respect for an amassing of wealth and power which would soon make her independent of men who would use her for her physical assets. She had accumulated wealth she had hidden from men like him; little baubles and trinkets, diamonds and emeralds, given her to win her favors. As a government agent and spy, she was amply paid to use her bodily charms to gain the intimate confidence of her lovers and loosen their tongues. The trinkets, favors of her marks, converted to cash, had been shrewdly invested, and soon she would be able to own him, to make him dance to *her* tune—if he wasn't in jail. And maybe she might find again the beautiful, simple life she had lost in her youth.

It had been a cruel life. When she was much too young to understand what she was losing, she had become part of a foreign intrigue, the pawn of men and power. Her duties had changed her life. Innocence had been sacrificed in the name of patriotism, and cynicism had conquered faith and happiness. Oh, to return to those idyllic days of her life when...but there was no use dwelling on the past. Her present was awaiting as the aircraft's wheels glanced against the pavement, recoiled briefly, and settled into a smooth roll. She noted with satisfaction the rented limousine was waiting.

After gathering up her purse, company blazer, and light topcoat, she walked forward to wait for the stairway to be lowered. Montrose did not look like much to her, yet its country appearance was appealing. There was something basically warm and honest about a rural town, something she trusted about its people, a trust born in her childhood.

"Greg," she said to the pilot, who let the stairway down, "you guys stay close. We have a tight schedule, and I hope we'll be flying around ten."

"Okay, babe. You do your thing; we'll be here for a quick getaway."

What are these people going to be like? she wondered, settling into the capacious rear seat of the limo. *The flight attendant is probably attractive, but the girl—is she some spoiled brat? What about this man? Married? Old, fat, and homely? That would be just my luck.* There was not much time for her musings for in a few minutes, the limo was cruising up the street next to a small park, occupying an oversized city block.

The park tugged at her heart because it reminded her of a similar park in her past. It was still early, so she asked the driver to stop. The trees, huge old trees, elms and cottonwoods just leafing out, beckoned. There were swings, teeter-totters, pipe jungles, and a sand box. The ubiquitous softball diamond took one corner, and picnic tables were scattered around, a few with nearby charcoal braziers. Her eyes were misty as she recalled happier days. The dew on the grass dampened her Gucci shoes, but the serenity in her heart was worth far more than a pair of shoes. The morning tranquillity, broken only by quarreling squirrels and chattering birds, overcame her sense of duty; she sat in a swing and pushed herself back enough to rock gently to and fro, her eyes sparkling with a happiness long forgotten. Oh, why was she caught up in the fever of modern life? Why not chuck it all and settle here and *live?*

Returning to the car, she admired the fine old Victorian two and three-story homes, dating back to the silver mining heydays, set back on generous lots lining the streets around the park. One on the corner, the one she was especially attracted to, proved to be the address she was looking for.

There were lights on inside as she mounted the steps to the large porch; somebody was up. She rang the bell.

"Jim, could you please see who is at the door?" Wilma yelled from the kitchen.

"Okay." He limped in the plastic brace to the door, opened it, then stared in shock and surprise.

"Jaime?" she asked, equally shocked, "C'est vous?"

"Oh, cheri, ma belle cheri!" he gasped, dropping to his knees with her. Neither could speak as each gazed fondly at the other. *He is more handsome than I remember,* she thought. *She is far more beautiful than when I last saw her,* he told himself. He reached to touch her face; she drew a hand across his cheek. In a sudden babble of French they began to catch up with each other.

Penny, standing to one side, was soon joined by Tania and Wilma. Walter was upstairs shaving. Tania watched for a few minutes, then cleared her throat.

"Jim," she said firmly, "don't you think you should introduce Su Lin to the rest of us?"

He did not look away from Su Lin's eyes, eyes which had always hypnotized him. His hands gently took her face and pulled it to him as he leaned to meet it.

"Mon cheri, Jaime, je t'aime," she said, her voice as soft and low as when she first said it to him years ago.

"Je t'aime beaucoup, ma cheri," he replied.

The kiss was light and long, and the fire of love he had for her, long held as a smoldering ember, blazed again within him. The kiss ended, they began to get to their feet. Su Lin, noticing his injury for the first time, helped him to his feet. He put his arm around her shoulders as they faced the others.

Wilma, Tania, and Penny were introduced, and, when the old doctor made his way downstairs, he was duly presented to Su Lin. Breakfast was nearly ready so they moved to the dining table.

For Tania this was a nasty turn of fate. She wanted one last chance to get Jim's attention, but he had eyes only for Su Lin. She wondered how this might affect his marriage, forgetting for the moment, what she wanted from him might have the same adverse effect. And she might as well face it. There was no way she could compete with the likes of Su Lin, a rare and exquisite beauty.

Tania manipulated the conversation to force Jim to talk about his wife and child, feeling this might cool Su Lin and remind him of where his loyalties should lie. He proudly showed his pictures of Jackie and Andrea to his old sweetheart, but it was clear to Tania, this had little effect on either of them.

Finally, much to Tania's relief, Su Lin wanted to hear about their escape from death. As their story unfolded, Su Lin realized there was little in what they were saying which reflected unfavorably on the company. They did not know of her recent bouts with the media and Lillian over the counterfeit parts, presently blamed for the crash. Jim's contention about airline seating should face to the back might prove costly, yet, in lives saved and law suits avoided, it might prove instead to be cost-saving. She didn't disagree with him and vowed to stay in the background and not upstage him.

Su Lin looked from one to another of her charges. All were noticeably thin, but they looked a very fit group otherwise. Penny and Tania were sporting new hairstyles Wilma had made with loving care. Each was wearing clothes Wilma had garnered from her friends, nice but not chic. Jim was trim, clean shaven, and decked out in slacks and a sweater. She would see that they obtained classier clothing when she took them shopping in Denver.

She could sense Tania's jealousy. Moreover, she couldn't blame her. Yet, he was married. It was a nice twist of fate which had brought her back to him, but, alas, too late. There had been too much in their lives since they lost track of each other; she no longer felt worthy of him. Their love had been too pure. *But what,* she wondered, *does that broad think she's doing with him?*

* * *

227

Jackie and Lori sat on the couch together, watching the TV coverage of the press conference. Lori held Andrea on her lap and pointed excitedly to Jim when he was on-camera.

"There's your daddy, sweetheart."

Andrea climbed off her lap and ran to the tube, putting her little hands on her father's image. Jackie, however, was disturbed by the way Tania clung to his arm. She also wished Jim was more vocal, instead of letting that hussy do all the talking. Not that Tania wasn't praising him; she was—enthusiastically. Penny was clinging to his other arm.

The press questions were unusually bland, Lori noted. She was unaware Jim had met the press representatives beforehand and warned that questions with any innuendo suggesting immoral conduct between himself and Tania would cause an immediate cessation of the conference. If the press really wanted to know how they got out, then keep it clean. Further, questions to Penny, deemed insensitive by Jim, concerning the death of her father or mother would likewise terminate this communication.

Doctor McCreedy gave the rundown on their injuries, presenting Tania's X-rays.

Although Jackie was glad to see her husband, she was afraid he might have been unfaithful. Lori, on the other hand was pleased with the whole interview. Their guy was really the center of attention, and Tania had done her best to make him a hero. That he was quiet and let others do the talking was simply his nature.

"She's very attractive," Jackie commented.

"Attractive, hell; she's beautiful!"

"She's trying to take him away from me."

"All I saw was a very grateful woman."

"Didn't you see how she was hanging on to him?"

"Sure, so what? I'd have been hanging on to Jimmy pretty damn tight, too, if I'd been through what she's been through."

"But he let her do it."

"What'd you want him to do, put his hand in her puss and push her away?...On live TV?"

"She looked like she loves him. He looked pretty fond of her, too, the way he put his arm around her."

"She may well be in love with him. I'm sure he's fond of her. Come on! Get real. They've shared an incredible experience from which they can only come out loving or hating each other. So, he's got another woman who loves him."

"It upsets me."

"Why? It doesn't upset you when he and I hug and kiss each other."

"Yes, it does."

Lori spoke slowly and deliberately, "After what you and I said and did last night, you can still say that?" She shook her head, unbelieving. "And Jimmy and I have been completely up front with you. Don't you trust anybody?"

Jackie twisted her face in disgust with herself. "No, I didn't mean it that way. It's just...I...I can't explain."

"You've known me for five years. All I've ever attempted to do, is help you, to enhance your relationship with Jimmy. You've known where he and I stood with each other from day one. I feel a little hurt by what you said."

"Lori, I said it without thinking."

"Exactly, it was what you *really* feel. You've been covering it up when you can consider your responses. Did you mean what you said last night? I meant everything, and I'm not sorry."

"I meant what I said. It's just that...I don't know. I'm worried about Jim and what he and she may have done."

Lori sighed, "Okay, let's settle one issue at a time. Last night I told you I love you, and you said you love me. Did you mean that?"

"Yes. Yes I did. You are very important to me. You've been a rock through this whole thing."

"The feelings I expressed to you are independent of 'this whole thing.' True, the joy we felt last night from Jimmy's calls triggered our emotional release to each other, but it was feelings building for the last *five years* I expressed to you, feelings I'm not ashamed of."

"No," Jackie paused, "I...I love you. I do."

"You sound uncertain. Jackie, for God's sake, spit out what's really on your mind."

Jackie writhed around, her face twisted. "Oh, I'm so confused!"

"What's confusing about last night? There was the joy and relief that the ordeal was over. We then realized how important each was to the other. So we held each other, and we caressed each other. We told each other of our love, and we kissed more passionately than we have before. We didn't have sex, and we didn't make exclusive commitments to each other—and we are not going to. There is nothing wrong about what we did or how we feel. I would gladly do it again...anytime.

"What hurts me is how I feel about you, but you somehow don't seem to trust me with Jimmy. He and I don't do *anything* behind your back. Please trust both of us."

Jackie looked down at her hands, ashamed of what she had said. If Lori had wanted to take Jim from her, she could have done it long ago. Instead, she was holding her marriage together. She nodded to Lori.

"Now," Lori patted her hand, "let's look at what's bothering you about Jimmy and the Richards woman. Can you see that she has damn good reason to love him? I mean, he saved her life, he saved her leg, he kept her from freezing or starving to death, he brought her out to civilization, and did all the things necessary to get help coming their way. And she watched him win that kid over. Both of us know how he is with kids. That's an awful lot for her to have only gratitude for. She *has* to love him."

"Yes. I think I can see that—"

"Can you also see that Jimmy has at least some reason to be very fond of her. Her looks do not count! He has to admire her fortitude through the whole thing."

Jackie did not answer.

"Remember," Lori prompted, "they have been through a very tough experience together. Don't you think they might want to express some feelings they've built toward each other?"

Grudgingly, Jackie admitted that might be true.

"Can you understand, in light of what we did last night, they might want to express some feelings to each other, in bed, without making a long-term, exclusive commitment?"

She didn't want to accept what Lori was making so plain to her. "Yes, but it isn't right. Jim would be cheating on me."

"You're absolutely right. But could you forgive that one time?"

"But what if it's not just one time? What if they've been doing it lots of times?"

"One time you forgive. Any more, and it's lawyer time. I don't feel they have."

"Why?"

"First, out in the wilderness, they've had a possible witness: the girl. Second, at the doctor's place, I don't believe they had an opportunity. But most important, love is built on trust. It was your possible distrust of Jimmy and me which was upsetting me. It is the possibility you can't trust Jimmy which is upsetting you. To hell with whether you can trust her or not, it's Jimmy who counts. Trust him! You *have* to trust him."

"What do you think I should do?"

"Do?" She looked reflectively at Jackie, "If I were you, here's what I would do. I would go to Denver prepared to hear a confession from Jimmy and be ready to forgive him. I would not jump all over him, accusing him of things he may not have done. I would let my own feelings of relief, of love, of desire overwhelm him. I'd hustle him into bed as soon as is polite, and get things going. Once well into it, I'd lie down on his chest, and I'd whisper into his ear he's going to be a father again. By morning, I'd be back in the driver's seat, and Miss Richards would be way back in his mind. Recognize, she might end up in the same position I'm in, but I think you can handle that." She reached

231

out, smiling, and patted Jackie's cheek. "That's what I think you should do."

Jackie returned the smile. God, she loved this woman! Lori could make everything turn out right. She took Lori's face in her hands and kissed her with the passion she had learned only last night. "Thank you, my love."

"Now, look, sweetheart, I want to warn you. When you walk in the front door with Jimmy, I'm going to jump his bones and be all over his mouth for a good long time. I don't want you to get all yanked out of shape, understand? You can *trust* me."

20.

When Su Lin, Walter, Tania, Penny, and Jim stepped from the plane in Denver, the media was there, like a pack of coyotes yipping and yelling, to record their every move. They went first to Joslins, an upscale clothing store chain in Denver. Su Lin presented her 'license to steal'—her company credit card—and the shopping spree was under way. While clothing was being selected and fitted, Su Lin arranged for rapid turn-around on the alterations, discreetly slipping three-digit cash to certain store personnel. It was, "Yes, Madame, we will take care of it immediately," or "As you wish, Madame." Always with an over-gracious, knowing smile.

With her charges more suitably attired in off-the-rack clothing, the remainder to be delivered to the hotel that afternoon following alterations, she treated them to a lavish lunch at a chic, downtown restaurant. Then it was off to the NTSB hearings in mid afternoon. Walter made arrangements at Children's Hospital for a scanner examination of Penny on Monday morning.

While the investigators wanted leads to why the airplane went down, they were no less interested in how these three people survived. Survivability of a crash is always one of the factors noted in any such investigation. Jim was on the stand for well over an hour, detailing what they had done and why. He diagrammed things on a blackboard, gave sample calculations, and finally promised to deliver a copy of a term paper he had written while at Cal Tech on this very subject. Lori had dug it out of his desk at work, and Jackie would bring it with her on Sunday. It contained a bibliography of over two hundred other papers on this and related subjects, covering research dating back over four decades. It had been Lori who had pushed him into writing the paper after their long discussion and library research. He was asked to return for more testimony on Monday morning, with his paper. While he hated to delay his return home, if he could effect some change in the regulatory agency's policies, it would be time well spent, a positive good coming from their suffering.

Su Lin and Tania sat together in the back of the hearing room, sharing their pride in him. Jim's quiet, completely assured manner as he testified impressed Su Lin. She leaned over to Tania and said in a hushed voice, "I remember when he couldn't even read his homework in class. Now look at him with no notes, and they're hanging on every word!"

"He told me about how you and he pulled out of your shyness together," Tania whispered back. "He still loves the you he remembers."

"Well I'm not the same person, and neither is he."

"Amen to that."

Walter, sitting with Penny, already had a high regard for Jim which increased as he listened. But he had another mission. He smiled to himself, feeling better and better about what he would do if the circumstances proved favorable.

Tania turned to Su Lin. "I don't know what your plans are for this evening," she whispered, "but tonight, he's *mine!*"

Su Lin looked into two blazing eyes. "He's married."

"Do you think I don't know that? After he got done discussing you and Lori—"

"Lori?"

"Someone you don't know, yet. All he talked about after that was Jackie and Andrea. I know he's married. But I have things I want to say to him, and I'm not going to get another chance with him alone. So, please, find something else to do after dinner."

Su Lin worried. As her company's PR agent, she didn't want one of their employees involved in a scandal. Tania had put Jim way up into the public consciousness, now she was threatening to rip apart her own good work. Su Lin was further concerned, lest he be blemished in any way; he was still the pure, wonderful young man whom she loved. No matter how she felt, this was hardly the place to make a scene; there were media cameras all over the place covering what Jim had to say.

And, yes, she still loved him. She deeply regretted not having gone upstairs with him to let her mother coach them through their first sex. Her introduction had come without her mother's soft voice coaching, in a shabby room, and under circumstances her mind tried in vain to forget. If...but there was no use speculating.

For the moment, she would not make waves. She would, however, require Jim to want to be alone with Tania before she would step aside and let them do whatever they wanted. Public relations was a tricky business. She was not their baby-sitter, but she could not let the media, who were dogging their every move, have a field day with Tania and Jim caught in a tryst. Yet, if Jim wanted the evening with Tania, what could she do? She could delay by involving them in other activities, but she couldn't prevent. The night was too long. The media had to be ditched as soon as possible. The limousine had to go. She excused herself to make some phone calls.

* * *

"Look," Lori said, handing Jackie a freshly ironed dress to pack, "You have something going for you she doesn't have."

"I don't know what that could possibly be." Jackie carefully folded the garment and placed it in the suitcase.

"Andrea."

"Andrea?"

"Sure. You let her go to him. Don't rush up yourself. Just let him take his time with her. You, baby, don't have any competition. Nothing she can offer can match what Andrea will do for you."

"If he loves her?"

"That's a data point we don't have, but we do know he loves you, and we know he loves Andrea. Andrea is the most precious thing in his whole life; *nothing* comes ahead of her; not you, not me, not even Su Lin. If he fools around with her, he stands to lose a lot. See, with love, what counts is what two persons *feel* for each other, and you don't need sex to convey those feelings. Jim, of all people, knows that because that's where he and I are at."

Jackie suddenly stopped her packing and looked up at Lori. It had bothered her for a long time, and now, with her much closer relationship with Lori, she was emboldened to ask.

"Lori?"

Lori stopped ironing to look at Jackie, "What?"

"Why did you refuse Jim's proposal? I've heard what you've said were your reasons, but you're too involved with me and Jim for those to be the *real* reasons. If we're going to be as close as we were last night, then I think you owe me the truth."

Lori carefully stood the iron up on the board, staring at it as she thought. She was about to speak when Jackie, filled with self doubts began to relent.

"No, look, maybe I have no right to ask—"

"No, I think you do. It's *your* marriage I'm screwing around with, so I think you have a perfect right to know...But, for God's sake, don't you dare breathe a word of this to *anyone*."

Jackie shook her head.

Lori sighed. "Okay, the reasons I gave Jimmy, while true, were really smoke for a problem of mine. Sure, I really didn't know who I was or what I really wanted. Stupid! We had been competing in all our classes, and we have been competing in our jobs, so nothing has changed there. And if I had married him, we'd still have competed, but I was afraid. I was afraid he would have wanted to settle down and have kids right away, and I had just finished layin' out big bucks and hard effort to train myself so I wanted a chance at my career. I realize now, he'd have given me that, and when we had kids, he'd have let me keep on with my career. But I didn't know that then—"

"Then why?"

"Daddy."

"Daddy? Your father? Didn't he approve?"

Lori shook her head, "No, he was all for it."

"Then I don't understand how he could be your problem."

Lori went to Jackie, took both her hands, and led her to the couch where they sat. "My father is career military. He lives and breathes service to the country. To him, there is no higher calling for our nation's youth than a career in the services— preferably the Air Force, of course."

"But I—"

"Mom and I were dragged from one military base to another, all over the world, always on the move, nothing permanent. I grew up surrounded by men who thought *they* were it, man! Like every woman should be glad to be fucked by one of them. And I was fucked by more than one. Sooner or later, I had to learn how to deal with that, how to defend myself, so I've had to become harder than them. And I don't particularly like the person I've become."

"It's your strength I most admire in you. You don't have to be ashamed of that."

"I admire you, Jackie. I would rather be more like you; gentle, maybe a little scared, but concerned about your life and your values, devoted to your child and husband, trying your damnedest to make a good home for your family. That's what I'd like to be."

"Oh, I'm too dependent on Jim...and you. I wish I had your independence."

"Do you know what all this independence gets me?...Lots of lonely. There are damn few men who can be comfortable around me. Oh, they want to climb on top of me in bed, but they're scared to death of me because they can't control me. That didn't bother Jimmy because he never wanted to control me; he loves me for what I am, no matter whether I like myself or not."

Jackie was silent for a moment. "So why were you concerned about your father?"

"Now don't get me wrong; I love Daddy. After Mom was killed by some political goon while we were overseas, Daddy and I have become very close. There isn't anything he wouldn't do for me. But...the son-of-a-bitch thinks women exist only to bear children, and children exist to grow up and become Air Force cadets! I don't want that for my kids!"

"You don't have to raise them to believe that."

"You don't understand. Daddy was ready for me to marry Jimmy and settle down and have kids. He would retire and get some place near us so he could drop by often and see us and the kids. He already has some tiny uniforms he wants to give my kids, if and when I have any. Can you believe that? So, you see, he would inculcate my kids with the idea they were going on to a military career from babyhood on. What chance would they have with a 'loving' grandpa like that?"

"So you turned Jim down because of him? Won't you ever marry? Can't you have a life of your own?"

"I kinda have it now. See, I can love yours and Jimmy's kids like they were my own, I can help you with them, I can teach them things, and I can enjoy watching them grow. There is nobody more precious to me than Andrea; I love her every bit as much as you do. If I could have, I would have shared nursing her with you. And since my daddy doesn't know about her, he isn't going to screw up her mind. Do you see?"

"That's no life for you, Lori. You should be able to have your own family—"

"That's what I've been trying to tell you: I *have* my own family; you, and Jimmy, and Andrea. I love all of you." She paused, looking at Jackie.

"Look. Jackie, let's face it. I'm using you and Jimmy. I'm horning in on your family. I want to be your 'sister'; I love you. I really do. I want to be close to Jimmy; I love him, and you know that. He's the only man I've ever respected. I want to be 'Aunt Lori' to as many kids as you will have. I'm lonely, and you are the *only* family I really have. I love Daddy...as long as he is on the East coast and I'm on the West coast everything is fine. But I don't want to be messed up in the military life ever again." Tears were beginning to dribble down her face.

"Oh sure, it's not what most women would accept. It's not ideal for me; it's an accommodation, but it works for me. But for it to work, *you* have to allow it. That's why I won't ever cheat on you with Jimmy; too much is at stake for me. That's why I didn't want to hear you talk of abortion; I want to love that child, too. And that's why last night was so important to me. I cannot tell you how happy it made me to hear you say you love me; it told me that it will continue to work for all of us. Jackie, dearest, please let this—my reasons—be our only secret from Jimmy." She squeezed Jackie's hands and let them go.

Jackie watched as tears fell down Lori's face. It all made sense to her, now. At length, she realized Lori was still waiting for a reply. She smiled and nodded, happy in her heart to have such a dear, dear friend. Her hand went to touch Lori's cheek, and, after she touched her, Lori took her hand and kissed it.

Lori stood, "Let's pack your sexiest lingerie, except for what you'll wear tomorrow."

"I wasn't planning to wear anything too provocative."

"That's where you and I think differently. You don't know what the situation will be there. I'd go prepared to get his attention the very first opportunity that presents itself. Say you go to the hotel to change for dinner; tantalize him, seduce him. That satisfied look on his face at dinner will be worth a lot. If he's been waiting like a good boy for you, reward him." Lori winked.

* * *

Su Lin shepherded her party into a very exclusive nightclub and restaurant. All were impeccably dressed, save the old doctor. Jim, wearing new slacks, a blazer and scarf covering a pure silk shirt, looked like a young, top Hollywood executive. Tania wore a rich, shimmering, deep violet, low cut evening dress; one she never could have afforded. She radiated beauty and confidence. Her perfume could only be sensed at very close range; a feminine trick she hoped to exploit to her advantage later in the evening.

Penny was also beautifully dressed, more like a teen-ager going to her first prom than an eleven-year-old. Jim, over Tania's and Su Lin's objections, felt she should have some reward for her exemplary behavior in the wilderness. A simple lemon yellow gown, trimmed with white lace, clung to her spare body. Jim had bought a white orchid for her hair. Tania had worked on her for some time at the hotel to get her to carry herself erect and proud. She was nervous with almost bare shoulders, and she looked sixteen.

Su Lin, hoping to divert Jim's attention from Tania, had abandoned her company uniform in favor of a very simple, but startlingly beautiful peach gown, contrasting with her black hair and black accessories with devastating effect. Her perfume was a light, exotic scent from the Orient. She held Walter's arm and turned every head in the room.

Walter, though not dressed for this kind of company, enjoyed leading Su Lin to the table. Never had he seen such a beauty. To have her on his arm was more than he could ever dream. He, however, was enjoying the not-too-subtle battle of the two women. Which would win? Then again, might Jim frustrate both; he seemed to be paying more attention to Penny. The old man was betting on him.

Jim had Penny on his left and Walter to his right. Su Lin and Tania sat together across from him. The conversation, interrupted for drink orders, was light, chatter about the day's events, comments about the restaurant and its patrons, and looking ahead to the days yet to come. Su Lin steered the conversation around to Jim's job. It was her purpose to keep him from thinking too much about herself and, more importantly, Tania. If he was busy talking about himself, he'd be less inclined to think about her.

Early on, Walter guessed Su Lin's motives. He might be an old country doctor, but he had a keen insight into people's minds. Sipping his drink, he was enjoying the evening immensely. It was, in his opinion, an unfair battle. Tania was no match for Su Lin, yet she had strong reason to try to win. Walter would not be surprised if Jim weakened sometime in the evening and succumbed to the charms of one of them. It would, however, disappoint him, for he had a reward for Jim he could only bestow if Jim could resist the temptations facing him. Since Jim was unaware of the stakes, it made the contest more exciting.

Jim parried Tania's attempts to discuss events of the recent past with side conversations with Penny about things Penny enjoyed, like her favorite musicians, movie idols, and so on. He engaged Walter in a discussion about fishing, and he also talked about his childhood in the Midwest, relating some anecdotes which Su Lin was familiar with. As he related these things, his eyes rarely left hers. He hadn't forgotten, had she? Su Lin could not hide her recognition of the events from him, though no one else could tell. But Jim, looking for the signs, knew he had reached her, knew he had told her he still cared very much for her. It was a message she had not expected to receive, and like the park, it caused waves of nostalgia within her. Though he never mentioned Su Lin as a participant, Tania was sure she had intercepted his communication, and she was a little hurt.

The subtleties of Jim's remarks, however, went past Walter. Without Jim's past history, he was unable to detect the love he was pouring out to Su Lin. He felt Jim was handling the situation admirably, ducking and darting away from both women, and several anecdotes were truly funny.

Penny enjoyed the evening, quietly eating, laughing at Jim, and talking about her favorite things. But the supreme compliment was paid her by a handsome young man, Todd, in his late teens, who, smitten by her beauty, asked her to dance with him when the band started playing. Tania almost choked when he asked. She was very happy for Penny, and proud of her when Penny, sensing she might give her age away by not knowing how to dance, declined but asked the boy to pull up a chair and talk with her. Was this her birthday? No. What was the occasion? Oh, nothing special. And soon the two were discussing their favorite musicians and other matters, oblivious of the adult contest being waged next to them. When it came time to leave, Todd helped Penny from her seat, and then, acting on an impulse, took her shoulders in his hands and kissed her.

"And I had to wait until I was fifteen for that," Tania confided to Su Lin.

"My first kiss came when I was fourteen," Su Lin replied.

"I heard about it. Jim claims it saved my life in the crash."

Su Lin blinked, unable to link the kiss to events on the plane. "There are few events in my life that are any dearer to me. Those were beautiful years. I'm glad he remembered them."

Tania grabbed her wrist and stared straight into Su Lin's eyes. "Believe this: you and that kiss are the reason Jim is the man he is today."

.

*   *   *

At the hotel, Jim took Su Lin's shoulders in his hands, preparing to kiss her good night. In a soft burst of French he told her would spend the remainder of this evening with Tania. She replied she would renew their friendship in Los Angeles when he was comfortably settled back in his home. Tania, her basic French, learned to aid foreign travelers and not quite up to theirs, was able to decode the gist of what they were saying. As Jim kissed Su Lin, she realized Su Lin had been trying to protect him, not to compete with her. She took Su Lin in her arms, kissed her cheek, and mumbled a soft "thank you" into her ear.

Jim was wary of Walter. Although the old gentleman had been quiet the whole evening, Jim had noted that little escaped his observation. At Tania's door, he held her close and whispered to her to wait by the door; he'd convince Walter he was going to bed. He gave Tania a slightly longer than polite kiss, said good night, and limped using a cane along the hall to Walter and Penny's suite. There he hugged Penny for a long time, complimenting her deportment for the evening. Recalling Todd's infatuation with her, he smiled, knowing it was a precious memory for her. He hoped she would have many more.

"W-was it okay to ask Todd to stay with me?"

"Honey, it was just fine. Did you have a good time with him?"

She blushed and nodded. "Is it okay if—if I dream about him?"

In spite of the awkwardness caused by the brace on his leg, he squatted to her eye level.

"No one can tell you what you may or may not dream. You may dream anything you want. He's a handsome knight on a white horse and takes you off to his fabled castle in the sky. He's a wonderful friend, a magician, a lover, whatever. Your dreams are yours. Without dreams, this world would be a terrible, terrible place." He hugged her again and kissed her cheek, "Good night, sweetheart. Sweet dreams."

Walter unlocked the door and opened it. Jim patted Penny's back as she entered the room. "Go get ready for bed. I want to talk to Dr. McCreedy for a couple of minutes." He closed the door behind her.

Turning to Walter, he took his hand. "She had a nightmare after the coyotes attacked me in which she saw me killed. I hope it does not recur."

Walter smiled, "All right. I can calm her down if she has it again."

"You know, Walter, she continues to amaze me. We've had only a few minutes of trouble from her the whole time, and all easily explained. She's a wonderful kid—"

"And you love her."

"Yes, like she was mine." There was no hesitation.

"In some ways, son, I wish I'd been as good with Marylou as I've seen you with Penny."

"Oh, come on! Marylou is a wonderful, sensitive person."

"I'm not saying she isn't; I'm just saying you have the harder case with her parents being killed. Wilma and I had nothing like you had to deal with. Penny seems to have forgotten her folks."

"She hasn't, and I won't let her. When we're alone, I remind her to think of them and try her best to represent them, to make them proud of her. I've gotten a few tears, but not as many as you might expect, and she's been great. Just super! What'd you think of her performance tonight?"

The old doctor smiled. If there was any plus side to ninety-five people dying on a plane, Jim with Penny was certainly it. "I expect we ought to say goodnight. Our little lady'll be wanting to get to dreaming."

The two men shook hands. "Thank you, Walter. Good night."

The Doctor turned as if to enter his room, then turned back. "It appears to me you have too many women chasing after you."

"Is that bad?" he winked, "Well, that's true. I love Su Lin from our high school days; I've never stopped loving her. I also love Tania; it would be hard to go through what we have and not feel close to her. But, my wife and daughter come first, and then Penny. It was kind of fun to watch them fight over me this evening."

"Never enjoyed an evening more," Walter agreed. "See you at breakfast, son." He smiled, then opened the door and went into his room. There would come a time to reveal his little surprise, he mused. A right time. But it would keep for now.

* * *

After he used the toilet and flushed it, counting on the noise to travel through the walls to Walter's suite, Jim ran the shower for several minutes. He quietly slipped out the door and silently moved down the hall to Tania's room. She pushed the door open for him to enter. The door closed. He took her in his arms and kissed her passionately, the kind of kiss she had long wanted from him. As she pressed her body into his, she could feel his desire for her.

244

The kiss ended. She gently stroked his face. "Now it's nearly over," she said softly, "and I wish it would never end. Tonight has to be for us; you and me—"

"Can only be good friends, my sweet." His voice was soft and sad as he looked longingly into her eyes.

"No! Lovers! Tonight. Just tonight."

He closed his eyes in frustration, then looked into hers, shaking his head slowly.

"Please," she pleaded, "I love you." She tried to kiss him again, but he moved his head aside. "Why? Jesus, I'm not asking you to leave Jackie. I'm not asking for more than tonight. Please, Jim."

He held her and looked into her eyes, longing, loving, hating what he must do. No pain, not even his leg, could compare with the agony he felt at this moment. To love, and not be able to love.

"By doing what I want to do," he said, almost whispering, "what you want me to do, tonight, I would lose Jackie, Andrea, any chance of helping Penny, and, my love, you. Jackie already suspects you and I are lovers."

"What? How can she?"

"The press conference this morning. You were a growth on my arm. She didn't miss that. She hardly heard a word either of us said. She asked some tough questions on the phone before dinner."

"Oh God! I'm sorry...You can't lose me, though; I'll stick through anything."

He slowly shook his head, "I know you would. But if my marriage were to come apart because I made love to you, I wouldn't want to see you ever again." He paused and gazed into her eyes. "Because I *do* want to see you again, as a very dear friend, I will not make love with you."

"Then why the hell are you even here?" Her frustration with him was complete. "Why are you holding me like this? Why did you kiss me like you did?" She tried to break from his arms, but he held her firmly to him.

"Because," he continued, softly and patiently, "I *want* to be here, to hold you, to kiss you." He looked at her tenderly, then kissed her cheek. "I love you," he whispered.

She reached up from behind his back with her arms, grasped his shoulders and pulled him close. Her chin rested on his shoulder as tears ran down her cheeks. Jim blinked back tears of his own.

"Jim, you've completely redefined what I'm looking for in a man. Just—just turned my whole life upside down, changed my values, changed what's important to me. I can't—can't even imagine life without you, now."

"I'm sorry, but it can't be."

"What if Jackie wasn't in the picture?"

"Are you sure you want to play 'what-if?' You might not like the result."

She heard the warning, but she was in a reckless mood, "Go on, what if?"

"Then I would have you, Lori, and Su Lin to consider. Don't underestimate my feelings for either of them. I might try to play all three ends, which might earn the wrath of all three of you, or I might settle for one and hurt the other two. But which one, I couldn't say. It wouldn't necessarily be you, though. Tania, I don't want to hurt your feelings, you're much too precious to me. Please?"

She hadn't considered the other women, and she understood each meant a lot to him. Maybe it was better this way.

"You said you loved your roommate...ah...Lillian, right?"

"Yes, she and I are very close."

"But you also said you do not make physical love with her."

Tania nodded, beginning to understand.

"Then please," he whispered, "accept what I can give you; don't spoil our last evening by demanding more."

He caressed the back of her head. She took her chin from his shoulder, bowed her head, resting her forehead on his shoulder. A minute or so later, she looked up into his eyes.

"Will you sleep with me like we have for the past two months?"

He thought for a moment, then just perceptibly nodded. Her mood changed suddenly.

"Come on," she said brightly, kicking her shoes off, "get your coat, the scarf, your shoes, and the brace off and get on the bed with me."

He took her face in his hands, like she had seen him do with Su Lin, stared into her eyes for a moment, then gently kissed her.

21.

Jim limped out of his room the next morning, heading for the hotel coffee shop where the group had agreed to reassemble. Walter opened the door next to him and let Penny out in front of him. Jim reflected it was a good thing he had wakened much earlier and quietly returned to his room for another hour or so of sleep. He bent to receive Penny's morning greeting; a kiss on his cheek. Placing his arm around her shoulders, he hugged her tightly, then straightened, smiling, to shake Walter's hand.

"I trust you slept well," he said.

"He snores worse than you do," Penny said.

"Wilma complains about that now and again," Walter laughed. "There might be something to it, I suppose. Of course, I never hear a thing."

Jim rubbed Penny's head, mussing her curls.

"Hey, I just combed my hair."

"You're beginning to sound more like a wife than a very sweet girl. When a man rubs your head, he's trying to tell you he loves you, but all you can see is he's mussed your hair. Well, I suppose you'll reach a stage where you'll simply swoon when the right mister somebody rubs your head in affection, like—" he grinned, "maybe a Todd?"

"He's too old," Penny closed him out with finality.

"Oooh!" Jim exclaimed, "And only last night you wanted to dream about him. What did he do wrong?"

"He—" she blushed and looked at Dr. McCreedy.

"Well? Come on," Jim prompted.

"He tried to make love to me."

"He tried to make love to you," Jim echoed. "And you think that's wrong."

"I'm too young for that."

"Oh, I agree. You are definitely too young for that. Just when last night did you tell him your true age?"

"I didn't."

248

"So, how was he to know you are too young? You were very beautiful last night. You looked and acted much older."

"He shouldn't be going around trying to put the make on girls."

Jim nodded, sagely, "That's true enough; he shouldn't be trying to make out. Honey, I think I'm missing something; just when did he try to put the make on you?"

"I dreamt it."

"Oh," Jim sighed, "I didn't miss it; you dreamed it." He sat on a little bench in the hallway, pulled her to him, and cupped her head in both his hands, staring into her eyes.

"Last night, when I said you could dream anything you wanted, that's still true. But, you cannot believe the person involved actually *did* whatever you dreamed. That's not right. The coyotes didn't kill me, and Todd didn't try to put the make on you. His only mistake was to misjudge your age, which actually is a great compliment to you. You looked older, and you behaved more maturely than an eleven-year-old.

"You're right, he is too old for you, or more correctly, you're too young to be dating yet. But *he* did not do anything wrong."

"So what? I'll never see him again."

"No, honey, that's not right, either. Suppose you met him again at the airport today. Are you going to put him down for something he didn't do and doesn't even know about?"

"No."

"Of course not. Really, Todd is a very nice young man. You, young lady, have to be very, very careful not to get your dreams and reality all mixed up. If you dream something you want to happen, then when you're awake, you have to work to make the dream come true. That's where many of the nice things in this life started—as someone's dream. It's okay to dream. Just don't believe people did what you saw them do in your dreams. Okay?" He smiled at her. She nodded. He kissed her cheek, then rubbed her head again, "Let's hope Dr. McCreedy will open the door so we can comb your hair out again."

*   *   *

Tania, as she put the finishing touches on her face reflected on her night with Jim. They hadn't made love, but she was more than satisfied Jim did indeed care for her very much. After she had gotten over her initial frustration with him, she had heard him tell her of his love for her, not an exclusive love because his feelings for Jackie, Andrea, Lori, and Su Lin were still as strong as ever. She realized she could never have what she most desired, him without any reservations, but he had made it clear he did not want the relationship to end; he wanted to continue to see her, to care about her like he did Lori. He had asked her to accept the same understanding he had with Lori which had enabled them to continue a very close relationship without interference with his marriage or guilt in either party's mind.

Tania was not certain she could become the kind of friend to Jackie that Lori had become, nor, as she reflected further, could she see how it would be to her benefit. If she couldn't have Jim, maybe it would be best to try and forget him. *Tania Richards! How can you be so dumb?* She could never forget him. But maybe she could go back to her life, be with her crowd, and invite Jim and Jackie to some of her parties. That could work. It would be a different kind of man she would be looking for now. She didn't want to ever lose track of Jim, her prototype, but she could never waste her life chasing a man she couldn't have. Although she had never met Lori, she did have a debt of gratitude for her, and she wondered how Jackie would allow Lori to continue with Jim. She resolved, however, she would try to establish some kind of friendship with Jackie to keep the ties with Jim and Penny open.

Excitement began to build as Tania finished her preparations. Lillian would soon be with her; she was arriving on the same plane Penny's grandparents were aboard. *Lil will be working, but she'll get off the plane and the other girls will finish the post-flight chores. How is she? Is she a lush again? I hope not...but I can understand and I'll forgive her if she is. Lil will be so great for me while I try to readjust my life without Jim and Penny. What am I saying? I'll have to see them from time to time.*

* * *

"Excuse me, sir. Are you Mr. Jacobs?"

Eric looked up at the large, attractive flight attendant, "Yes."

"And are you going to meet a survivor from flight 238?"

"Yes, my granddaughter. Is something wrong?"

She displayed the biggest grin he had seen in months. "Well, hi! I'm Lillian Bromley," she extended her hand to him, "My roommate, Tania Richards, was with your granddaughter. It's real great to meet you, Mr. Jacobs. I'm so excited, I can't wait for this thing to land; she sounded so great on the phone."

"Penny sounded very enthusiastic, too. She's all I have left since my daughter was killed on the flight and my wife died a few days later."

Lillian was shocked. "Oh, what a downer! That's awful! Look, if there's anything any of us can do to make your trip more pleasant, just push the call button. Boy, we'll come a'hoppin' to help."

"Thank you. It was nice of you to stop by." Eric returned the warm smile Lillian poured all over him.

"Hey, no problem. Now, hang in there and have a nice trip. I just know you're goin' to like my Tania when you meet her; everybody does. And I saw your little girl on the tube. She is so cute!"

Eric chuckled. Lillian's runaway enthusiasm was getting to him, too. "Thank you, again. Miriam and I love her very much—" He stopped, realizing he had used his wife's name as if she was with him.

Lillian patted his hand, "That's okay. It takes time. Don't you apologize. I gotta get back to the tourist section, now. We'll see each other in Denver. Okay?"

* * *

Two gates down from the flight crews' lounge, the plane from Chicago pulled up to the jetway. After many passengers had disembarked, a passenger agent helped Eric from the jetway. Penny ran to him.

"Hi Grandpa!"

Eric took her in his arms, smiling, and kissed her cheek. Strobe flash units blinked during the embrace.

"Oh, Penny, you look so wonderful!" His voice cracked with emotion.

"Where's Grandma?"

His smile faded, replaced with sadness. He knew he would have to tell her, but he had hoped, somehow, it wouldn't have to be so soon. He stroked the head of curls.

"Sh-she died a few days after your plane went down." He hugged her as tightly as his frail arms could hold her. "I'm all you have left. I'm sorry."

Though she wanted to be with Jim, suddenly love of family overwhelmed her. Miriam was a kindly person who had loved her from the day she was born, and she loved her grandmother. Tears began to fall from her cheeks as she held her grandfather tightly. Too many of her family had been lost in recent months.

Eric looked up at Jim and Tania waiting. He patted Penny's shoulder.

"I think you have some friends waiting for you to introduce them."

Penny released her hold on him, wiped her eyes with a hand, reached for Tania, and introduced her. Eric took Tania's hand and told her he had met Lillian on the plane.

Penny took Jim's hand. "This is Jim, Grandpa. He's neato!"

Jim took the old gentleman's hand, "Jim Hoskins, sir. I'm sorry to hear about your wife."

Eric shook his hand. "The news of Penny's and Maude's deaths was too much for her."

Jim nodded. "It would be a considerable blow, coming so soon after Penny's father's death. I'm glad Penny didn't die. She's full of life, and she's been one tough little trouper."

"Yes. I'm afraid I won't be able to cope with all her youthful vigor. I'm Eric Jacobs, Jim, and I am in your debt."

At this moment, Lillian burst from the jetway and screamed, "TANIA!" She dropped the handle of her luggage cart, which turned slowly on the floor, and rushed to Tania, crushing her in a hug. In her enthusiasm, she lifted Tania free of the floor and spun around with her. The flash bulbs went crazy.

"Oh my God!" she croaked with emotion, "I can't believe I'm holding you! If I'm dreaming this, please don't wake me."

She pulled back from her hug, looked at Tania, and crushed her again.

"How are you doing?" Tania gasped.

"I'm clean! I made it all the way without it."

Tania grinned and kissed her on the cheek. "I-I can't tell you how happy I am for you."

"It was Sara. She and the AA gang. I-I never could have made i-it without them." She was crying. "W-will you look at me? Just a b-big crybaby. Oh d-damn, you l-look good!"

By now, other members of the flight crew from Chicago were crowded around them. Each took their turn hugging and kissing Tania, and the excited babble of their voices filled the area.

"Where is this big hero of yours?" Lillian asked.

Tania took her hand, led her to Jim, and introduced him. Lillian immediately grabbed him in a hug and began kissing him again and again.

"There," she said, kissing him after each word, "isn't...anything...I...wouldn't...do for you." Her lipstick covered Jim's face.

"Hey," Tania laughed, trying to pull her roommate from Jim, "Lil!...ugh...Lil, leave some for his wife, for God's sake!"

Lillian pulled back, "You're *married?*"

Jim grinned and nodded.

"Oh, Christ! I'm sorry."

Tania finished the introductions of Jim to her friends, and then introduced Penny. The captain of the flight took Penny into the jetway to show her the cockpit, promising to bring her back to the flight crew lounge. Tania completed the introductions of Eric and Walter and the crowd started down the corridor to the nearby lounge. Tania allowed Lillian to help Jim while she helped Eric.

"Where are we going for dinner?" Lillian asked, "I know this real neat place on the west side what serves some great Hasenpfeffer, venison, and Rocky Mountain trout."

"Lil!" Tania laughed.

"Did I say something wrong?"

"What do you think we've been living on for the last two months?...Rabbit, venison, and trout!" Laughing, she opened the lounge door.

"What the hell is *she* doin' here?" Lillian screamed when she saw Su Lin in the lounge. She had to be restrained from striking out at her.

"Lil, cool it!" Tania commanded, holding her arm with the clenched fist. "She's our PR agent and handling all our arrangements."

"Yeah? Well she and I have been goin' at it all across the country."

Su Lin approached Lil calmly, "Hello, Lillian. I'm happy your roommate wasn't killed. I've heard so many wonderful things about her." She took Tania's hands from Lillian's arm. "You were right to be upset at losing her."

Lillian glared at her but refrained from pulling away from Su Lin's grasp.

Su Lin released her hand. "Lillian, has your job caused you to do things you really didn't believe in?"

"Yeah, damn right. So what?"

"So it is with me. I am *paid* to represent the company. That doesn't mean I have to agree with what I'm asked to do any more than you. Actually, I feel you and your campaign have accomplished a lot. I hope the courts and the investigators will continue until this blight is removed."

"But...but—"

"Today is a happy occasion for all of us. My high school sweetheart is the man I saw you, on the TV, put your lipstick all over. Why don't you and I put this ugly mess aside and enjoy our reunions?" She held out her hand to Lillian and smiled.

"Just what have you been up to?" Tania asked.

Several persons started to fill her in on her roommate's crusade. Through all the babble Tania's pride in Lillian began to grow. Her eyes glistened as she listened.

"And the union is offering Lil a job with them," somebody said. "She's become quite a leader."

"And," Su Lin added, "the corporate wheels came just this close to firing her," she held two fingers a little apart. "But, I, as their PR agent, mentioned to them how the media would just eat that up and never give them a minute's peace. Lillian, I think you are bulletproof for the moment. But don't get too cocky."

Suddenly it occurred to Lillian Su Lin is not the enemy! She impetuously put her arm around Su Lin's shoulders and squeezed. "I'm really sorry for all the shitty things I've let my mind think and my mouth say about you. Thank you for being bigger than me and helping me."

Jim and Eric sat next to each other on a couch. Walter, anxious to tune in on their conversation, sat next to Eric. Noting Eric's obvious frailty, coupled with the death of his wife, Jim felt there was indeed a chance Penny could be adopted.

"Mr. Jacobs, what are your plans for you and Penny?"

"I don't know. This all came up so suddenly. Her call Friday afternoon was so unexpected and...and so wonderful!"

"I'm happy she was able to make it."

"She looks very well for what she's been through."

"She was injured. Dr. McCreedy is afraid she may have to have an operation to remove some adhesions and scar tissue in her abdomen before it can cause trouble."

"Oh, I'm sorry to hear that. I am only three weeks out of the hospital, myself. I probably shouldn't have come here, but I'm the only one named in Maude's will left to care for her. I'm afraid I'll have to put her in a foster home; I require a day nurse to care for me."

"You take it easy; she's well cared for at the moment. Dr. McCreedy," he nodded in Walter's direction, "is her temporary guardian until the Court can determine who should get her. He and his wife are fine people."

"Did I hear you mention your daughter's will?" Walter asked. "My daughter's the judge handling Penny's case, and she needs the will."

"Yes," Eric turned toward him, "Maude mailed it and many other personal papers to us before she left Los Angeles. I have the copy with me. The original is still in Los Angeles with the attorney."

"Fine. Could I talk you into traveling to Montrose with me to present it to my daughter?"

"I don't know if my health will permit. Maybe after a few days of rest."

"Of course, sir. We have a day or so of business left here, including a scanner examination of Penny tomorrow. I'm afraid Penny won't like having to fast this evening," he laughed, "she's been eating everything in sight."

Penny and the Captain entered the room.

Jim, heartened by Eric's comment about a foster home for Penny, decided to press ahead.

"If you can't care for Penny, would you entertain the idea of me and my wife taking her into my family?"

Eric turned to Jim, shaking his head in wonder, "Oh, you are so kind! I couldn't ask you to do any more, Mr. Hoskins. You've already done so much for us."

"I don't think you understand. I'm asking you if you would allow me to adopt her. I want her. I love her."

Eric's eyes widened, "Oh...I see."

"I haven't had a chance to discuss this with my wife yet. I'm hoping she would want to do this with me. I'd like you to think it over, meet my wife, talk to Tania, to Penny, and to Dr. McCreedy."

"Are you Jewish?"

"No, we're not," he answered, thinking fast, "But, if you wish, we would see she attends a synagogue near us. I'll take her there myself."

"That's more than her own father would have done. I would like to be near her."

"I'm sure you would, and you should be. Could we interest you in California? You could be close to Penny, and you could be outdoors more. We'd bring her by as often as you like."

"Well, I should find a good retirement home; I can't take care of our apartment by myself."

"Give me time to get settled back at my home and job, and Jackie and I will research places for you to consider."

"My, my," Eric shook his head, wonderingly, "you are a determined man."

"When it comes to Penny, yes. If you're going to put her in someone else's home, I want it to be my home. Look, you chat with Walter while I see if I can spring Tania loose for a little bit." He got to his feet and limped toward Tania's group.

"What's the matter with his leg?" Eric asked.

"He broke it a few days back. Now, I've only known the man going on three days, but were I wearing your shoes, I would be listening to him. You can learn a lot by just watching Penny and him together, like I have. Tania'll bend your ear on the subject of them for hours, if you let her. How do you feel?"

"Tired. I noticed it took a lot of effort to leave the airplane. It takes some time to get over a heart attack."

"Jumping Jesus! Why on earth didn't you say something?"

Walter motioned to Su Lin, who was checking out her charges, to come to him.

"Yes, Doctor?" she purred.

After first introducing Eric to her, he requested a wheel chair and oxygen for Eric. When asked why, he replied, "Mr. Jacobs has just come from a low altitude. He is not strong. I think we should do everything possible to keep him alive for his granddaughter...Tell them 'stat' when you order the oxygen."

He nudged Eric as Su Lin left on her mission. "You don't find a lady like her every day." He watched Su Lin slide gracefully through the crowd. "Now, there's nothing to fret about. Just rest easy."

"Do you feel oxygen is necessary?"

"Absolutely! You shouldn't have been permitted on the plane without it. Tarnation, man, we're a mile above where you come from...There'll be no fee for my services."

"Doctor, you are most kind."

"I'm going to make some changes in Su Lin's accommodations, too. You'll room with me; I'll put Penny in with Jim and Jackie and their daughter. They have a nice suite."

"Won't that be an imposition on them?"

"When it comes to Penny, nothing is an imposition to Jim."

"When his wife gets here, won't they want to be alone?"

"I expect they might want to enjoy the pleasures of each other's company. They can close the door. Penny'll mind their daughter for them. She's a fine girl." He watched Jim and Penny meet part way across the room. Jim patted her reassuringly on the shoulder and smiled. Penny put her arms around his waist.

Walter nudged Eric and nodded his head toward Penny and Jim, "See that?"

* * *

As her plane touched down, Jackie tried to remember what Lori had coached her. Let Andrea go to him. She remembered, but her deep-seated suspicions took hold of her; her husband had succumbed to the charms of that man-hungry Richards woman. How could she greet her cheating husband? She knew him; he could not hide guilt if he tried. She would know if he'd been playing around. Lori's message about understanding and forgiveness was lost on her; she was prepared to hear the worst. Yet, even as she was convinced he had strayed, she could not deny the love she held for him, the longing, the overwhelming desire to have his arms tightly around her. Maybe, she reflected, Lori was her only true friend...but she desperately wanted Jim. She gathered her things together, her mind in a state of confusion.

As she left the jetway with Andrea, she caught sight of Jim and bent to her daughter, pointing, "Look, there's Daddy!"

Andrea ran to Jim, yelling, "Daddy, Daddy!"

He crouched low. "Come on, Lilliput!" he yelled as he caught his flying daughter in his arms, and swung her high over his head. "Hi, sweetheart!" he grinned. She giggled as he lowered her down to kiss her cheek, her arms tightly encircling his neck as he hugged her, and he whirled around and around with his precious daughter. She saturated his senses. His cheek sensed her fine hair and her soft moist cheek pressed against him. His nose savored the slightly sweet odor of her hair and body while his neck felt the strong tug of her arms. One of his arms bore her weight while the hand gripped the thigh of her firm bare leg. His other hand pressed on her back holding her to his shoulder as he heard her rapid breathing. The pain in his leg was totally forgotten. Strobe flash units fired incessantly, photographers trying to catch the pure essence of joy in each happy face.

Penny, watching the uninhibited display of love and affection, had pangs of jealousy. Tania, sensitive to her feelings, put a reassuring hand on her shoulder.

"Remember," she whispered in her ear, "she's *his* daughter. It doesn't mean he doesn't love you, only that he hasn't seen *her* in a long time."

Penny's expression changed. Smiling, she went to Jim when at long last he lowered Andrea to her feet and beckoned to her. She took Andrea's hand when he introduced them. This, she hoped, would be her sister.

Andrea wanted no part of Penny; she had eyes only for her daddy. She tried to pull away, Penny held her hand firmly.

"Daddy," Andrea wailed, trying to pull her hand loose.

"Wait, Andrea," Penny soothed, "he wants to greet your mom, too. You stay with me. Please?"

And now it was Jackie's turn in his arms; she couldn't think any more. All she knew was she had waited what seemed a lifetime for his embrace, and it felt good to be in his arms again, secure, protected. She kissed him with hunger and passion, only to find a stronger hunger, a hotter passion within him. Rarely had he held her so tight. Her tears of joy mingled with his, and minutes flew by without their knowledge or concern. The ubiquitous cameras and flashes could record but a portion of their embrace.

It was Tania's turn for jealousy, jealousy she knew she had no right to have. *Okay, get a grip. He isn't going to be mine. But if I'm going to see him, I have something I must do.* She shook off her feelings of jealousy and composed herself, waiting to be introduced.

Walter watched the reunion with a certain detachment, sitting in a seat with his arms spread out across the backs of two adjacent seats. He glanced at Penny and Andrea, noting Penny's control of Andrea, while at the same time trying to establish a relationship with her. He smiled. The girl certainly wanted to be a part of Jim's family, judging from the intensity of her effort to make friends with Andrea.

Andrea, seeing her father and mother all wrapped up in each other, realized they had no time at the moment for her, so she turned to Penny.

"You a friend of my Daddy's?" she asked, her eyes wide in wonder.

"Yes," Penny smiled, happy Andrea would talk to her. "He saved my life, and I love him."

"I love him. He's *my* daddy."

"You have a real great daddy. Would you like me to be your friend, too?"

Walter realized both Jim and Penny sensed their goal was achievable. Eric was back in the employee's lounge, under Lillian's watchful eye, deep in consideration of what Jim had proposed. He had talked for some minutes to Tania and learned the highlights of the ordeal. He had seen Penny's obvious love for Jim, and his quiet affection for her. Walter doubted Eric would deny the opportunity to place Penny with a family who really cared. It all came down to how Penny and Andrea would get along, and if Jackie would accept Penny into the family. He smiled as his attention returned to Jim and Jackie; Penny was certainly trying to put her best foot forward.

Jim relaxed his hold on Jackie, remembering he had some introductions to make. He beckoned first to Penny and introduced her to Jackie. Penny still held Andrea's hand, shy and uncertain; this was her biggest test. Jackie noted Jim's reassuring hand on Penny's back.

"Hello, Mrs. Hoskins." She took Jackie's extended hand.

Jackie smiled, "Hello, Penny. I guess you've had quite an adventure with Jim."

The smile encouraged her. "Yes," she responded with improving confidence, "he's a nice man."

Jim laughed. "I was 'neato' to her grandfather, I'm only 'nice' to you." He looked down at Penny, "It's all right, honey. She isn't going to bite you."

Penny smiled, shyly, "Mrs. Hoskins? Would it be okay if Andrea slept with me in my bed tonight? I'll take real good care of her, and we could become better friends."

Jackie was surprised. She looked quickly at Jim. He nodded, smiling. She had been wondering what they would do with Andrea while he and she caught up with each other.

"That's very sweet of you, Penny. I think that would be fine." All indications she had were that Jim loved the girl very much; she was beginning to see why. Ideas began to form in the inner reaches of her mind.

Jim next introduced Walter, explaining Walter's guardianship of Penny. Jackie was delighted with the gentleman's western twang. She knew, from Jim's phone calls, the good doctor had treated Jim's broken leg and put all three up at his home. Trying to imagine what his wife was like, she said she wished she could see where all this took place. Walter promptly invited her to come back to Montrose with him. He knew Jim would want to go there to be on hand when Eric gave Marylou the copy of the will. A little hesitant, characteristic of her shyness, she looked at Jim, then accepted, not knowing of the other business to be conducted.

Finally, Jim looked in Tania's direction and nodded. Tania walked to them, smiling. He kept his arm around Jackie's waist and tightened his hold slightly as he made the introductions. Jackie took a deep breath as she faced Tania, who appeared even more beautiful than she had on television.

Jackie's tension was high as she coolly accepted Tania's extended hand. Tania was relaxed, noting the apprehension showing in Jackie's expression. *She really believes Jim and I are lovers.*

"Hello," was all Jackie could say.

Tania smiled, "Hi. You and Andrea were about all Jim talked about in the cabin. You're a lucky woman." She stiffened a little with resolve, "Could we talk alone for a couple of minutes, please?"

Jackie reacted, fear of the worst things she had imagined about Jim and Tania leaping forth in her mind. She glanced quickly at Jim for some hint of what Tania might want to discuss, but his face was blank; he didn't know. She released her arm from around his waist, filled with anxiety.

"Honey, why don't you and Dr. McCreedy take the kids across the hall to the snack bar and get them some ice cream or something."

Without a word, Jim and Walter herded Penny and Andrea out of the gate waiting area. Tania guided Jackie to a seat and sat next to her, twisted around to face her. Jackie stared at her, very suspicious.

"Thank you," Tania said quietly.

"Why must you talk to me alone?" Jackie asked crisply. She might as well get it all out in the open now.

"Because," Tania started uncertainly, "because I don't think you trust Jim. I'm sure you don't trust me."

Jackie nodded, "Should I?"

Tania smiled, "I really don't know how to say this. As you may have observed, Jim and I have become good friends during our ordeal. Good friends, Jackie, but *only* good friends."

"But on television—"

"I know. On television I—I came on like he was mine. That man—your husband—saved my life in so many ways, and he saved my leg. I feel I have a right to tell the whole goddamned world how I feel about him."

"Which sounded like you love him." Jackie's voice was hung with icicles.

"I do—"

"And now you're going to tell me you've slept with him?"

"I have, but—" Tania began to fidget.

Jackie's anger came to boil, "I don't know why I'm even talking to you, you—"

Tania interrupted her, holding both hands up in a stop sign. "Whoa! Slow down! You're on the wrong runway!" she insisted. "We love each other, yes, but we are *not* lovers! We're more like a very close brother and sister. Please, Jackie," she pleaded, "you *must* believe me!"

A look of confusion appeared on Jackie's face. "But you slept—"

"In the one adult sized bed, with our clothes on, holding each other, trying to stay warm. Penny was in a youth bed in Jim's sleeping bag."

Jackie stared at Tania, coldly at first, but then it began to sink in what she had said. Slowly she began to relax. Tania watched her expression soften. Jackie drew in a deep breath, raising her chin, and then lowering it suddenly as she understood. "Oh," she exhaled.

Tania was still tense; she had more to say. "Now, let me tell you about last night."

Tension gripped Jackie again. "What about last night?"

"We spent the night together," Tania continued, quietly, "on my bed, dressed as before, holding each other in affection...And we discussed our feelings for each other and those around us."

Jackie took a breath, getting ready to speak, but Tania raised a hand to stop her.

"Let me finish, please...Jim has certain priorities: You and Andrea are in front of all others, Penny is right behind—"

"Penny?"

"Yes, and I am, I think, in roughly the same category as Lori or members of his family. If I am to be completely honest with you, then I have to admit if I thought there was any chance of winning Jim away from you, I would certainly give it my best shot. But Jim won't permit it and made me see how totally destructive it would be to both of us, the children, and all those around us. Now," she sighed, "you know everything between Jim and me."

Jackie looked at Tania, and then down at her hands, feeling guilty for what she had been so ready to accuse her. She wrung her hands, wishing to God she had listened more carefully to Lori who had been right again.

"Why," she asked meekly, "did you feel you had to tell me this?"

Tania relaxed with Jackie's attitude change. "Because Jim has done so much for me. Would I be returning his favors by letting your suspicions wreck his marriage? He and I are friends...and we want to continue to see each other...as friends, but only with you present. He's your man; for God's sake, don't doubt him!"

Tears began to build in Jackie's eyes. It was a happy occasion; there was nothing left to mar it. She began to rise from her seat.

"Thank you," she smiled, eyes glistening. "Let's go over to the kids."

"Thank you," Tania replied. "I hope you'll see this as an effort to become your friend, too. Could we become friends?"

Jackie looked hard at her. The woman actually had done her a great favor, for now she had nothing but joy to be reunited with Jim. She smiled and extended her hand to Tania.

"I'm sorry for the terrible things I thought about you. Let's give it a try."

As they started to walk out of the waiting area, Tania glanced sideways at her.

"Has Jim ever told you about his high school sweetheart?"

"You mean Su Lin, the girl whose picture he carries around?"

"Yes."

"What about her?"

"You're about to meet her."

"She's here?" Jackie's fears began to reassemble. "Is she as beautiful as her picture?"

Tania nodded, "More. We are talking about a world class beauty. She's gotten better with the years!"

"Why is she here?"

"She's my company's PR agent. Jim and she still have a thing for each other, but I don't think she wants to upset his marriage. She spent the whole evening last night," Tania giggled, "trying to protect him from me. He told me they want to pick up their friendship once he's back in Los Angeles, but on the same basis as what he has with Lori or me. Don't get spooked about her like you did with me."

"He told you about Lori, too?"

"We had a lot of time to do nothing but talk. I heard about Su Lin, eating rabbits with fur on, Lori, and you name it. I even think I know you pretty well, which is why I wanted to clear the air right at the start." She nudged Jackie and nodded at the snack bar. "Look at your husband."

Jim had placed Andrea on a stool while she was eating her ice cream. Penny, licking her own cone, was trying to help Andrea. Jim had a hand resting on Penny's shoulder, and mopped up dribbles from Andrea's mouth with a napkin in his other.

"There's a happy man," Tania observed.

"What's to become of Penny?"

Tania stopped walking. "I'm glad you asked." She talked to Jackie for a few more minutes. Finally, they joined Walter, Jim, and the children. Both women were smiling, so Jim assumed things went all right between them. Andrea was somewhat of a mess from her ice cream. Jim picked her up, and they started walking toward the lounge to join Eric and the others. Tania took Penny's hand as they walked slowly, Jim favoring his leg.

"Dr. McCreedy," Jackie said, "Tania was telling me she has to have surgery on her leg, and that Penny may need to have some scar tissue and adhesions removed."

"Yep, that's probably true," Walter replied.

"She said she was kind of hoping she and Penny could have their operations at the same time and share a room at the hospital."

"I expect that'd be very helpful to Penny, having someone who's close, like she is, with her. Abdominal surgery can be quite painful."

"Well," Jackie continued, "do you think it could be arranged so Jim and I could take Penny with us to Los Angeles for her operation and recuperation?"

Tania quickly squeezed Penny' s hand. "Stay cool," she whispered.

Jim's heart jumped with excitement, "Gee, honey, that's a really *nice* idea!"

Walter grinned. "Well," he drawled, "Marylou and I kinda figured along these lines. She knew Penny's grandpa wouldn't be able to handle her, but we kinda had to see more about Jim and how you might take to her. Now, Wilma and I would love to have her with us, but she belongs with Jim. With Mr. Jacob's consent, Marylou's prepared to draw up papers for you folks to do just what you suggest, and I don't see why she shouldn't."

It was too much for Penny. She broke from Tania's grasp and rushed to Jackie, wrapping her arms around her. Tears of happiness wet her face as she hugged her. Jackie was at first surprised. Then she put an arm around Penny and smiled at the others.

THE END

J. Howard Speer, Jr.

ABOUT THE AUTHOR

J. Howard Speer, Jr.

Howard Speer, a retired mechanical and electronic engineer, worked 40 years in the Los Angeles aerospace industry. He was a sought-after member of many proposal teams at McDonnell Douglas. He has one technical paper published in the IEEE Power Electronics Specialists Conference 1981 Record.

Howard's outside interests and activities provide him a rich back-ground of experiences to use as settings and actions within his fiction. He has traveled to all but two of the States, plus Canada, Ireland, and Kwajalein in the Pacific. Vacations in the Sierras, Utah, and Colorado provide settings for his novels and a novella. Experiences as a member and a leader in Boy Scouts with first aid and camping are sprinkled into his characters. He also uses experiences in fishing, model airplanes, auto repair, and photography.

Speer holds a BSME from Northwestern and an MSE from UCLA. He is married and lives with his wife in Estes Park, Colorado.

Printed in the United States
6382

9 780759 620445